LOVE

IS THE

ULTIMATE WINNER

ROMESH CHOPRA

PARTRIDGE

A Penguin Company

Partridge books may be ordered through booksellers or by contacting:

Partridge India
Penguin Books India Pvt.Ltd
11, Community Centre, Panchsheel Park, New Delhi 110017
India
www.partridgepublishing.com
Phone: 000.800.10062.62

For Nivedita, Gaurika and Sumit Chopra.

CHAPTER 1

Chief Engineer, Prem Chand Rustogi along with his retinue of Superintending Engineer, Executive Engineer, Assistant Engineer and two Junior Engineers, was on the inspection round of the housing complex being built by the Housing Development Corporation of Delhi, popularly known as HDCD. After every two minutes, he was berating the government contractor and occasionally his juniors under whose jurisdiction the construction work was being carried out.

"Is this how you have constructed the walls? Are these walls, or the trunks of a banana tree?" He fumed and rubbed his nose.

"You have not used even half the quantity of cement as per the laid down guidelines."

And then he cleared his throat by making a loud sound.

"And the lanterns you have used, I must say that I am scared lest they should not fall on me and take my life."

All this was part of a well thought of drama on his part. It was a well known convention that the chief engineer would at first fire the contractor left and right and would find fault in everything and in the evening, Rs. One Lakh will reach his home, neatly packed in a new box, a costly one, and it would always be received by his wife who would always tell the contractor that the *Sahib* has gone to the club and would not be back home before 11 o' clock.

The way the contractor was being submissive and taking all the criticism into his stride, it gave him the pep to entrap him for more money, may be another fifty thousand or even more.

"Surely sure, I will bring in the improvement." The contractor spoke in English.

It was hard for him to check himself from laughing, whenever the contractor spoke in English.

Harbans Lal, the contractor was known for his fluency in English, with no concern for the grammar.

"I am surprised who approved you as an 'A' class contractor. You are not fit even to be a cobbler. You must have given huge bribe to gain this status. That is why our country is not progressing."

"Sir, I wow to follow all the instructions you given."

There was silence for quite some time. The chief engineer had started panting and was concerned about his blood pressure going high. He took a tablet to control it and this time resumed his lecture in a low key.

"Look Harbans Lal, I am not personally against you, but I can't tolerate any thing which is substandard. NEVER. I work for HDCD, which stands for Housing Development Corporation of Delhi and do you know what is our slogan . . . . our catch word, 'WISELY WE BUILD THE CAPITAL OF INDIA.' So, no compromise on quality. No, Never." And then he threw his eyebrows smugly upwards.

"But government *ji.*"

"Don't interrupt me. Even when I was just an assistant engineer," he maintained his low key, "Where quality was concerned I never compromised, NEVER. On this point I even dared to fight with my superiors. And cared two hoots for my annual progress report, but anything below standard . . . . I never let it go. No, never. Therefore, some of these structures have to be dismantled and you . . ."

"This way I will be ruined, has some of the mercy over me."

"No way, I can't fathom how in the first place my staff approved of it. They had closed their eyes, I suppose."

"Sir *ji*, I agree that there are some weaklings. I will do the ratification with your wise and able guideless."

Before, we proceed further with our story, it may be mentioned that at the time of partition of India, Harbans Lal was studying in class 8th in a village school. After he came to India, due to utter unfavourable circumstances, he could not continue his schooling, though later on he studied up to intermediate privately. He had lost all his family members during the riots, and had to struggle hard to make both ends meet. Nevertheless, he had the talent, will-power and the pluck to rise in life. He loved to speak in English without caring a fig for the grammar.

After taking another glass of water, the chief engineer by closing his one eye said, "You have no other choice than to comply with my orders."

"But sir, it is not as bad a work as you claim him to be."

"It is hundred times worse than that . . . And you are not going to hoodwink me with your sycophancy. Look, my name is Prem Chand, and Prem in Hindi means 'love', and I love those who do good, honest work, who are forthright . . . . who do quality work. And those who do substandard and shoddy work . . . . Listen", he shouted dramatically, "MY name changes to HATE CHAND."

"I will do my best and will give you no chance to complaint."

"This you promised last time also. Instead of any improvement, your work has further deteriorated."

"I am doing my utmost."

"You are doing your the worst." The chief engineer thundered. Now he was really angry. But inwardly, he was pleased with himself as the things were working as per his plan.

On the other hand, the contractor was musing that he would have to cough up more money . . . . 25,000 . . . or 50,000 . . . but more than that he was not going to agree.

"You are doing, Mr. Rustogi, much moiré exaggeration in finding the faults out of my work. Government *ji*, quality work is very dear to me and I work hard on it."

Mr. Rustogi flew in rage and his mouth became frothy. Pacing up and down, he said in a mincing tone, "So, you the great Harbans Lal dares to argue with me . . . . no you will see what I am going to do with you . . . . I am going to suspend you and I will see to it that you get black-listed."

Now Harbans Lal also lost his shirt, and he mimicked his tone, "Is it your father's concern. It is the HDCD and not the Honourable Rustogi Housing Development Corporation. Understand you."

The chief engineer blasted, "Shut up you son of a bitch . . . . You a runaway third rate refugee, I will finish you . . . you . . . . you . . . son of a whore." He shouted at the labourers, "Stop the work."

"Continue the work," Harbans Lal roared.

The work continued.

"Now I show you, who will finish whom," He spoke in a low controlled voice.

With blood-thirsty eyes, he walked towards the Chief Engineer with measured steps. Previous to that he always stood at a distance from the Chief Engineer as a mark of respect as per the Indian tradition. "Be of assure from now onwards I am not going to give you any money of bribe, not even a *nikka paisa* [small coin] and also you don't know, what harm I can done to you . . . you don't know . . . be careful . . . I've proof of your malpractices with autography and photography, BOTH, *bothum-both*."

"And this is my gift to you." And he whacked his face with the back of his right hand. The Chief Engineer was stunned; he was just going to fall on the ground, but for the timely help of his Executive Engineer, and who looked at his boss like a sportsman who has just won a medal. But inwardly, he cursed himself. *What a sight it would have been seeing his boss lying flat on the ground!*

"And you don't know the real Harbans Lal . . . you swine, he won't speak a word against the honour of your respectable parents . . . or your wife and children . . . because he is the son of noble parents . . . but he may take them for a visit to your mistress house, who lives in 3/18 Shangara Nagar."

The Chief Engineer was stunned. He was put to utter shame in the presence of his subordinate staff, and then he got this final blow.

"I've even effed her," Harbans whispered in his ears, but loud enough for others to hear. This blatant lie had the desired effect on him. He shuddered with fear when he found himself and his staff surrounded by the contractor's workers with piercing eyes and toned up muscles, he sensed some imminent trouble.

Suddenly, out of the blue, yelled the executive engineer with affected bravado, "You have hit a government officer on duty . . . you've gone against the law . . . we will see to it that you spend rest of your days in the *sasural* [which means the jail in local lingo]."

Harbans Lal squeezed the executive engineer's mouth with his thumb and four fingers and said, "You unpaid parrot of this dirty-drains' mongrel, I will dig you in under this very ground, fully of you . . . and nothing will happen to me . . . you don't know me, I am very close to a renowned gang, very dangerous, of Bombay and they have their branch office in the Delhi also . . . if I decide to tell you their name, you are going to piss under your pants . . . you all of you . . . now utter the word of 'Sasural' even once again . . . then I am going to cut your tongue and will put it in your shirt-pocket . . . say 'Sasural' . . . come on . . . say it . . . say again." This bluff made all of them nonplussed.

"Sorry", said the executive engineer with folded hands; his jaw was paining badly. The executive engineer was really shit scared of Harbans Lal.

Harbans called his assistant, Ram Kirat, his man Friday and instructed him that all of them must not be allowed to leave this place before having their meals, because he was against wastage of food. It was an immoral act to waste food, when in our country millions of people can't afford two meals a day. He also instructed him not to offer them scotch which he had specially bought for them, and then said, "Offer them butter milk instead of whisky. And plenty much of it."

All of them stood glued to their ground. They felt flabbergasted to decide what their next step should be.

With folded hands, Harbans Lal said, "You will oblige me by eating my humble meals. I may have behave like rogue at times . . . have to . . . this line of contracterism is such, but I am also the son of noble parents who always said, 'A guest is like an angel in your house, so says the Rig Veda', that's why I won't let you go having before eaten meals."

Like lambs they went towards the contractor's office, where meals were to be served.

Just like a typical Punjabi, Harbans was whimsically thinking, "whose face I saw in the morning that all this happened today." Just when he was thinking about this bad omen, he saw Mr. Sudan, the Superintendent Engineer, rushing towards him with long hurried strides.

"I have come to tell you, I am with you. Hell to this *Bania*, I am never going to abandon you. You have always been so good to me."

"Come, let's sit and talk."

"No, I'VE TO RUSH BACK. I told the chief engineer that I am going to the loo."

"Okay, then your commission is restored . . . with 25% bonus extra."

"Thanks, but no bonus. I am not a Bania, I am a Brahmin."

He started going back, then turned, and came close to Harbans Lal and hissed in his ear, "You have really effed him hard. Bravo!"

Then without waiting for a reply, he rushed back to join his colleagues. Sudan, unlike his late father could adapt himself to any given situation and he was gregarious by nature. He always felt tormented that after the partition of India, his father could never adjust to the new and unfamiliar surroundings.

Harbans Lal felt assured that he has won half the battle. He just needed one of them to be on his side, of course preferably Mr. Sudan whom he genuinely liked. So far money was concerned these people won't bother about their self respect with the exception of Mr. Sudan and they would bow to his terms and conditions.

Harbans Lal was deeply perturbed; he simply could not withstand if somebody called him a refugee. *He always thought when we have not opted to leave our well-established houses in our own country to seek shelter in some other country; why, have we got the tag of the refugees?* He hated it and it was not acceptable to him.

While leaving the construction site, the three of them decided to meet in the evening at the executive engineer Kashmeri Lal's house. That was the safest place to discuss the gravity of the matter, as Lal's wife who was a school teacher, having two tuitions besides teaching job in the school, was always too tired to take any interest in others' affairs. Whereas Rustogi's wife was by temperament very inquisitive, even a hint of what happened this afternoon would have been good enough for her to ask question after question and then she would shower them with her invaluable suggestions and advice. She had the mastery in this art to poke her nose, when the other person wanted to be left alone. She was indeed a penny pincher by nature. She never considered bribery as a sin or a crime. She called it '*the above earned money*' and this is the main attraction of a government job, otherwise it is more paying to open a shop. She always nagged her husband that he was not bringing home enough 'above earned money'. That way her father, a retired excise inspector was much smarter than him. And she even cajoled her husband to learn a trick or two from him.

However, her father always advised him, "Do not listen to this stupid daughter of mine, as she is a true replica of her mother in these matters. Better be always on the safe side. If the job is intact then some extra money is always there. If one loses his job, then there is no salary and the extra money is out of question."

It was she who had goaded Rustogi to draw out as much money from the contractor, as he could. This money she was going to spend on the marriage of her eldest sister's daughter. The reason why he agreed was that he himself was a very greedy man, besides, whenever he brought the extra money to his wife's satisfaction, she did not moan for a fortnight in bed during their love-making.

Drinks were forbidden in Sudan's house. His wife belonged to a staunch Arya Samaji family and her father was a well known leader of the Arya Samaj. In their families nobody ever took any bribe and also they never gave any. Both they considered, are sins of equal magnitude. By not even giving the bribe often they had to suffer many obstacles in their work to be accomplished. But they never did budge. Also, they were strict vegetarians and teetotalers.

It was decided that they will sit over drinks and the expenses will be shared, but Kashmeri Lal knew that he will have to bear it alone. As the chief engineer will conveniently forget about it and he will not dare to ask the Superintendent Engineer to pay, as in one's career it is always beneficial to please one's immediate boss, as it is he whom he is to report to and his annual appraisal report is written by none else than him. Therefore, he won't ask the Superintendent Engineer to give his share. He knew that the chief engineer has all the power to harm him but nothing good can be expected out of him.

At 8 pm sharp, they met in his house. Punctuality was a rare phenomenon with them, but today it was a question of their lives, jobs, and above all the kick-back money.

Kashmeri Lal poured the pegs. They started drinking in silence. Nobody said 'cheers'. The atmosphere was so morose, melancholic and depressing that they were at a loss what to say. Ultimately, as he was the host, Kashmeri Lal broke the ice. "As my father used to say there is a solution to every problem."

"Have you any?"

After a long pause thus uttered the executive engineer, "The way his workers surrounded us . . . . I was so scared."

"Even I was scared . . . . for the first time in my life." The chief engineer rubbed his nose.

Before that you have been scaring others, thought Kashmeri Lal, it was long due to you, you daughter fucker.

Then suddenly Sudan uttered, "Since I had no direct confrontation with Lala Harbans Lal . . . still I was apprehensive . . . . you can never tell about these people . . . . I thought they may not even spare me. So, somewhat even I was scared. But not the way you two were."

"I thought I am the chief engineer, they dare not touch me. But when I looked at his blood-shot eyes, I was worried and scared, for the first time in my life."

Kashmeri Lal got fed up with his chief's utterance of 'for the first time in my life', so he decided to change the topic.

"As my father used to say, there is a solution to every problem."

"And what is that, will you bark it out?"

"Let bygones be bygones, we should try to be friendly with the contractor once again. It is a question of our life, honour and some money."

"But how?"

"One of us should approach him with a white flag."

"But who?" The chief Engineer asked, and then added, "Certainly not me. I am really scared, though for the first time in my life." And he vigorously rubbed his nose.

"You instruct Mr. Sudan to do the needful." Kashmeri suggested.

"I am ready to instruct him."

"I am ready to accept the chief's instructions."

The atmosphere became somewhat light and only then their hands moved towards the plates to eat snacks.

When they were having their third peg, the chief shuddered, "And he was saying that he is close to some Bombay gang who has their branch office in Delhi. Was it a bluff to scare us?"

"May be or may be not . . . . from experience I know that all, almost all of the property dealers, builders and contractors have some ruffians on their pay-rolls . . . . their work-culture is such that they use them when they need them off and on," Mr. Sudan said.

Kashmeri Lal burst out, "Sir *ji*, one should never take any *panga* with them and moreover with a man like Harbans Lal, he has steely hands . . . . and . . . ."

The chief started rubbing his nose, now even more vigorously.

This time Mr. Sudan did not let him complete, "Don't forget Mr. Rustogi, he had been always polite, humble and generous with us. This side of his character with which he came out today was never known to us."

Actually, by saying so he had pinpointed the chief's fault without making it explicit. Mr. Sudan then added, "He had been always full of fun and had been respectful towards us. Did we ever insult him like that before? We belittled him in the presence of his men. We rebuked him as if he is a riff-raff of the society. Don't you agree Mr.Rustogi?" Mr. Sudan diplomatically used the word 'we'.

He never called his chief, *Sir*, because he got his promotion out of turn, thanks to his political connections, which he could never digest.

"Yes, I agree. We should not have behaved like this. It was our mistake, not mistake but blunder . . . . big blunder." And he rubbed his nose.

After their fourth peg, they departed. They had little appetite for the meals because of the impending worries, though they had hope still, as Mr. Sudan was an amicable character. He knew the art of what to say, when to say and how to say.

While waving the chief good bye, Kashmeri murmured silently, *'we will share the expenses, ... you mother fucker . . . . sister fucker . . . . daughter fucker.'*

CHAPTER 2

When Harbans Lal entered his house, his wife Rani was eagerly waiting for him to tell him something sensational.

"Do you know that doe-eyed girl, who always appeared innocent and guileless, has eloped?"

"Not with me."

Rani giggled and then said, "First, let me prepare tea for you, and then I will tell you the whole story. It is very juicy."

"Look Rani, I am very busy. I will listen to your juicy story in the morning . . . . I have a lot of work to do . . . It's a question of Rs. two lakhs . . . . please do not disturb me . . . . I may have to work till late at night."

Rani, though she was not stingy, but would not even waste two rupees.

"*Accha ji* [okay], wake me up when you want your dinner."

He went to his study room and bolted the door from inside. Today, he wanted to be in his own company, drowned in his deep thoughts of nostalgia.

He was on his third peg. He was in a pensive mood; the awful nostalgia was an unpleasant burden on his mind. His mind was roaming in his village Daman Kalan, in District Montgomery, renamed as Sahiwal by the government of Pakistan.

His father, Lala Gurdita Mal Pasricha was the sole village shop keeper, who sold all sorts of goods required by the villagers. He was known for his fair dealing and because of that people from the nearby villages also used to buy from his shop. He was also a money lender, but a kind-hearted one, who at times waived off the entire interest if someone was helpless to repay; but never the principle. It always remained in his books, called *bahi khata* [a kind of register to maintain accounts], even when there was no hope of its recovery. He had his farm land also, which he never ploughed himself. It was always given to the landless farmers on crop sharing basis called *batai* [crops sharing]. He always charged less than the prevalent rate, as he believed that it was the tiller who was doing the real hard work. That way nobody ever cheated him. Whenever his folks advised him to charge more, his standard reply was, 'God has given me enough. The almighty can fulfill our needs, but never the greed.'

The village had some two hundred houses. The land was fertile and the villagers were sturdy and laborious, as such nobody was poor. He was one of the few who were considered rich as per the local yardstick. That is why he was called Lala, which means a well-off man.

Every one in the village had a pucca house. There was not a single house made of mud, called *jhonpri;* everyone went to the fields to ease themselves in the morning, as people usually did not have a proper toilet inside their houses. Separate areas were roughly marked for gents and ladies and it was never violated, the punishment was severe beating until the culprit became almost unconscious. Children up to the age of 5 could go to either side. The village had mixed population of Hindus, Sikhs and Muslims. And they lived in peace, good will and harmony. There was great camaraderie and fellowship amongst them. Punjabis by nature are both belligerent and friendly. There were occasional fights and of course with the choicest abuses. Almost every abuse contained an act of fornication. Even in day to day life, hardly a sentence was spoken without an abusive word. Nobody bothered whether their daughters, sisters and mothers were listening to it. Wives had plenty of quotas of abuses from their husbands. And it was taken casually by them. They abused even when they felt romantic. Such as, 'today you are really, sister fucker, looking beautiful', and it pleased the woman immensely and she altogether forgot that she was called sister fucker also. This practice happened even during their love-making.

These fights always attracted spectators and it was great fun for them, but what appeared that they would become sworn enemies forever, was altogether forgotten within a few hours, as if nothing had happened earlier.

Women had mostly their quarrels while baking the *rotis* [loaves] on *a tandoor*, a king size oven. Their abuses contained mostly the execution of their rival's fathers and mothers. Sisters, sons and daughters were spared. During their spats, their hands never rested because it was their duty to feed their families in time. And no roti ever got burnt even partially, as they had remarkable twofold concentration.

In Punjabis, in their parleys, obsession with death is common both amongst men and women, such as, *I am dead, I will die, if you do it, you will see my dead face, on my dead body, may your father die, may your mother die,* [again sons, sisters, and daughters are spared], *you husband eater, Nee, dead one* [for daughters, sisters and wives], *Ooey dead one* [for sons and brothers]. All these phrases are never taken seriously.

Every child was beaten once in three to four days. Girls were not beaten by their fathers when they attained the age of ten. As the girl-child grew, her beatings became less and less. Even otherwise, they are mostly beaten by their mothers, who check themselves from beating their sons. Sons are always considered special, as they are an asset to the family; and the daughter a burden. Sons are better fed than the girl-child. A girl is treated grandly if she happens to be the only child of her parents.

Wrestling and kabbadi were the sporting events and they were played with great enthusiasm and sense of competition. Boys played *gilli-danda* and football and flew kites during the season. The young kids played hide and seek with great verve and noise.

Young girls played with *gittas* [small stones] or some games involving a rope. Once their chests developed, they hardly played any game.

On festive occasions, there were wrestling and kabbadi matches against the teams of the adjoining villages, and were played with great fanfare, frenzy and excitement. There were shouting and counter shootings. Whenever a team got a point or had the upper hand, there was a riotous uproar. The losing team always abused the winners for using unfair means which was taken lightly. In the end, there was a common *langar* [community eating] where people ate squatting in rows. Thereafter, lots of jokes were narrated; mostly bawdy ones only when women were at a distance.

The village also boasted of its ten matriculates. One rose to the rank of Police Inspector, one became Subedar Major in the British Army. One retired as *Bade Babu* [head clerk] from the district courts. They were the esteemed ones.

Whenever anybody passed matriculation, there was the performance of drum beating and Bhangra dancing outside his house, and sweets were distributed in the entire village by the boy's parents.

Baisakhi [the harvest season] was always celebrated with great zeal. It was the common festival of Hindus, Sikhs and Muslims. Everybody wore new clothes and there was a lot of dancing and singing. People went to the nearby river or canal to cleanse their body and soul. It is celebrated on the 13th of April every year. It was on this day that Guru Gobind Singh, the tenth guru of the Sikhs, created the Khalsa Panth in 1699.

Harbans poured another peg, he was in deep thoughts, and the reminiscence of his past was on his mental screen.

He was the eldest son of his parents. He was very fond of his younger sisters, and was very protective towards them. At the time of the partition of India, Durga was fourteen, and the youngest sister, Rupa was just six years old. She was named so, because she was very pretty. She was called Guddi because she looked like a doll. Harbans was a student of class 8th at that time. Durga studied only up to class 5th. It was enough education for a girl-child in that era; so that she could write a letter back home after her marriage, and read the holy books of Gita and Ramayana.

He was quite a good student, but excelled in sports; especially in sprints. Nobody could ever beat him, even those who were elder to him. His school was at a distance of three miles from his village, and daily he walked down to his school. It was a middle school only up to class 8th.

Guddi was in 2nd standard, and her school was at a distance of only one mile from her home; it was a primary school. She was only five, when she joined the school; otherwise villagers sent their kids to school only when they were seven or eight years old. Some kids even went for schooling when they were nine or ten years old. People were not much inclined towards the education of their wards. Guddi was studying in a girl's school, co-education was unheard of at that time. If introduced, it would have been vociferously opposed. The youngest to go to school was Prema's son Bishna. He was only four years old when he started going to school, he cried hoarse if he was not allowed to go to school. He was his only son after the birth of five daughters. Prema daily dropped his son to the school on his bicycle. His wife went to the school every day to breast feed him, lest her son becomes hungry and may not become a weakling. She never minded walking to the school three miles to and fro, every day. She was a sturdy *jatni* [belonging to peasant class].

Guddi was a very bright student. She had a photographic memory. She used to tell her brother, rather proudly, 'One day I am going to speak English like you.' Harbans Lal was simply crazy to be apt in English language. Nobody could ever judge including himself that he always spoke grammatically incorrect English.

Summer was at its peak. Hot winds had started blowing even after the sunset. People were sweating. Suddenly Lord Mountbatten, the last Viceroy of India, announced the dates of formation of the two states of India and Pakistan. Pakistan was to get its independence on the 14th of August and India on the 15th of August. Why the date was fixed for India on 15th of August for India? Was it taken in consultation with the Indian leaders, who had consulted renowned astrologers of the planetary situation of *Rashis* [star]? It may be so, because it is still happening in India to know the planetary positions of the stars for important decisions and events.

Lord Mountbatten had done no home work to arrive at such an important historical decision. Of course, he was guided by his institution, which created a mammoth devastation. It was well known that the *Gora Angrez* [The White English] did meticulous planning for the execution of any important political step, invariably this they did for their own good and convenience, and when it was beneficial to them. India indeed progressed under the British regime, but only in the areas where it was advantageous to the British. Apart from that, they took everything casually, rather too casually. They never thought how the great exodus of Hindus and Sikhs will be carried out from West Punjab to East Punjab and from East Bengal to West Bengal. Likewise, the arrangements for the safe passage for Muslims who were going to the newly created state of Pakistan; that is in West Punjab and East Bengal.

What will be the arrangements to carry their household goods to their new abodes? How will they be compensated for their properties, farmland etc.? For many, their cows, buffaloes, camels, horses and oxen were their very livelihood. How cumbersome would it be to carry them out to far off places? They were hardly able to sell their live-stock; or at best at the rate of pea nuts. How could they take their livestock along with themselves? Say, from Trivandrum to Dhaka?

During British regime, India was never governed by half wits. Many of the Indians admired their administrative skill, but alas, this much decorated Admiral behaved like a bovine, to say the least. The British must have thought that you want to oust us, then go to hell. And hell it was for many unfortunate Hindus, Sikhs and Muslims. The most devastating occurrence was that they decided to belittle each other's religion and attempted to enhance the prestige of their own religion by looting, killing, raping and arson.

Riots had spread like wild fire, especially in Punjab, U.P., Bihar and Bengal. When Mountbatten took over, law and order had already broken down in many states, but got awful momentum during the Muslim Leagues campaign, in August, 1946 in the city of Calcutta, in which more than 5,000 people were killed and many more injured. Anybody could murder anyone. No FIRs, no court cases, no police investigation took place, and of course it had the religious sanction. History is full of such instances where religiosity has created havoc with mankind. Perhaps the Almighty was busy somewhere else that it continued happening for many months. Or was it his wrath for our sins? Or was the Goddess of Nemesis satisfying herself for her law of their conscience locked in the cupboard? Even a lion won't touch any animal within his retribution? This free for all continued with more and more vigour day after day. The murderers and marauders felt elevated after their fiendish heinous acts, with no sign of repentance or remorse. It increased their hunger to do it more and more. An animal never kills for pleasure, it kills only to satisfy its hunger, or when it feels threatened. But the human race had become more beastly that would put to shame even a beast of prey. Killing, looting, and rapes became a sport and a great fun for the inhuman humans. Such dastardly brutes felt that they were enriching the prestige of their religion.

There was much less bloodshed in Sindh in West Punjab, and there were hardly any communal disturbances over there, because the Hindu and the Muslim Sindhis had close cultural and amicable relations with each other for centuries, another reason was that of their common mother tongue, the Sindhi language which made them close and friendly with each other which is altogether different from the Punjabi language. Incidentally, it had no script of its own and was mostly written in the Persian script. The Sindhis are known for their love for good food and trendy clothes and their zeal to enjoy life. Many of them stayed in Pakistan. In India, one can rarely find a poor Sindhi, or doing some menial job. They are one of the most prosperous communities in India, mainly because of their business acumen.

Also, in the Himachal region law and order was more or less under control with the exception of some sporadic incidents in the villages. The Muslim population was sparse in this region and most of them were *Gujjars* [the milk men]. Most of them migrated to Pakistan. The Himachalis by nature are soft spoken, docile, amiable, non violent and hard working. They are tough, but not rough. Before, the partition of India, a major segment of Himachal was a part of the undivided Punjab. After the partition, entire Himachal became part of East Punjab. After the further division of Punjab, it became a separate state in 1966.

Of course, there were many instances when people saved the lives of those who belonged to other than their own religion. At times, it was with great imminent danger to one's own life. Many true God-fearing Muslims saved the lives of their Hindu brethren, but they could not do much for the Sikhs, because they were conspicuous by their appearance. Likewise Hindus and Sikhs also saved the life of their Muslim friends. This decreased the magnitude of slaughter to some extent.

Some sane people thought that the date of independence for the two countries should have been delayed, first all arrangements should have been made for the safety, welfare and settlements of the millions of migrants, but they did not come out openly for the fear of being considered traitors or the sycophants of the British Empire. Even B.R. Ambedkar, known as the father of the Indian Constitution, wanted it to be delayed but for a different reason, for the cause of the *Dalits*, who lived in constant fear and intimidation of the upper caste Hindus and lived in unpleasant and miserable conditions. They were given the tainted name of *Acchuts* [the untouchables] by them. He was so disgusted with the Hindu caste system that he converted to Buddhism along with his many followers. In this matter, he did not trust Nehru and Gandhi and even had no liking for them.

People in Harbans Lal's village were leading a normal life, because of the communal harmony in their village, but it could last for a few months only. They were aware of what was happening in both sides of Punjab as well as Bengal. U.P., Bihar, Madhya Pradesh, Rajasthan, Bombay and Gujarat were other prominent sensitive and troublesome areas.

Not too many Muslims in the Hindu majority state of Hyderabad ruled by a Muslim Raja, called the Nizam of Hyderabad, opted to migrate to Pakistan.

Still to be on the safe side, volunteer guards in Harbans Lal's village started their vigil by taking rounds and rounds of their entire area. Five strongly built men during day time and seven or eight during the night were deputed for this duty.

The Hindus and the Sikhs of the village started bolting their doors from inside their homes during the night, which they never had done before during the summer time.

His friend, Rabba's father Hamid Ali Khan who was the Lambardar of the village, used to boast, 'Nobody dare raise his finger against our village, otherwise I am not the son of a Pathan.' But he still advised, 'Better be safe than to feel sorry.'

The most horrid dilemma was for the Muslims, whether to opt for India or Pakistan? Many of them went to Pakistan reluctantly. Even in one family, some of their members stayed in India, while the others marched to

Pakistan. In that way, Muslims were the worst sufferers. This kind of plight one cannot forget all his life. For them it was not only division of India but also division of family. This was not the case where the Hindus and the Sikhs were concerned. History has no such parallels.

The motivated bickering and tussle for political advantage and supremacy between Mohd. Ali Jinnah on one hand and Nehru plus Gandhi on the other was beyond the comprehension of the common man. The three of them had blind followers in plenty. A Mukand Lal, for that matter or a Rehmat Ali or a Sardar Jagtar Singh of course had heard their names and that's all, rest they did not understand what really their political philosophy was all about. These great leaders hardly cared for the feelings and views of the common man, but they were always too ready to shed tears for them. In that matter, they were really seasoned actors. After the creation of the two nations, Nehru and Jinnah lived in palatial bungalows provided by their respective governments. But the likes of Mukand Lal, Rehmat Ali and Jagtar Singh were on the roads, without a roof on their heads . . . hungry, dazed, and with no future, and with hardly any hope. Gandhi indeed lived like an ascetic, always traveled in the third class and Sarojini Naidu used to say that he is the most expensive third class passenger, and this Messiah of the downtrodden after his unfortunate death, is peacefully resting in a land worth millions and millions of rupees.

It is true leaders like Jinnah, Nehru and Gandhi felt deeply tormented about what had happened during the riots; murders, looting, arson. Later on, they did their best to rehabilitate these unfortunate refugees and made camps for them in their respective countries for the provision of food and shelter, but conditions in these camps were miserable because of the rampant corruption. The largest camps in India were created in Kurukashetra and Delhi. Situation in the Delhi camp was better, because Nehru took personal interest for its proper functioning. But it was too late, far too late.

Gandhi was busy for the welfare and the safety of his Muslim brethren in Calcutta, which was abhorred by the Hindu radicals. And he was shot dead by Nathu Ram Godse, a Maratha Hindu Brahmin for that very reason.

It is debatable whether forcible abductions of girls, rapes, naked parades of mothers, sisters, and daughters, were at the behest of the local police or they preferred to be silent spectators. It happened, in both this side and that side of India. Some females jumped into the wells to save their honour. Some were killed by their own male members.

The Christians remained silent spectators during this turmoil and were free from any harm.

It is erroneous to say that every Muslim went to Pakistan willingly. Obviously, many must have left for Pakistan for the safety and security of their families. Some must have gone there thinking that they won't be able to live freely and comfortably in what they thought would be predominantly a Hindu state. Surely, some must have opted for Pakistan thinking that they will live their life according to the tenets of Islam, in the land of the pure.

While being involved in these thoughts, Harbans Lal was least aware that he had finished four pegs. He poured another peg. Suddenly, he started looking at his glass intently and started talking to himself in a sort of hallucination. *'Oey Harbans Lal, our great leaders or the so called great leaders could not see through what was lying in the eyes of the Gora Angrez. They were chiseled bastards. Ooey Harbansia, what are you doing . . . . drinking after drinking? Will this fifth peg of yours make you happy? Forget the past . . . it is of no use . . . absolutely, have some sense. In the morning, you will have a big hangover . . . . and very severe head ache . . . . you will look like a pig . . . and you are behaving like one . . . . Really . . . . past is past . . . . go went gone . . . Be a man . . . What will your father and mother say sitting in their heavenly abode . . . 'Our Harbans has become a drunkard' . . . . if you drink more . . . you won't eat . . . . lose your appetite, and your loving mother always said, 'Food should never be wasted, it's a sin' . . . and your dear wife didn't press a button and lo, the food got prepared . . . . she did labour to cook with all her love and care . . . . don't be a weakling . . . get up and eat.'*

He quietly went to the dining table, because he did not want to disturb his wife. It did not matter to him whether the food was hot or cold, he was totally unmindful of this fact; such was his mood.

In the morning, his wife was livid with him for eating cold meals and not awaking her. He gave her a fake smile. Then he went to his study room to look at the bottle and to know how much he drank last night. His wife could never know that her husband had always opened two bottles; one he kept on the table and the other under the table. She had become so obese that she could not bend to see the one under the table.

She came back with a mood of confrontation, "You drank so much last night that you were not able to finish your last peg . . . . shame on you."

Harbans Lal grinned and said very confidently, "First of first, if I was so drunk, I would not have taken my meals, and secondly, you always advise me no to have more than two pegs or maximum three pegs, on health grounds. So, when I was going to have one more peg, I got reminded of that, and I didn't drink it and left it unfinished, my butter-pot."

"Hai, may I die! Why I am so suspicious by nature. Shame to Me!"

CHAPTER 3

Sudan's family had shifted to East Punjab four months before the eruption of riots. His father was politically percipient; he could foresee what was going to happen. With the influence of his maternal uncle, he got himself transferred to a comparatively peaceful city of Bhatinda, in what was going to be the Indian side of Punjab. Although his uncle and other relations dissuaded him from leaving Lahore, they argued that everything would get settled down after sometime and nothing untoward was going to happen.

For centuries that they lived in Lahore, there had always been communal skirmishes off and on, but they never lasted long. His counterpart, Naib Tehsildar Daulat Ram was too happy to be posted in a place like Lahore. So he welcomed Pyare Lal Sudan and assured him of every help to settle down in Bhatinda. He even vacated for him two rooms of the government accommodation he was occupying, without accepting to share the rent. All this he was doing because he was skeptical that Sudan may not change his mind and get his transfer orders revoked. He was well aware of the fact that Sudan belonged to an influential and well-connected family of Lahore, as such getting his transfer orders revoked won't be any problem for him. Moreover, one who had lived all his life in the big city of Lahore won't be able to adjust in the élan vital of Bhatinda. He would find life too dull and drudgery in this small remote city. So the ongoing Naib Tehsildar Daulat Ram handed him the charge in just two days and the very next day he left for Lahore along with his family with bag and baggage. He was not even bothered for the admission of his three sons and one daughter in schools. Being a Naib Tehsildar, it won't be any problem for him, he surmised. Indeed, his children got admission in the schools of his choice within three days of his arrival at Lahore.

Daulat Ram's prognosis proved to be correct. P.L. Sudan could never adjust with life in Bhatinda. Nothing attracted him so far this place was concerned. Life here was utterly monotonous without any literary or cultural activity. He even started hating the local dialect, which was as a matter of fact with lot of fun and vivacity. He always missed Lahore very dearly. He often quoted the Punjabi phrase *Jhiney Lahore nahin dekhya oh jamiya hi nahin* [he who has not seen Lahore has not been born]. Here, not being born connotes that his life is worthless. Once, when he was passing through the local bazaar, he felt like eating samosas and he ordered for the same. While eating the samosa which he did not relish, he murmured, *'This samosa and the samosas of Lahore, No Match!'*

He left the rest of it uneaten and started missing Lahore in a frenzied reverie. In the evening, his wife served him daal and four chapattis, he just ate the daal and kept the four chapattis under the table and decided to offer these to a cow in the morning. Often he was indulging in this practice without the knowledge of his wife. If he could not find a cow in his morning walk, he offered these chapattis to some street dog. He knew that if he didn't do it, his wife would create a scene by knowing that he was not eating properly. Moreover, he never liked to displease her, as she was whole heartedly devoted to him. As a result of it, he started losing weight. The only time he felt cheerful, was when someone patiently listened to his tales of Lahore. He was always full of them. People started calling him *Lahori sahib*, and he never minded being nicknamed so.

One day, he told his wife that he had to work on an important file, which he was to submit to the Deputy Commissioner in the morning. As such, nobody should disturb him. And he also asked his wife to prepare some snacks for him, as he was not feeling really hungry.

When during late at night, his wife went to the Loo, she saw that the lights of his room were still on. She went near his room which was bolted from inside and heard him murmuring something. It was not a new thing for her. He did it so often even when he was awake. She thought when would her husband learn to forget about Lahore? Lahore is past, we have to live in the present. There is no way out, absolutely. She gave a twist to her head and went to her bed.

Sudan was in a deep reminiscent mood. He started to talk to himself in a reverie, *'Oh, my dear Lahore!? Where have you vanished!? No place on earth can match our Lahore . . . . oh, the great . . . the wonderful Anarkali Bazaar . . . . the eateries and the dhabaas of Lahore . . . . the mouth watering preparations. The horse drawn tongas and their decorations . . . . what a ride and so cheap! Our city was the well known centre of art and culture . . . . it had a well established Film Industry . . . . the beautiful Cinema Halls . . . oh the eye-catching beauty of the Historical city called Lahore . . . Oh the tomb of Nurjehan surrounded by beautiful gardens . . . . its famous schools and colleges . . . . the mushairas [Urdu poetic symposium], where every well-known Urdu poet felt proud to participate. Oh, the great hustle-bustle of the Congress session of 1929 presided by Pundit Jawahar*

Lal Nehru, which he attended with such enthusiasm when he was just a student of class 8th and the tremendous roof-shattering applause when he proclaimed, 'Total Independence for India' . . . . Hoey hoey hoey . . . . its beauty . . . its splendour surrounded by its well maintained beautiful gardens . . . . The Anarkali Bazaar, the typical full of fun atmosphere of my Vachowali . . . oh, my beloved city, why have you abandoned me?' He cried like Christ at the cross and yelped.

In the morning, when the children had already been dispatched to their schools, Tripta thought that as he had worked till late at night, so it is better for him to have some more sleep. At about 9 am she recollected that Sudan Sahib had to submit some papers to the Deputy Commissioner, so it's appropriate to wake him up, otherwise he will be scolded by the big boss. She knocked at the door, but there was no response. Then she shouted, 'Sudan Sahib, *main kiya ji, suntey ho* [I am talking to you, are you listening?], you are getting late, very late', again there was no response. Then she started trembling, fearing some calamity might not have happened. Then she started banging the door in frenzy, but nothing stirred. She rushed to the home of her kind neighbour to seek their help. They also banged the door much forcefully, but there remained the dreaded stillness. Ultimately, as there was no other alternative, the door was broken open with the help of two strong men. He was lying peacefully dead on his bed. There seemed to be no suicide attempt, obviously to all of them he had died in his sleep. Someone rushed to call a doctor. An adha of whisky [half a bottle] was found on the table. One third of the bottle was empty. Normally, he never drank more than two small pegs and that also very occasionally.

The doctor came, he checked his pulse and heart beat and declared, "It is a case of heart failure." He took his fee and left.

After the cremation and the kirya ceremony, Tripta Sudan decided to find a job. At the time of the death of her husband, she was only twenty eight, her eldest son Suresh was eight, younger son Satish six and daughter Suraksha was only five years old. A long battle to survive and to give proper education to her children was her immediate concern. She had studied up to intermediate. Actually, she was married a year before her inter exams and she cleared the same after her marriage.

Triple M came to her rescue. The real name of Sudan's immediate boss was Murli Manohar Manchanda, but he was popularly known as triple 'M'. He managed to get her a job as a teacher in the local primary school. The pay was Rs. 75 per month with an annual increment of Rs. 2.5, besides she was to get a pension of Rs. 25 only, because her husband had only 15 years of service that is why the pension was so meager.

By and by, all the gold she had was sold. She kept only the necklace which her husband had presented her on their first night. She was a proud woman and had never sought any help from her relations. It's another matter no one came forward to offer her any support, not even lip sympathy. With the passage of time everybody forgot about her. She also started taking private tuitions, and she was not paid more than Rs. 15 per tuition. She did not even have any household help, but her children did help her in the household chores. Even the little Suraksha made her contribution in this respect. They were a close-knit family and they never talked to anyone about their plight, and they never grumbled.

They were allowed to stay in the government accommodation for six months. Normally, a deceased government employee's family can continue to occupy the government quarters for a maximum period of three months only. But thanks to triple M who was a gutsy man, he manipulated the rules to let them stay for three more months. He also kept the vacancy of the Naib Tehsildar vacant during this period, so that the new entrant might not make claim for this accommodation. Later on he managed to get them allotted an evacuated Muslim house at a very cheap rate of rent of Rs. 7 per month which was to be paid to the state government. Their financial position was so precarious, that sometimes the arrears of the rent got accumulated up to six months, but triple M saw to it that they do not get a notice to vacate it for non-payment of the dues. No government official harassed them in this regard, also such was the reputation of her late husband, who was honest, diligent, and forthright but with full of human kindness. And above all, he never accepted any kick-backs.

For her peace of mind, Tripta often went to the nearby local Gurudwara. Though she belonged to a staunch Arya Samaji family, yet she had an unflinching faith in the Sikh Gurus. She always wore a *Kada* which is one of the five articles a Sikh must wear, as per the tenets of Sikhism as laid down by Guru Gobind Singh, the tenth Guru who created the Khalsa Panth on 13th April, 1699, on the auspicious day of Baisakhi.

There she met Sardarni Manjit Kaur. After a few days of meeting each other, they became close friends. Her husband Sardar Niranjan Singh was a prominent member of the local Shiromoni Akali Dal. He was 6 feet 2 inches tall and of strong built but was very soft spoken and kind hearted. Whenever he passed through his street, he always walked with a bowed head looking at the ground. That was the reason he could recognize very few women living in that locality. He was a big landlord who owned acres and acres of cultivated land. They were living in the next street in a very big house. They had two buffaloes but never sold the milk. After meeting their requirement, the rest of the milk was always given freely to the poor. It was beyond their dignity to sell milk, they could not even think of it.

Tripta and Manjit started visiting each other's house quite frequently, but it was Manjit who went to her friend's house more often. After a few visits Manjit could smell that Tripta was living under acute financial constraints. She wanted to help her without hurting her pride. She told her that they had two buffaloes who gave more than twenty seers of milk every day. And they never sold milk. So it would not make any difference to them if she sent to her house 3 to 4 seers of milk, through her servant. Tripta refused flatly, but of course politely.

"Then you will accept *lassi* [butter milk] from our house."

"Please, no."

"Look Tripta, nobody in this town sells *lassi* when butter is squeezed out of it."

"I can't accept it like that, please try to understand."

Manjit totally ignored her and went to her house and she came back with a jug full of *lassi*. She wanted to bring some home-made sweets for the kids but knowing Tripta's nature, she decided against it.

"Times are changing. Tomorrow people may even start charging for drinking water. Then I will also start charging for *lassi*. I may even open a shop." And she laughed.

"Manjit for God's sake, take it back, it is meant for your kids."

"If you are not going to accept it, then pour it on my *sir* [head]."

Both of them laughed.

They drank tea, chatted for half an hour. Then Manjit left because Tripta had to go for her tuitions.

There were times when Tripta's family poured salt and red chilies in the lassi they got from Manjit's house and had their meals by dipping loaves in them. It substituted as vegetable for them.

One day, two trader brothers along with two ruffians, came to Tripta's house and started banging her door and when she came out, they asked for the money for the purchases she had made from their provision store on loan, which she had not been able to pay for the last four months. Tripta begged them not to speak loudly lest the neighbours should hear it. And she promised them with folded hands that she would make payment of half of it the very next month, but they became even more rowdy and abusive. In the meantime a young girl who lived nearby Tripta's house, rushed to Manjit's house. She guessed only Manjit aunty can come to her rescue. She rushed to her house and knocked at their door. It was Niranjan who opened the door.

The young girl ejaculated in a huff. "Uncle, uncle, some goondas have come to beat Tripta *masi* [aunt]." Niranjan was at that time wearing a vest and a *kacha* [a typical shorts worn by the Sikhs].

"*Putar* [Son], you try to detain them . . . . I am just coming." And he went inside.

Young girls are also called putar affectionately by the Punjabis.

The more Tripta was entreating them to be kind to her, the louder became their curses.

Then everybody heard a thundering voice. "You dogs of stinking drain . . . I have come to serve you very nicely. I'll see who dares to threaten our sister." He was waiving a naked *kirpan* [sword], and had not even changed his clothes because as per his judgment there was no time for it.

Seeing Niranjan Singh rushing towards them, the four of them ran back like fugitives.

"Brother, it was my fault . . . . I could not pay them back." There were tears in her eyes, and she was sobbing like a child.

"You go inside. Don't worry. I'll handle it." He patted her softly twice. She felt stirred.

She obeyed him and went inside. Still tears were flowing from her eyes. The touch was fatherly, of love, care and deep concern.

Images came to her mind as if Baba Nanak was consoling her 'henceforth you will never feel helpless and alone. I have sent my own true guru ka piyara to rescue you, for your safety, and for your security. Don't weep my child. Look at me! Your worries will be taken care of my child.'

For the first time since her husband's death she was totally at peace.

Niranjan went home to dress up properly. He knew the two brothers. They had their shop in the main bazaar. He asked Manjit for the keys of their car.

"Where are you going? You were telling me that you are going to stay at home the entire day and rest."

"You go to Tripta *behn* [sister], she needs you, and don't leave her even for a minute till I return."

"*Hai*, what happened to Tripta?"

"I will tell you when I come back." And he left.

Manjit rushed towards Tripta's house. On the way she started envisaging that something bad had happened. As her husband rarely ordered her like that. In a tense situation or during some crisis, he was always a man of a few words and invariably during such a situation he acted very swiftly. Then she realized that she was sans her *Chunni*, she rushed back to her house and wrapped the *Chunni* over her breasts and started shouting as she literally ran towards her friend's house.

"Tripta I am coming . . . Tripta I am coming."

When Tripta narrated her about the whole incident, Manjit went to the bathroom, took out a thick stick called *sotta* with which women in Punjab wash their clothes by thrashing them with it, "Well, *sachi*, I am going to break their legs with this *sotta*."

"No Manjit, no, it's my fault. I couldn't make the payment . . . . it's my fault."

"But you never said I am not going to make the payment. They thought you are alone . . . . none is there for you. Don't call me a Sardarni if I don't take the revenge from them with interest."

She wanted to rush out with the *sotta*, but Tripta clasped her forcefully with the continuous request to take it easy.

Suddenly Manjit loosened up. "Oh ho, my Sardar ji instructed me to stay with you and not to leave you even for a minute. Never mind, he has gone there and he is going to mince them into meat. Be sure of it."

When Niranjan reached their shop, they had already put down the shutters of their shop and were about to leave. On seeing Niranjan they tried to run away.

Niranjan shouted, "Don't you run away." And then he showed them his bare hands and gestured that he was carrying no sword. Both of them came to him and fell at his feet, such was the dread of Sardar Niranjan Singh.

"You have the strength to kill us with your bare hands . . . . please, please in the name of Vaheguru, please for the sake of God pardon us. We never knew she is your sister, Sardar Sahib."

"Yes, she is my sister, my beloved sister. But try to understand one should never behave like this with any lady. Especially, if one happens to be a helpless widow!!"

Both of them caught their ears with their hands.

"We promise, we shall never do it again. Never, again."

"Okay, let bygones be bygones. Open the shop and let's have a friendly talk."

Like obedient followers, they opened the shop, and dusted the chair for him to sit, when there was no need for it.

"How much she owes you?"

"Nothing Sardar Sahib, nothing."

"We always pay our debts. And don't waste my time."

"Four hundred and twenty seven rupees."

"Here are five hundred rupees . . . . rest you can keep as your interest, if you so wish."

"Never, never," said meekly the elder brother.

Niranjan Singh was somewhat pensive for quite some time, and then he started tapping his right knee and then finally said, "From henceforth you will charge her only 60% of the amount payable and the rest 40% I will pay. But you are not going to disclose it to anybody including my wife."

"But in case she starts asking why we are charging her so much less, then what should we say?", asked the younger brother.

"Look . . . *hoon* . . . . she . . . . is a very self respecting woman, this sister of mine. Okay . . . . make it up to 70%. And if she asks you any questions, you simply tell her that you have been overcharging her for a long time. So to make amends from now onwards, we are going to charge you at the wholesale rates and the rest leave it to me."

"That's a fantastic idea, very convincing," said the elder brother.

Then he went to Tripta's house and assured her that he had settled everything and she didn't have to worry for anything. Later at his home he told his wife everything, but that 70% deal he kept it to himself.

"May you be my husband in seven births?" And she kissed him passionately.

"You have excited me, come let's play the game."

"That is for the night, you rogue."

She ran to the kitchen to prepare lunch.

Niranjan Singh heard her humming some song. He simply adored her. *'Love thy wife that is one of the preachings of Sikhism.'*

Tripta came to know that Niranjan Singh has cleared all his dues which she owed to those shopkeepers. She went to her friend's house to make a part payment. Niranjan Singh heard it and before Manjit could say anything, he interrupted, "You have seen my anger, which means I am not a good man, but at least let me be a good brother." And he folded his hands. And then he rushed out.

And on her pay day when Tripta opened her purse and Manjit smelled that she was going to pay her, she said, "Look Tripta if I accept the money from you and then my Sardar ji would break my bones by making love to me all night. He is like that . . . He is a very virile man . . . . have some mercy on me."

CHAPTER 4

Niranjan and Triple M were close friends. They often had their drinking sessions where they didn't let any other person participate, because during these sessions not only they had their bawdy jokes, which were often narrated by TM, but they shared their secrets and confided in each other. Neither of them ever betrayed each other. The post of the Tehsildar was a coveted one and it was a power to reckon with in the government machinery. But Niranjan never used it to his advantage, though TM would have been too happy to be of any service to his very dear friend.

Niranjan sent a message to TM that he will come to his office at 7 pm and they would have drinks, besides he was to discuss an important matter with him. Mostly they drank in his office, they rather preferred it. TM's wife always made a long face when they drank in his house. And if they chose to drink at Niranjan's house, Manjit interrupted them after every ten/fifteen minutes on one pretext or the other, and often with the humble advice 'to drink within the limits.'

Niranjan reached TM's office exactly at 7 pm.

"Why have you brought the bottle *Niranjana*, you want to show me that you are very rich? I have already sent my peon Ramji Lal to the market for the same." said TM with friendly annoyance.

"Okay, it won't happen next time . . . . Today I have some *Programme* with my Sardarni . . . I thought suppose you are busy . . . or simply not in the mood to drink. So I brought the bottle."

Programme was their password for love making.

"Better I sleep in the office, mine won't even let me touch her after the drinks."

They started drinking and Niranjan came to the point straight way. "Look Manchanda, sister Tripta is financially in a very bad shape. We must help her."

"I know it, but what can we do when she is not ready to accept any help?"

"I have come with a proposal."

"And what is that . . . ?"

"How much pension is she getting?"

"Rs. 25"

"Only this much? What is this mother fucker government doing? *Thoo* [he spat]."

After a pause Niranjan said, "And her salary must be very meager."

"That is true."

"We must do something. Okay, you tell her that government has increased her pension up to Rs. 200."

"She will never believe it."

"Okay, let it be 150."

"Even that she is not going to believe."

"100?"

"Nope."

"*Then your mother's head.*" Niranjan felt irritated.

"50 or 60, she may believe."

"Something is better than nothing."

"I will tell her that government has increased her salary by Rs. 48 with Rs. 12 as dearness allowance. That means Rs. 60 in total."

"But she must be looking at the documents while signing."

"She never does that. She has *sixteen annas* [a unit of Old Indian currency, here it means hundred percent] faith in me."

"In case, she comes to know about it?"

"Oey Sardara, then we will fall on her feet and request her to let us help her."

Both of them laughed and started their drinking session, but their topic remained the same how to help Tripta financially.

On Sunday, Triple M and Niranjan went to meet S. Bachittar Singh, who was the Chairman of the Bhatinda Municipal Committee. He was a leading member of the state Akali Dal and a close friend of both of them.

Niranjan told him that a close relation of his wife was working as a teacher in the municipal primary school for girls and after three years of service, she was just getting Rs. 82 and eight annas as salary.

"Is this justice? What interest will she take in teaching our young daughters, when she is getting such a meager salary? See her record and here is the letter of recommendation from the school headmistress. You must raise her salary."

"That is not in my hands."

"You can have the money from me."

"Your money can be spent on the books, copies and slates for the poor students only."

"I know your power. You can give her promotion . . . indeed that is in your hands." Triple M said.

"Let me think to find out some way."

"Don't think, please act," insisted Niranjan.

"Well, that has to be approved by the Board members of the school."

"I will manage that." Niranjan assured him, "but what promotion can be offered to her, Bachittar Singha, you are a man of the government, and I hardly understand anything about such matters."

"Let's say junior headmistress." Triple M suggested.

They all agreed.

"What is her name?"

"Tripta"

"Kaur?"

"No, Rani."

"Then, we must help her, as we Akalis are often accused of being biased against the Hindus."

Next Saturday, Niranjan invited five members of the board to his home. He did not invite the one lady member, a social worker, intentionally because everything was going to be maneuvered over drinks.

Two were from the Congress Party, one from the Bhartiya Jansangh and two from the Akali Party. One member of the Congress Party, a local advocate did not turn up, as he was to attend his gambling session, where he mostly won. There was hearsay that he earned more from gambling than from the legal profession.

Niranjan poured the pegs, and many varieties of meat including *tandoori* chicken of which the Punjabis are very fond of, were served.

When they were having their fourth peg, Niranjan after giving a little brief about the matter handed over a paper to them. "It is a small matter. Sign it quickly and let us not spoil the party."

Four of the members signed it promptly. The fifth member of Jansangh, Kasturi Lal Sharma started reading it.

"She is not an Akali *putra*. She is a Hindu and her maternal uncle is the president of the RSS, the military wing of your party, in Ludhiana." And then Niranjan pushed down his right shoulder with some force.

"Hi, hi . . . . who can say no to you, Niranjan Singha." His shoulder ached

Niranjan took his hand off his shoulder.

He also signed.

After a week, Tripta got the appointment letter. Her salary was fixed at Rs. 225, with an annual increment of Rs. 10.

Tripta threw a party where close friends along with the families of Niranjan Singh and Triple M were invited.

After six months, thanks to the efforts of Triple M, the government of Punjab gave her the ownership of the house she was occupying against the claim of the property her late husband owned in Lahore, now in Pakistan.

She stopped taking private tuitions altogether. She even engaged a part time maid. She never looked back. Now she was going to concentrate on the education of her children. Luckily, all three of them were very bright students.

She could never forget what happened two days before Diwali that year, when Manjit came to her house carrying a big bundle.

"What is this?" Tripta asked.

"These are humble presents from a Sikh family for their very dear Hindu sister."

"You know it, Manjit, I won't accept it. You people have already done so much for me which I can't repay all my life."

"You *sadi boothi* [Burnt Face, a typical Punjabi expression, kill joy], I knew it that you will behave like that, but if I take it back, my Sardar ji will throw me out of the house and my rivals will start clapping."

"Manjit, my dear friend, you are so good to me. I cannot repay you in seven births. Tell me, have I done anything for you or your family even once? I can't accept it, please try to understand."

"I dissuaded my husband, because you're *sadi boothi*, you are very proudy, but he won't budge. He is standing outside, go and tell him directly."

"*Hai Ram*, why have you not asked my *Veerji* [brother] to come inside? Curse on me."

"Brother, I can't tolerate that you should spend so much money on us."

"People say that Niranjan is one of the richest landlords of this town. What is the use of my richness if my nephews and nieces do not wear some nice clothes on Diwali, then what sort of *a mama* [maternal uncle] am I? I will feel like a *Kansa* mama, if you do not accept our humble presents."

Tears started flowing from this sturdy Sardar's eyes. She wiped his tears with her Chunni and embraced him. It was a divine embrace.

What sort of a sister I am, I always make you unhappy. Manjit calls me sadi boothi and rightly so.

"My other sisters also behave with me like this and you are no exception."

Her eldest son, Harish was very inquisitive by nature. Without taking her mother's permission, he opened the bundle. There were two pants and two shirts for each of the two brothers and four beautiful frocks for the youngest Suraksha.

"There are four frocks for Suraksha. Wow."

Niranjan said with a smile, "Our doll should not know the spelling of hardship. One can't say what will be her fate when she goes to her real home. She must get better treatment in her maternal home. Where is my tea? I am not going to leave without having tea."

"May I die, I have no manners. I will just bring it."

Tripta brought tea along with some biscuits and *namkeen*.

After taking tea, Niranjan put a ten rupee note on the table. It was a custom amongst respectable Punjabi families, that parents avoided taking even a glass of water in their daughter's house. Some elder brothers who treated their younger sisters like daughters, also behaved like this. Normally, if a glass of water was taken, they gave 4 annas, for tea eight annas, and for meals one or two rupees. Those who were affluent gave much more.

"Eight annas are enough."

"Say it again and today I am going to behave like a real Sikh."

"*Veer ji* [Brother] please, I should not accept more than eight annas."

He put one ten rupee note on the table and said laughingly, "Say it again."

Tripta saw another ten rupee note in his hand.

Tripta raised her hands, "I accept the defeat . . . . can't fight when my brother is 6'2" tall."

"This 6'2" tall man feels like a pygmy before his sisters' sense of self respect."

"Never try to confront him, he is so bull-headed."

Niranjan left soon after.

The way she calls me sadi boothi, I simply love it. There is so much camaraderie and sense of closeness in it.

They chatted for another one hour. Manjit felt proud of her husband. She also left thinking, *'today I must give him a wonderful Programme.'*

CHAPTER 5

Manjit and Tripta visited each other's house now more frequently. If Niranjan was present in the house, he would simply greet her and ask her, 'how are the kids?' And he then quietly left them alone.

The date of betrothal of his eldest sister's son was fixed two days before Lohri, one of the most important festivals of Punjab, which is celebrated on 13th January every year. People gather around a huge bonfire lit with the use of wood and dried out cow dung. There is boisterous merriment with lot of singing and dancing of Bhangra and Giddha [typical vigorous Punjabi dances]. Invariably, Lohri gets started with the song:

Sunder mundri ey
Tera kaun bichara
Dulha Bhati wala

It is in praise of Dulha Bhati wala, the folk hero of the Punjab, a la Robin Hood, who rescued the abducted girls and then married them off and even spent money on their dowry.

They had invited Tripta also, but she said that she won't be able to make it because of final exams of her children. But Manjit was not ready to accept it.

Manjit told her, "If you go, I go. If you don't go, I don't go." She said it loudly by thumping her foot on the ground.

Actually, Tripta did not want to go because she had the apprehension that she might not be accepted by Niranjan's sisters and she would feel like an alien in their house. She felt that it was a no-win situation with Manjit's insistence, so she finally agreed.

When they reached Niranjan's sister Darshan Kaur's home, his other two sisters were already waiting for them near the main gate. Darshan did not let Tripta enter the house and said loudly, "*Nee* Harjit, where is the *katori* of oil? You are always late at the right moment."

"*Biba ji* [elder sister], it is there right in my hands."

"I guess I have gone senile with age! Tripta dear, you are coming for the first time to our home. Let me do the *tail chowna*." And she poured oil on both sides of the door, and then turns by turn all the three sisters embraced her.

Tail chowna is a ceremony performed to welcome a very important guest who enters someone's house for the first time. This practice has been continuing in Punjab since time immemorial.

"*Veer ji*, you have done us a great favour by bringing dear Tripta to attend the function."

Tripta felt overwhelmed with the respect they had bestowed on her. Then his three brothers-in-law patted on her head with love and blessings and wished her, '*Sat Sri Akal.*'

Then the ladies started chatting. Suddenly, the eldest brother-in-law shouted "Darshan Kaurey, first ask them for *tea-shee* and then have your silly talks. The best *maal* for eating must be given to sister Tripta."

Everybody laughed.

"I am really a mad one. *Hai*, when will I learn to behave?"

In the evening the betrothal ceremony was performed with great pomp and show. The bride's party had brought a truck full of sweets of different varieties, fruits and other gifts. The first *ladoo* was put in the boy's mouth. The fiancé or the bridegroom is called a *Munda*, which literally means in Punjabi a boy; even if he is more than fifty years old, still he is called a Munda. Then a bundle of currency notes was presented to the Munda along with other gifts. Next was the turn of the parents and other close relations. A suit and money was given to Tripta also; they were especially instructed to do so.

Suddenly, Tripta said, "Why have I been given 22 rupees, when others have been given 21 rupees?"

"To break your pride, you mad one." Manjit laughed.

There was uproar of clapping and shootings of joy. *"Choti masi Zindabad, choti masi zindabad."* The kids roared.

For the first time since partition of India, Tripta was out of her shell and started dancing and making noise along with others. She was surprised at her own behaviour. There was deafening noise of celebrations. After all it was a function of a Sikh family. In this part of Punjab, if a Sikh spoke in a low voice, he was looked at with awe and astonishment.

If the whole world had been like the warrior community of the Sikhs, loud speakers would never have been invented. There would have been no need for it.

Yamla Jat, the renowned folk singer was a special invitee. He had come with the condition that nobody would drink while he was performing as it broke his concentration. He regaled the audience with his typical Punjabi folk songs. His song, 'main majhe di jati, gulaboo nikka jiya', was a super hit.

It was about the story of a tall well built girl whose husband was lean and of a very short height. Such ill-matched marriages used to happen, when close friends decided the matrimonial alliance of their son and daughter, when they were just small babies. Sometimes, close friends used to decide to marry their offspring when they were pregnant; of course if one had a son and the other a girl. It was a word of honour, no ceremony was performed, this vow was taken and it was invariably so often honoured. Betrayals were rare.

Girls had no say regarding their acceptance of their life partner in matrimonial alliances. They were taught house hold work, sewing, embroidery, weaving of pullovers and cardigans at a very young age. It was considered very useful to become a successful house wife and they were too keen to learn it. Much more importance was given to it than to academics. A working woman was looked down with disdain, unless she worked as a teacher in a girl's school.

The boys thought, whosoever their doting parents chose for them must be the best for them. Surprisingly, they never even felt to talk about it. Besides, they had unfaltering dogged faith in their parents. And sometimes all this was decided by the grandparents without even trying to know the opinion of the boy's parents. So often the couple had not even seen each other before their marriage and that also on the first night when the boy lifted her *ghoonghat* [a kind of veil] and gave her a present for *moonh dikhai* [for looking at her face], as during the marriage ceremony she remained in her *ghoonghat*. At times, friends from both sides helped the couple to have a look at each other, mostly in the market place and that also at a distance that they could not even say hello to each other. The boy looked at the girl with full eyes and the girl looked at him with half closed eyes due to shyness and modesty.

Love marriage was a very rare phenomenon, which was looked down upon with outright condemnation by the society. It was much appreciated in the movies by people and they clapped for the lovers, and cried for them when due to adverse circumstances or opposition the lovers got separated. It was so rare when both sides gave their consent to a love marriage, still they preferred to keep it as a secret, lest their wards should get defamed. It would also become difficult to marry their other children because of the ensuing defame. If a girl eloped with her lover, she was forbidden to enter her parent's house. After the birth of a child or two some reconciled with their daughter, but some remained her sworn enemies throughout their life. There were honour killings, though it was often the boy who was murdered, in some cases even the girl was not spared. It was not uncommon when both got lynched. If a girl had some fun before marriage she never admitted it to anyone, rather she spoke against such acts on moral grounds.

There could be occasions when a couple decide to elope but developed cold feet at the last minute.

There is an English adage, the whole word loves the lovers. But in India it is the other way round especially amongst the Punjabis and the Haryanvis.

The passion for revenge amongst the Punjabis, especially amongst the village folk has no limits. There would be murders and counter murders at the appropriate opportunity, for which sometimes they were on the lookout for years. And this feud continued from one generation to another generation. The main cause for such occurrence was mainly for three reasons, *jar, joru and zamin* [money, woman and land], there would be court cases which lingered on for years and years. There could be eight to ten murders because of one of these reasons. The only one to be benefited from these happenings was the lawyers.

After the ceremonies were over, Niranjan's sisters Harjit and Gian Kaur along with Tripta sat on the sofa and chatted for some time, then decided to retire for sleep. Darshan Kaur had already gone to sleep because she was dead tired handling the hectic activities during the day. Hardly anything came to their mind to chitchat while sitting on the sofa. These rustic women were never really comfortable sitting on the sofa, and Tripta was too self conscious to start a topic. They went to the bed room where four cots were laid down for them to retire for the night.

"Come to my bed for a little while as I am not feeling sleepy," Gian Kaur said. They went to her bed.

"What sort of a man is our brother? He is not comfortable in communicating with even his own sisters. Today when I asked him 'how do you like my new necklace?' Without even looking at it, he simply said, it's beautiful."

"Looking at your necklace also meant looking at your . . . you know what," giggled Manjit, "And they are so big."

"I am not going to cut them for your satisfaction."

They started chuckling by putting their palms to cover their mouth, lest others should get disturbed in their sleep.

"Shame on you, Harjit! You speak out no matter what comes to your mind," said Gian Kaur.

"Is he bashful with you too, Manjit?"

"Bashful with me? *Meri jutti!!!* [My Shoe, means who cares] You can't imagine what he does to me in bed. He breaks my bones . . . and crushes mine you know what," said Manjit with mock annoyance.

There was a loud laughter, then realizing that it was unbecoming of them to laugh like that in the dead of night. They altogether closed their mouths with their palms but continued giggling.

"What is happening?" Shouted an old man sleeping in the court yard, "Let others sleep."

They kept quiet for a while. And then suddenly, Gian Kaur asked, "And how was your first night, Manjit?"

"It continued from evening till morning. In between, there were some intervals to normalize the breathing, and some rest, but no sleep."

She had asked her about this question umpteen times and always got the same reply and she always enjoyed listening to it.

"And what about now . . . ?."

"The shop is open seven days a week, except on govt. holidays," promptly replied Manjit,

"And what is it now in your case?"

Harjit dramatically heaved a sigh and then said, "There are more rest days than working days . . . I always have to open the batting when I am in the mood. At first I excite him and then I refuse him and he starts begging for it."

"And then *tan tana tan*," Manjit teased her.

"Of course."

"What about you, Gian Kaur?"

"I am not going to talk about it . . . . you shameless *randis!!* [whores]," replied Gian Kaur, "it is meant to be performed, not to be openly talked about."

"*Wad bhandey wich* [enter into the utensil, it connotes go to hell]."

"You have already littered six children, when is the next one due?" Asked Manjit putting her one hand on Gian Kauri's belly.

"I think the land is no more fertile," Harjit added.

Gian Kaur gave her a gentle slap and abused her.

"*Kutti randiey* [You bitchy whore]!"

"And what happened on your first night, Harjit?"

"For the first three nights my man was out even before opening his score."

"And on the fourth night . . . ?" Manjit queried.

"On the fourth night when he was playing so well, and I was bucking him up, suddenly he was out before scoring his first half century, but some of his shots were just fantastic."

"And later on . . ."

"With practice he became a good dependable batsman, but he could never guess that it was I who was coaching him slyly," replied Harjit with a wink.

"*Hun bas wi karo, khasma noo khanieyo* [Better stop it now, you eaters of husbands]."

When she was a child, Harjit used to play cricket with the boys of her *mohalla* [street] and she really played well, but at the age of ten she was forbidden to play cricket with the boys, and the other girls in the area had no liking for cricket, still her obsession with cricket never subsided.

After a pause Manjit asked, "Harjit, what do men talk about when they have a sitting like this?"

"The same as we do."

"*Hai,* these men are really shameless!" Gian Kaur heaved a sigh.

Suddenly, everybody started yawning. They went to their respective beds to sleep, without wishing anybody 'Good Night'. It was not the custom to do so. It was thought unnecessary.

Tripta was not feeling sleepy at all. She started missing her husband and their days of blissful married life very badly, although she had become asexual and had suppressed her carnal desires. She started floating in the world of romance and ecstasies, unmindful of her surroundings.

But deep down, she felt miserable and full of remorse.

After some dillydallying, Harbans Lal finally agreed to meet Sudan, after five days of that incident. Harbans Lal told him that he could guess why he had come to meet him, and it was on the behest of the Chief Engineer. Sudan nodded in affirmative.

"You have come with a proposal to do compromise."

"You are absolutely right."

Harbans Lal told him that he would be ready for a compromise only if it suited him. It must be an honourable one. He also told him that he would pay him 25% more of what he had been paying him earlier and only 50% of agreed payment to the C.E., and not even a penny more. And above all, he must stop his stupefying visits once for all.

"He won't come again," assured Sudan. "Between you and me, he is simply terrified of you."

"That suits me fine."

Then Sudan told him that he has come to tell him which he could not even think of.

Harbans kept quiet, he thought Sudan was up to a new trick.

"Actually I don't want any commission at all."

"Why be it so? I hope you are also not scared of me."

"But you won't tell them that I am not getting any money from you."

"You want to switch over to honesty living, but you don't want to be known honest man?

It is surprising me."

Then Sudan told him how they were helped through thick and thin by his father's boss Triple M and Uncle Niranjan Singh. Today all three of them; his younger brother and sister are well placed because of their selfless help; and his mother's single-minded devotion towards her children.

"So, there are Sikhs in your family. I do like Sikhs because they are large hearted."

"Actually my father and my uncle Sardar Niranjan Singh had never met. His wife Sardarni Manjit Kaur and my mother became very close friends, more like sisters. And our own relatives never bothered for us. Uncle was like a patriarch for us; very humble and a man of few words. Do you know he was 6'2" tall, very strongly built but very shy, especially when he had to face a woman, be it his own close relation. Such an adorable character! Today, if he asks me to jump from a mountain; I will do it *Harbansia*. BELIEVE ME . . . . our own relatives never really cared for us and when we became well-placed, they tried to renew the relations, but I said get fucked by a dog! We don't want to have any bond with you. Although I did not use these words like that but it connoted the same meaning. My mother supported me."

"God does send his angels to you, if you deserve it. I and my dearest friend Vijay are also very close to each other the same way. Both of us were helped by an unknown Christian, who himself was facing terrible financial crunch and they never showed it. They were like angels to us. There were others also who gave us love and care. My own cousin humiliated me and I beat him and that is a long story, I will narrate it some other time. What a man . . . what a man your uncle was! I am ready to kiss the very earth at which he treads. If such a man asks me to stand on one leg all the night; I will do it and with a smile on my face."

Sudan embraced him and kissed him on his cheek.

Suddenly Harbans Lal shouted, "Oh *munshia*, go to the market and bring the best of the food and also for yourself and in plenty."

Sudan entreated him that they would sit together some other day because he had an urgent work.

"Sudan *Bhutni dia* [son of a ghost] . . . I will break legs of yours if you go without meals . . . try to do it and you will see the fun . . . You don't know this Harbans Lal of Mintgumery. He always pronounced Montgomery as Mintgummery.

It is typical of Punjabis to show their deep love and affection by abusing and threatening of physical harm. They are basically very emotional and simply can't hide their emotions.

"And you *double Bhutni dia* . . . I am going to stay even if you change your mind."

And they laughed like kids.

After third peg Harbans Lal was suddenly nostalgic.

"There were riots, disturbances everywhere. Anybody could kill anybody else, but life in our village was very peaceful and normal. Hamid Ali Khan was the *Lambardar* [the village head] of our village and his son Rabba was my closest friend. Khan Sahib was well built and of medium height. He was amiable, generous, and full of humour, but if anybody dared to hurt his pride, he pounced back like a ferocious tiger, which are the characteristics of a Pathan. Their families were socially close to each other. He was very smart and down to earth man. Khan Uncle decided that during day time, five men will guard the village by taking rounds of the entire territory of their village against any untoward happening. And likewise, seven to eight men were to do this job during night. They were armed with guns, swords and cudgels. Nothing untoward happened for about twenty days. The day vigil was almost abandoned but the night vigil continued. People in the village used to boast 'nobody dare raise his black eye against our village and if anybody dared to do so, we would gouge their eyes and put them in the sister fuckers arse.' The night vigil was reduced to six but usually four or five turned up . . . . on that eventful night only three turned up."

His father lamented, "Why only three . . . . and there is not even a single gun man." He was in the habit of counting them and then reporting it to the Lambardar as desired by him. He thought of reporting it to the Lambardar there and then but his wife suggested better do it in the morning. He agreed.

During the dead of night, the three of them on guard, surmised that they were unnecessarily wasting their time,

"Let's go home and please our wives."

Quietly they left.

It was a foreboding for a catastrophe to happen.

Out of the blue, Harbans Lal started hitting his forehead, as if in a delirium. "No . . . No . . . I must forget it."

And he kept quiet. They continued drinking in silence. After sometime, Harbans told him that it was better that he did not talk any further about this tragedy.

As a matter of fact he had never talked to anybody about his heart-breaking story, even to his closest friend Vijay. Whenever he recalled these past events, he would become gloomy for days together.

Sudan could understand everything, he caught Harbans Lal's hand and said, "Better, we don't."

Their drinking continued and Sudan started talking shop so that the conversation could continue.

All of a sudden, Harbans started talking about his village. This time there was a glow on his face.

"Life in the village was wonderful. I used to be very mischievous, always full of pranks. I was the best sprinter in the entire village. No one could ever beat me. We used to climb up the mango and guava trees and relish the fruit and when the owner came rushing towards us, we used to jump down and run away. Surprisingly, I never got hurt and when the owner of these trees complained to my mother, she always said, 'Don't worry brother, when he comes home, I am going to twitch his ears and make them red.' And she paid him back more than the amount of his losses. That is why our mischief was never reported to my father. And when he left, she always chuckled, 'He is my *Krishna Kanhaiya*, he is bound to do some mischief. But why he has this aversion to butter??'

Of course, she always chided him when he came home, though mildly."

"And then there was this girl, Gulabo."

"Gulab [rose]?"

"No, Gulabo, she was named so by the boys because of her rosy cheeks. I have altogether forgotten her real name."

"I used to pick up fights with other kids . . . but never with Gulabo . . . We really always clicked. Whenever I called her 'Gulabo', she never minded but if anyone else called her so, she retaliated fiercely. When she was about nine or ten years old, her father prevented her from playing with the boys."

He finished rest of his peg in one gulp.

"It happened a few days before I left my village, for never to put my foot there again. I met Gulabo after many days, as she often remained confined to her home. Just to start conversation, I happened to ask, how is your school going on?"

"I have stopped going to school. Father does not allow it."

"But why so?"

"He says I have grown youthful."

"Grown youthful?"

At that time I could not understand it. I was too naive.

She said, "Even for the summer, it is too hot." And unexpectedly she removed her Chunni from her chest, and wrapped it around her head and smiled coyly.

"Indeed she had grown quite full of youth. I looked at her young breasts like a thief. They were small and rounded and so beautiful. My legs started trembling in excitement. I felt the urge to fondle them, but lacked guts. Her breasts started heaving; she looked deeply into my eyes. I felt mesmerized. Instinctively she held my hand and smiled and said, you know boys and girls in the village go to the sugarcane fields stealthily." She was silent for a few moments and then added, "When nobody is around."

I was really puzzled, I asked, "Why?"

"To wrestle together, you fool." She giggled and ran away.

"I stood there for quite some time trying hard to understand what she meant."

"So she was your first love."

"Perhaps . . . . of course, yes."

"And later on, did you have any . . . any other girl friend in your life?"

"She was only one I could do converse easily . . . a few girls really liked me, but I always developed cold feet . . . . as a young boy whenever I tried to talk to a girl my ears go red . . . . and what about you?"

"I had been quite a sportsman and my first sexual experience was with a woman of forty. Her husband was a drunkard. She told me that he had become useless in the bed, as he has lost his current."

"And where did you do it at first?"

"In her own home."

"What about her children?"

"Yes, they were standing there and clapping when I was on top of her! . . . . To them she was a very religious and pious lady. She fasted on every Tuesday."

Both of them had a hearty laugh.

"Actually they had gone to their school."

They had finished the entire bottle and decided that enough was enough.

They continued embracing each other and "okay bye, see you . . . . good night." They continued doing so, then ultimately his faithful driver dragged them to the car to drop them home. On the way, Harbans said,

"Don't worry Sudan . . . . my driver brings your home to your car in the morning."

On reaching home, when his wife opened the door, she could not notice that Harbans was trying to stand erect but all in vain, as the driver had shielded him with his bulk. He told his wife that the Sahib had taken his meals in a party thrown in his honour, and was feeling very thirsty and asked her to make *shikanjvi* for him with lot of sugar in it. This he did as he needed to gain time. He almost had to drag him to his room, and hurriedly took off his shoes and socks and made him lie on the bed. When she brought the *shikanjvi*, he took it from her.

"I will give it to him. Sahib has to give me some important instructions for the morning assignments, and in private."

With great difficulty, he managed to change his clothes. He himself drank the *shikanjv*i and left.

Next day he was generously rewarded by Harbans Lal for the services rendered.

Sudan's' wife did not speak to him for seven days.

CHAPTER 6

When Harbans landed at Amritsar, he had high fever and was shivering. He slept on the roadside by making the bundle of his clothes as a pillow and he kept one hand in his pocket where he had kept his money, lest somebody should steal it.

When he woke up, he found himself lying on a cot. He just couldn't remember how he came to this strange house. He hurriedly put his hand in the pocket and to his relief the money was there, intact. In the meantime, a lady came with a cup of tea and when she saw him half sitting and half lying, she started praying, 'Oh, *Issa Masih* [Jesus Christ] your compassion for the sick and the poorest of poor is great. You are the true Saviour of mankind, O' Lord, I had this faith that the poor boy is going to be alright, when he is under the care of the greatest of Physician. O'Lord. Glory be to thy name. Amen.'

She told him that her husband found him lying on a pavement on the roadside and moaning deeply and seemed to be almost unconscious. He brought him home and he had regained consciousness after about ten hours. He had a temperature of 104 degrees. *Actually it was 106 degrees; she lied about it as she did not want to scare the young hapless boy.* At that very time, her husband came carrying some fruits. On finding him recovered, he also profusely thanked the Lord Jesus Christ. He introduced himself as Kenny George and his wife Maria.

They had two children, who had gone to the school. Kenny was a painter by profession who had more off days than working days during these days of turmoil. In that era of disturbances, people like him had scant work. Maria worked as a nurse-maid in a local hospital. They had fallen on bad days and were finding it very hard to make both ends meet. They were living in a small two room house near *Pingal Wada* in Ram Talai. The house had no living room.

Pingal Wada was established by a saintly man, where lepers and people with vulnerable skin diseases are taken care of, who were neglected or abandoned by their own kith and kin, were treated and looked after. People of Amritsar donate generously to Pingal Wada; apart from money; clothes, bed sheets, blankets and quilts etc. There are people who donate some money regularly every month. Lately, another *Pingal Wada* has been established near Putli Ghar.

Harbans got up and told them that he intended to go to the house of a close relation who lived in Chatiwind. They firmly told him that they won't let him go until he had fully recovered and out of danger; otherwise their Lord, their Saviour would be disappointed with them.

He recovered after four days and wanted to go, but Maria insisted that he must stay with them for two to three days more, lest his ailment relapsed.

After two days, Kenny dropped him on his bicycle at Chatiwind. During this journey he had to stop five to six times to fix the chain which slipped when he paddled a little too hard. It was quite an old bicycle.

With great difficulty he was able to find the house of his cousin, as he did not know the house number and it took him almost an hour to locate it.

After he found the house, he knocked at the door with great excitement, in those days very few people had door bells outside their houses. Somebody shouted from inside the house, '*Vey*, who is there?' It was some lady's voice.

"It's me, Harbans."

Then a lady came and asked him, 'who he was' by opening the door a few inches. He could only see a part of her face.

"I have come to meet brother, Roshan Lal." The lady went inside without caring to reply to him. She told her husband that some boy had come to meet him. He seemed to be a refugee and looked like an *uthaigira* [shop-lifter].

The man came out and closed the door from outside. "Yes!?"

"Namaste *Bhaji* [brother]."

He neither invited him to come inside the house nor said anything. He just kept mum.

"It seems that you have not recognized me."

"No, I've not," he replied sternly in an unfriendly tone.

"I am Harbans . . . Harbans Lal."

"Oh, *Atcha Atcha* . . . Right now I am going out for an important work . . . . in which refugee camp are you staying? I will definitely come to meet you. Leave the address with my wife, after I go."

And without waiting for a reply, he gently closed the door and went inside.

Harbans was taken aback and stood there for quite some time dumbfounded.

He remembered his *Taya* [father's elder brother] used to visit them with their entire family. He would himself stay there for two to three days only, but his family always stayed there for a month or so. His parents always treated them very nicely, thinking that they were part of the family, Roshan Lal was the first born son in their paternal family, because of that he was always treated more favourably than the others. He was also special favourite of his mother, who dotted on him. They had not visited them for the last two years because of the disturbances.

Harbans was seething with anger, the way he treated him indifferently. He was his only hope in this alien city. He searched here and there for a stone and found one. He threw the stone with full force, striking the door. There was a loud bang.

Roshan Lal came out rushing.

"How dare you behave like a stray dog!" He yelled at Harbans Lal.

"Your father owed my father three hundred rupees . . . . I have come to collect that. If you decide to pay me right now, I am ready to forget about the interest." Harbans Lal shouted at the top of his voice, as he wanted the neighbours to listen to that, which no Punjabi would like, as it goes against his honour.

"In today's conditions . . . . in these days of disturbances, nobody owes anybody any money," he replied firmly but in a low voice.

"Then I have an important message for you, come near me, please." Harbans Lal pleaded with mock politeness.

Roshan Lal was relieved that his cousin was not going to pick up a quarrel over this money matter, otherwise his neighbours, who were according to him, mean and petty minded, would gather around and start enjoying the fun. It would be a great merriment for those wretched people. He came close to him, and said in a domineering tone, "Whatever you want to say, do it fast. I've no time to waste."

Harbans closed his fist and gave him a hard blow on his jaw and then kicked him on his balls.

Roshan Lal started writhing in great pain. He looked around, but no one was there to see him treated in such a humiliating manner. He staggered back home, trying to suppress his moaning. Nobody had seen him beaten by a boy much younger than him, was his only consolation.

Impulsively, he ran away from there, apprehending his people may not beat him up to take the revenge. He started towards his home . . . . *His home . . . . was it his home? For the present, he could consider Kenny uncles' home his only available shelter.* It was at a distance of about three miles from Chatiwind. After running for about two furlongs, he stopped running, when he became sure that no body was following him, he started walking leisurely. He felt tired and lifeless, energy had literally sapped out of his limbs. He dragged his feet towards home. He felt thirsty and hungry. He decided not to go to any eatery as he wanted to save money. He had to think hard about the future. He drank water from a *chabil* on the way.

If they were demeaning people like Roshan Lal, there were also kind-hearted generous people who offered free food to the destitute displaced people; with compassion and friendliness. There was no dearth of such people in Amritsar. The Amritsarias are by and large full of love and compassion. He stopped to eat from one of such places, but decided against it. It would have been at the cost of his self-respect.

He reached home and pushed open the door. In those days, generally people did not bolt their homes from inside during day light, with the exception of the rich. He lied on the cot and looked at the ceiling with dazed eyes.

Kenny uncle came to him. He was in great spirits. "You are so lucky for me my son that you can't imagine what luck you have brought to this house. It is because of you and with the blessings of Lord Jesus that you are like a good omen to our house, to bring us out of financial predicament. You won't believe Harbans, what I am going to tell you . . . I have got the contract to repaint and rewrite the boards of an entire market . . . . They have given me two hundred fifty rupees as advance." And he showed Harbans the currency notes with the enthusiasm of a child.

Vijay, who later on became Harbans' partner and closest friend, was already there. Kenny also treated him like a son. He was also a refugee like Harbans whom Kenny had helped to settle down.

"Then, there is going to be a treat," said Vijay.

"Definitely, there is going to be . . . And it will be right now."

They went to the market and entered *a halwai's* shop, and Kenny shouted, "Two plates of *samosas* each."

They relished the *samosas* with lot of *channas* and *chatni*, especially Harbans as he was feeling very hungry. After they cleared the plates, Harbans said, "Chacha, you won't mind if I have one plate more, they are so tasty."

"Chacha will mind, if you don't have another plate."

After they had eaten the other plate of samosas and were having tea, Vijay asked, "What are you doing at present?"

"Nothing."

Vijay had instantly liked him, and he offered him to stay with him. It was to serve two purposes, one was to kill loneliness and the other was that he would feel more secure. He told Harbans that he was paying Rs. four as monthly rent, but he would charge him only rupees one and a half as the latter was without work.

"No, it should be fifty-fifty. Why should you pay more?"

Vijay told him that as he was elder to him. So, he was supposed to be obeyed by him, as per the Punjabi tradition.

CHAPTER 7

Next day Vijay and Harbans went to the vegetables and fruits wholesale market. Harbans surveyed the entire market before buying different kinds of fruits. Vijay suggested to him not to buy those of highest quality, because if he was not able to sell the entire purchase, he was going to lose lot of money. He added that he was not suggesting that he should buy some cheap quality stuff. It was better to adopt the middle-of-the-road path, neither too costly nor too cheap.

Harbans Lal argued that he wanted to create a reputation for himself as a vendor, who always brought top quality fruits and vegetables. And his rates would be reasonable and he would never overcharge some and undercharge others. That was how his father had established his business.

After making their purchases, they hired a Rickshaw and Vijay asked the Rickshaw-puller to take them to a posh colony, as only there Harbans would be able to sell them.

"To which place?"

"Choice is yours."

"Are you new to the city?"

"Yes, brother."

"Then we take you to Lawrence road area."

After about ten minutes of the drive Harbans felt thirsty and asked the Rickshaw-puller if he could get some water to drink from some place.

"*Lao ji*, then we take you to the *Thandi Khui* [a well of cold water]. It is not water but *Amrit* [nectar]. The one who has not drunk its water, has not been to Amritsar at all. The well is situated on the Mall Road, opposite the road is a beautiful garden called *Cumpany Bagh* [Garden]." It is how people pronounced Company.

The three of them drank the water.

"What a taste . . . it is really Amrit," said both of them. It gave them feelings of spirituality.

"Well, this is the place where I am going to start my business."

Harbans gave him two rupees as the fare. He returned him eight annas of his own. Harbans gave him two bananas to eat.

"How much?"

"Free!!"

"This can't happen. It is the *Bhoni time* [first purchase]. *Atcha*, here is *a pouli* [four annas]."

He sat with them for a few minutes, they asked for each other's names. Jinder, the Rickshaw puller told them that the water of this well remains cold throughout the summer, that is why its name is *Thandi Khui.*

"It is all because of the blessings of the great Gurus." And he left paddling and singing a Punjabi song of a hit Punjabi movie.

By 7 pm, Harbans was able to sell all the fruits. He had made a profit of Rs. 6 and he was in great spirits. If somebody haggled over the price, his well-thought of standard reply was 'I can give you one guava or one banana free, but the price remains the same.' Some took it, but some refused it.

Within days his reputation spread. His regular customers just asked about the rates and some just wanted to know the total amount. He always spoke in English with the rich and the educated class. Girls always liked to buy fruits from him, because of his pleasant manners and good looks. Just after a few days he got a two-wheeled cart on hire basis at the rate of eight annas per day. Soon, he started buying fruits worth 50 rupees, and it never happened that he could not sell all his purchase.

He also asked Vijay to start selling vegetables sitting by his side, as he was earning just rupees two to three by ironing the clothes, but he was content with his meager income and he declined politely. This made him think that Vijay was hiding something from him as he always complained that his hand ached for ironing the clothes, yet he said 'no' to his proposal. He was disappointed with him, but he kept it to himself.

Vijay had one small steel trunk and he always kept it locked. He never even once opened it in the presence of his room-mate. He always kept his money in the trunk, whereas, Harbans kept all his money under the pillow. Vijay never saw him counting his money in the morning. One day he requested Vijay to keep some of his savings in his trunk, but he remained quiet for some time and then said, "Let's go to the market to purchase a trunk, as you badly need one." And there and then, they went to the market and bought a trunk which was of a bigger size than the one Vijay was having.

By and by Harbans started liking the city of Amritsar and he was even fascinated by the narrow streets of this city, but not Vijay. He always liked open areas. And he missed his home town Sialkot terribly. Harbans liked and loved this city, though he always missed his village. People were bubbly with a glow on their faces. They simply loved good food and good clothes. They knew how to live and enjoy life, and had positive outlook towards life. If one wants to live nicely, he should befriend an Amritsaria and learn from him. Surprisingly, most of them pronounced their city as 'Ambersar' and a local was not called an Amritsaria but an Ambersaria. Punjabis by nature economize the use of their lungs power and change the word the way it can be easily pronounced with minimum effort. So Lyallpur [renamed as Faisalabad] was pronounced as Lailpur, Lahore as Lhore. Likewise station, lorry, box, mandir, exercise are spoken as tation, laari, bux, mandar and excise. Even in names, Satish becomes Stish, Sumit as Sumat, Vinod as Vnod.

The Sikhs being a marshal race have an obsession with army ranks. So, their sons are named as Kaptan Singh, Major Singh, Kernail Singh, Jernail Singh and Fauja Singh. Lieutenant and Brigadier ore left out, as speaking out these words puts strain on their jaws.

After them staying together for two months, Vijay saw their luggage lying outside their rented house and a big lock on their door. In his bewilderment, he could not spot his trunk. He felt as if life had been taken out of his body. He almost started running towards his home. He felt relieved when he saw the trunk lying behind Harbans Lal's legs. He felt resuscitated.

"What happened?"

"We have been chucked out."

"But what is the reason?"

"The landlord wanted to raise the rent."

"How much increase did he want?"

"By rupees two."

"It is nothing."

"It is 25 % more."

"But for God's sake, it is only rupees two and you should have agreed."

"I said 'big no', it is exploitation and I never let anybody exploit me."

"It is fucking no exploitation." For the first time, Vijay had used an invective.

"It is."

"At least you should have consulted me."

"This Harbans Lal of Mintgummery not consults even his fore fathers when he taken a right decision." He replied in English to show Vijay that if he can speak English, so he can also.

Just then a Tonga came and just when they were putting their luggage in it, Vijay asked, "Where are our cots?"

"I have sold them."

"Oh, God! You have really gone mad."

Vijay was seething with anger and he wanted to beat him.

"Some where."

"But for heaven's sake, where is your bloody some where?"

"I am not going to tell you . . . . you are not behaving properly."

Vijay thought that there was no use of arguing with this asinine rustic boor, so he kept mum.

On the way, they did not utter even a syllable and Vijay kept his sullen face bowed down.

The tonga reached near a neat and clean street.

Harbans started walking towards a house along with his luggage, Vijay languidly followed him and Harbans climbed the stairs of the house and opened the door. It was a one room accommodation with a separate bathroom and a latrine. Punjabis in those days could not bathe in the same room which was also used for a toilet. They simply could not stand it.

"This is our new home." Harbans bowed.

Vijay hugged Harbans and started jumping with joy.

"It is simply princely accommodation, but why did you not let me know it beforehand?"

"It was an impulsive decision . . . . and you take so much time to take a decision, your every step is taken with caution."

"That is true."

They celebrated their house warming by drinking a bottle of beer and surprisingly, it was Vijay's decision. It was the first time in their lives that they had taken any alcoholic beverage.

They felt drunk, did not have their meals and slept.

In the morning, when he got up, there was a smile on his face. Harbans had already left for the *mandi,* he always reached the *mandi* [market] before 5 am, otherwise the fruit of best quality was not available.

In the evening, when he came home, Vijay was already waiting for him. Harbans Lal shouted at him to come down, as he had seen that the lights of their room were on. He had brought a table and two chairs. They took them upstairs.

"How much did it cost?"

"It is none of your business."

"I must know . . . I am going to pay my share . . . ?"

"You can't afford it." Harbans Interrupted.

"I can well afford it."

"It is full stop. No further discussion."

"Okay. Now it is my turn to say, full stop."

He opened the sideboard. There was a stove, a bottle of kerosene oil, some crockery, glass tumblers and some utensils.

"From where did you get the money? I guess you took loan from someone. I know it well that you can't afford. I must pay all the money."

"You said 'full stop', now abide by it."

Then Vijay prepared tea for both of them and put some *namkeen* in a plate. In the mean time, Harbans was thinking that he would find some modus operandi to make the payment.

While taking tea, Vijay asked him how much was the rent for their accommodation. He replied that it was 15 rupees per month.

"Just by paying eleven rupees more, we could live nicely . . . why didn't I think of it before . . . . I am such a fool."

"But you will be paying just rupees four."

"Why so?"

"Simple. With your meager income you can't afford."

Vijay spoke after a long pause, "You know it that I never open my trunk in your presence. There is some reason, why I do it so."

"Lately it also came to my mind, but it hardly matters."

Vijay kept silent for some time and then started narrating his story.

"Just listen, before we boarded the train from Sialkot for Amritsar, my father gave separately some money to each member of our family. It was his idea that if all of us survive, it is great, otherwise the one who survives must have some money for his basic needs for some days, and he should not feel helpless for want of it. He also managed to book seats for us in different compartments, so that in case we are attacked, all of us don't get killed without any survivor. There was so much rush in the train, the seat reservation had no meaning. I am going to cut out the details, it is so painful to talk about it. In the entire train, there were only fifteen people including me who had survived. Sometimes, I wonder why they did not kill the driver and the guard of the train, because after the raiders had their feast of the murders, the train continued moving."

"Perhaps, they wanted more chances for loot and murders in the train."

"Perhaps, well, I had two thousand rupees with me."

"Two thousand rupees, that is quite an amount!? That is why you don't open your trunk when I am present."

"I had successfully camouflaged that I was dead, actually, our entire family had rupees twenty thousand in total. Twenty minutes after the marauders had left, an idea struck my mind, I started searching the luggage and the pockets of those who were dead, honestly thinking, that there was hardly any chance that this money will go to the coffers of the government, it will be grabbed by unscrupulous people and there has never been dearth of such people in our country. Till today I have no qualms of what I did on that day. I collected another seven thousand rupees, if I found gold I did not touch it, lest it may create problems for me later on . . . . by nature I am a very cautious person . . . . I stopped this searching business thinking that I have already too much money in my possession to handle, and with too much money I may not be harassed by the police. They may even deprive of all my money. I put portions of this money in all my pockets and the major part of it I put in my shoes. When the train reached Amritsar, I was helped by the police to search for my family . . . . when they found that I have lost all of my family members, they were very sympathetic with me. As I had some wounds and bruises, they took me to a hospital, but before that they gave me food to eat, it was nice food and they refused to let me pay for it. I was taken to a hospital for the treatment of my wounds. I was allotted a bed in the general ward and there I met Maria George, and I told her that I am not going to occupy the bed. She was astonished, as it was very difficult to find a bed in any hospital as they were already over crowded. I told her that I have a close relative who lived in Tarn Taran and he was a doctor. I would prefer to be treated by him."

"Tarn Taran, where is that?"

"As if I know, I had just heard the name . . . . how, I don't know, may be because of its famous Gurudwara and I entreated her to find an accommodation for me just for one day, saying that you are just like my mother and even lied that she resembled her. She made a sign of the holy cross and began praying for me and then she gave me her address and a letter for her husband."

"Did you go to Tarn Taran?"

"No, I did not even know where Tarn Taran is."

"When Maria aunty returned home in the evening, I fell on her feet and apologized for telling her a lie, and admitted that I had no relative living in Tarn Taran and told her that I did not want to remain in the hospital, as the atmosphere over there was so nauseating. I confessed and even cried."

"Take it easy, there are people who prefer death than to be in a hospital."

"I had fake tears when I was crying, it was all acting . . . . suddenly I started thinking . . . . ousted from our own homes . . . our own land, the land of our ancestors . . . . it has become an alien land . . . . why so . . . . catching a train to go to a place which never had any connection in our lives . . . . family being murdered . . . . my parents, my brother and my sister, who did not even know these rogues, had no enmity with them, had done them no harm . . . . murdered for what reason, for what cause, for what purpose . . . the one and only fault was belonging to another religion. My heart got burst and I cried out."

"I can understand that." Harbans said stoically.

"And they started consoling me whole heartedly, even their son and daughter enthusiastically joined them in this venture. I felt touched. That gave me a purpose to live, and I saw my brother and sister in the young kids. Maria aunty hugged me with motherly compassion; Remember, you called me mother in the morning, the Lord wanted it to be so . . . . it is he who sent you to us. He is the true Saviour."

"I stayed with them for ten days. Aunty herself took care of my wounds, cleaned and bandaged them; her hands had such a cooling effect. I sensed clearly that they were just able to eke out their living. So, one day when aunty had left for the hospital and kids had gone to the school, and when I felt that Kenny uncle was going out, I stealthily put a hundred rupee note outside the door and lied down on the cot pretending that I was asleep; I even snored mildly, did it mildly so that they don't suspect when they don't find me snoring again. After he had left, I went outside; the note was gone and it made me happy and for the second time in my life after we had to abandon our home that I thanked God."

"When was the first time?"

"When I saw the dead body of my sister with badly wounded hands, her clothes were intact . . . . she was young, beautiful and had just turned fifteen . . . . I felt unburdened, it was a great relief and I thanked God. Please don't ask me to explain."

"Please don't, I can understand . . . I was not that lucky . . . saw her naked . . . completely . . . my own sister . . . in our own house . . . she had killed one of them . . . must had gotten her chance, her two hands were lying scattered on the floor. I decided to stay in Pakistan till I find the killers of my entire family, even if I had to become a Musalman. Religion meant nothing to me. I had only one aim in my life to kill those bastards . . . . And I found them, and butchered them with their own sword . . . . and . . . . and . . . . let us stop all this . . . . its reminiscence kills my very soul."

They kept quiet for a long time, then went to the market, bought bottles of beer and packed food. This was how they got used to beer whenever they had bouts of nostalgia.

While drinking they discussed only their future plans to start some business, as they had plenty of money in their possession. There was no further mention of their melancholic past.

In the morning, Harbans did go to the whole sale market, but did not feel like buying anything. His past was haunting him and he was in a nostalgic mood. The unbearable anguish weighed heavily on his mind. He tried hard to forget all about it, but just could not.

On that ill-fated day, he was sleeping on the roof of his next door neighbour. In rows after rows, the houses in the village had joined roofs with a common wall. It was done to show closeness and solidarity with one's neighbours, besides it was economical. He and his friend Lalli always alternately slept on each other's roof. They loved to chat with each other before going to sleep. Lalli often talked about girls, which used to enhance Harbans' curiosity. They always had a glass of milk before going to sleep, as the mothers in the village considered that it had two fold advantage, it is good for having a sound sleep and it makes a man healthy.

Earlier his entire family slept on the roof, but when his sister was growing into a filled up lassie, his parents decided to sleep downstairs. The youngest Guddi always slept with her mother.

At midnight, Harbans felt the urge to pee and when he went down, he saw the most horrible and blood-curdling scene of his life, which was going to haunt him all his life. His mother and father were lying slain; huddled together, and his sister naked, raped and killed and her two hands were lying bleeding on the floor. Also lying on the floor was the body of a stranger, a bearded man with a shaven head. The two hands on the floor made it clear that his sister had killed the villain when she got her chance, obviously when he expected it the least. He heard some strange voices coming from the last room.

He hurriedly went upstairs and pushed Lalli vigorously, "Wake up, wake up."

Lalli, while rubbing his eyes with his hands to get out of his slumber, asked. "What happened?"

"Our entire family has been killed . . . . and we must take our revenge."

Lalli asked him to hide in his house, and first of all they must save their lives, but he was unrelenting. He even dragged him to come down but Harbans pushed him away. Lalli ran down stairs to his house.

He was thinking fast, what should be his next step, come what may, he was going to take his revenge. *'I am not going to spare these loathsome rascals.'* He came to the edge of the roof to have an inspection of the situation and found a woman clad in a burqa outside their door, he could immediately judge that she must had camouflaged his parents to open the door. He picked up a heavy stone and struck it on her head with full force and she shrieked with pain. People had started keeping stones in their homes and on their roof tops as a first line of defense.

On hearing her cries, two men came out of the house and saw her bleeding profusely and moaning in great pain; she put a piece of cloth in her mouth to subdue the sound of her crying in order not to wake up the neighbours. One was a hefty strongly built man and the other was tall and lanky. Harbans hurled a few stones on them also and then jumped from one roof to the other roof and they chased him from the ground level with naked swords in their hands and also they were carrying bundles in their armpits. It continued for quite some time and now the three of them were at a distance from the village. When they could not catch him, they put down their bundles, so that they could run fast. Harbans could see that they lacked his stamina, so to tire them he decided to run in a zigzag manner. They thought that they were not being able to capture him because of the burden of their sword, whereas the boy had no load with him to carry. Therefore, they kept their swords aside and ran with full force to get hold of him, but they were no match for him.

This is what he wanted, to discard their swords. Though, he was totally devastated, yet his mind was working clearly and fast. He further decided to enrage them to make their minds befuddled. Thus he shouted, "Your mothers must have slept with dogs to give birth to you depraved minds."

"You infidel, you will see what lesson I am going to teach you, better than what I taught your sister. Ha, I deflowered her when she was dying, she had to pay the price for killing my *jija* [sister's husband]." The hefty man shouted back.

"You must have been trained thus by your naked sisters and mothers, and in full public view, for them to clap in appreciation."

"*Madar chod* [mother fucker], I am first going to sodomise you, before I cut you into pieces and I will present your head to my sister as a trophy."

"You must have learnt from your father when he made your sisters bend down to have the fun."

They continued running and abusing each other for another half an hour. All three of them were out of breath then. The two marauders sat on the ground to even their breathing and discussed with each other how to entrap him. They lied down to revitalize their energy.

This was the moment for Harbans Lal. He dashed past them with full steam. They were bewildered by his move. They immediately got up, and chased him with all their might, but he was way ahead of them.

AND WHEN THEY SAW THE SWORD IN HIS HAND, they retreated and took to their heels to save their lives.

Harbans reached near the hefty man first and entangled his right foot in that man's left foot and he fell on the ground and then he kicked him hard on his buttocks.

He began pulling his own ears, "Please forgive me this time . . . . please . . . . please . . . . I swear I will never do it again."

"You won't be able to, this I assure you." And he killed him savagely.

He then started searching for the other person, who had hidden himself in the nearby cotton fields, Harbans knew that it was the only place where he could find him. After about twenty minutes of his searching efforts, he could hear the heavy breathing, as it was dead of night, a slight sound could not escape one's ears. He cautiously moved towards there from where this sound was coming and after another fifteen minutes of search, he finally found him and dragged him out by pulling his hair.

"I did nothing . . . . he would have killed me if I had stopped him . . . . he is a butcher by profession . . . he is a number one *madar chod* . . . . everybody calls him Zalim Khan because of his cruelty . . . . I am totally innocent . . . . Please bestow your mercy on me . . . . I have a large family to support."

Harbans was listening to him patiently because he wanted to know if anyone else was involved in it, may be someone from his own village. He asked him with affected politeness, "On whose instigation did you come to our house, just tell me that?"

"It was only Zalim Khan . . . . One should never have a friend like him . . . please show your kindness on me . . . . that was my big mistake . . . . you can have all my things."

"You have the guts to say that, All My things! Wah! Bravo! I am sure you will never do such a mistake again." He beheaded him with one stroke.

He had one more score to settle, that woman who was the key to this satanic crime. He started walking fast towards his home lest she runs away. He was then not scared of anything or anybody, the two murders had emboldened him. He reached his home and saw her lying down. He raised his sword to lynch her and then thought better of it, he thought that it was unmanly to kill a woman. Then the picture of his dead sister emerged in his eyes. Out of sheer uncontrollable anger he kicked her, she did not even stir. She had already bled to her death.

He went to a nearby well, washed his hands and face and started walking towards the main road in a dazed state of mind. He saw a cart coming, it was his father's close friend Rehmat Ali who was going to the market to sell his yield of vegetables. Wheat and cotton was the staple crop of that area and vegetable farming was done by Muslims mostly. He stopped his bullock cart and when he saw him in blood stained clothes, he was sure that some calamity had happened. He decided not to waste time by asking questions, he would do so once they reach the market.

Rehmat always wore a *tehmad* instead of pants or pyjamas, hardly anybody in the village wore pants. He took out his *Kutcha* [long cotton underwear] and asked him to put it on and discard all his blood stained clothes. He mechanically put it on, it was damp with human sweat.

After some twenty minutes of traveling, a military truck stopped ahead of them and then it retreated back.

Some Gurkha soldiers climbed down from the truck. Rehmat got scared to death, but not Harbans as life or death had little meaning for him.

They started purchasing vegetables from him, as they were fresh and the farmers always sold them much cheaper than the market rates. When they were going to make the payment, Rehmat requested them with folded hands, "I don't want any money, but take this boy to India safely. He is a Hindu, son of my dearest friend . . . . when it is a question of helping someone, his father never discriminates between his Hindu and Muslim friends."

After some discussion amongst themselves in their mother tongue Nepali, they agreed but still made the payment for their purchase.

Rehmat took Harbans aside, emptied his pocket and kept just two one rupee coins for himself and the rest of the money he forcibly gave to him, and said, "Please take it, I owe your father much more," then hugged him and prayed for him in Arabic. The Gurkhas were watching him intently, they greatly admired him and saluted him for his humane generosity. They helped the boy to get into their truck.

In this great exodus-ii, people moved in *Kafilas* [caravans], Muslims from India to Pakistan and the Hindus and the Sikhs to India. It did not affect the Christians, and there was very little migration amongst them. They remained safe and were not harmed, attacked or killed by the Muslims, Sikhs and the Hindus. Even their chapels and churches were not defiled.

In these Kafilas, people walked on foot, some were on their horses and a few were riding on the camels, and some traveled in their bullock carts, but most of them were marching on their foot with no clear picture of their destination and despair was written large on their faces, saving their own and their family's lives was of utmost importance in their minds. Some of their animals were abandoned for lack of food and water, some poor animals also died because of this unfortunate reason. One could see a number of carcasses of these animals lying on the roads.

Some kind hearted Muslims offered them food, but the Hindus and the Sikhs were reluctant to eat it, fearing that they might have not mixed poison in them. Realizing it, many of them offered baskets full of carrots and radish, which were readily accepted.

At times, they were also attacked, in which case it was mostly the Sikhs who braved it out with their *Kirpans* [swords]. The Hindus were not in the habit of keeping any weapons with them, mostly the only weapon they had in their homes was the kitchen knife, and that also was not sharp enough. Some few rich Hindus had rifles and guns for their hunting pastime. In these attacks, the worst sufferers were the young girls and women whom they could abduct. Beauty was a curse in the scenario of that time.

When they left their homes to join some Kafila, people carried much more from their homes than they required for their sheer basic needs, but by and by they threw away their goods to lighten their burden and load, as they were too fatigued to even drag their feet. The worst sufferers were those who were too young and the old. Some could not withstand this torturous ordeal and fell sick, some died because of lack of medical care. Some completely lost balance of their minds and became crazy, some even totally insane. Some women wept when they could not feed their babies, because of acute under nourishment, their breasts dried up. But the Kafilas continued moving along towards an unknown and unplanned destination. Almost everything was available lying scattered on the roads, and it was there for your asking. On the way, the Gurkhas collected a few things for the boy which they thought he would need once he reaches India. They gave him shirts and pants to wear and an old pair of chappals. They made a bundle of these articles they had collected for him and gave it to him. He was now a man with some property, alas!

Finally, they reached Amritsar and before dropping him, they collected some money amongst themselves and thrust it in his pocket.

Thus Harbans Lal reached free India, but his mind was in shackles.

He was standing on a road, which road, he didn't even know the name. Soon, the sky was full of thick and dark clouds, and in no time it started raining cats and dogs. He did not even realize it for a while and he got completely drenched, he was simply too dazed.

Then he recollected that he had not seen his youngest sister, dead or alive.

CHAPTER 8

They ruled out the idea of purchasing a house as others may not become suspicious, from where they got the money, because one was ironing the clothes and the other was selling vegetables and fruits. They went to different bazaars to find a shop on rent for starting their business. They found out a shop near Hall Bazaar and a card board fixed on it with 'To let' written on it and just below it was the scribbled address of its owner.

They enquired about the owner from the adjoining shop keepers, as suggested by Vijay, his father often quoted the Russian proverb: Trust, but must verify. Amritsarias are very forthright and out spoken people. He told them that the shop actually belonged to a Muslim, who fled to Pakistan. This Gupta claims that he owed him more than the current market price of the shop; as such he says the shop belongs rightfully to him. He is well supported by the local police, as the sister's phallus has been well grease their palms by this *sala bania*. If they are given the bribe, all the sister fuckers government officials are hand in gloves with the daughter fuckers crooks and charlatans. Where is the freedom for us, the real freedom is with these people? Corruption is going to flourish in our country. *They did not realize that they now had freedom of speech in Free India.* The reason of their ire was that they had to give money to the different inspectors of the different departments of the state government, as they had the power to harass them and make things difficult for them to run their business. It was popularly known as *The Inspector Raj.* This menace continued till Rajiv Gandhi, the Prime Minister of India curbed their powers and it is now of lesser evil.

The ancient King Manu divided the Hindu society in four castes; the Kshatriyas, the Brahmins, the Vaishyas and the Shudras. With the passage of time the vaishyas, the trading class, started being called *bania*. Punjabis call them *baania*, and a Brahmin is called *baman* and the feminine version is *bnaini* and *bamni*. Sometimes these words are used in the derogatory sense. The bania title is also given to a stingy and miserly man, similarly a man who has the mentality of a taker or who always wants others to spend on him is nicknamed as baman; often the prefix of sala is added to it as, 'sala bania or sala baman', be he of any caste. Sala actually means wife's brother, but it is always used in the demeaning sense. All the four main castes are further divided in many sub castes. Inter caste marriages are most of the time unacceptable and there are honour killings or banishment from their society which in local lingo is called *Hukka paani band,* because of that. Amongst the really educated and enlightened people and the higher stratum of society, inter-sate or inter-caste marriages are not taboo; with the passage of time for this class of people this caste system has lost its domain.

THIS CASTEISM HAS DOOMED INDIA IN MANY WAYS.

They went to meet this man called Phool Chand Gupta, the so called owner of the shop. Phool Chand told them that he won't charge a penny less than Rs. 150 as rent per month and he must be given three months rent in advance.

They haggled over the rent as well as the advance again and again, as per their plan, as they wanted to show him that they had financial constraints. He finally agreed to take only one month's advance and they shook hands.

"Fine, 15 days advance right now and the rest 15 days advance will be paid after 20 days." Harbans announced.

"The entire advance must be given right now, otherwise the deal stands cancelled," Gupta shouted.

Their entreaty, pleading and cajoling continued for another thirty minutes.

Finally after much discussion, Phool Chand agreed to take 20 days advance and then and the rest 10 days advance after 15 days and they shook hands.

"Sir, let's discuss the rent now," Vijay said.

"But that has been already agreed upon; one fifty per month and not a penny less."

"You did mention it sir, but we have not discussed it." Vijay said with effected politeness. Again discussion over the quantum of rent continued for about an hour. Phool Chand's determination dwindled and he agreed to charge them Rs.118 as rent. Once again they shook hands.

Only when the deal was finalized, he shouted to his wife to bring three cups of tea.

She brought half filled three cups of tea of small size.

"If you don't mind, I am feeling somewhat hungry," Harbans said.

"Bring some thing to eat . . . . you have brought bare tea only, what will the guests think? You have drowned my nose." Gupta yelled at her with disdain.

She promptly brought three biscuits in a steel plate. One of the biscuits was slightly broken. Gupta surveyed the plate and left the broken one for one of them to eat.

"Sir today is an auspicious day. We have made the deal. It is a bad omen to eat a broken biscuit . . . . one should not start a business with bad foreboding." Vijay said.

"*Madarchod*, when will you learn to treat the guests properly? Replace the biscuit and put the broken one in your *maa di bund* [mother's arse]."

They had their tea. Once more they shook hands.

When they were at a distance from his house, they laughed and laughed.

They went to a *dhaba* [eatery] to eat something. Harbans found that Vijay was hardly eating.

"You are thinking something?"

"Yes."

"What?"

"Gupta may not doubt us; there was something in his eyes."

Vijay looked to be scared.

"When will you leave this your suspicion nature?"

"I can't help it."

After they had paid the bill, Harbans caught his hand and said, "Let's go."

"Where, let me know?"

"No where else but to Gupta's house."

"But for what?"

"I am thinking on that."

They reached Gupta's house and knocked at his door.

"Now, what is your problem?"

"Sir, we have a request to make," Harbans replied.

"And what is that?"

"Please . . . please, reduce the rent by rupees ten."

"No, And No and IT IS No." Gupta roared.

"Okay . . . . at least rupees five . . . . five rupees mean nothing to you." Harbans fell on his feet and caught his right leg with his hands.

"It means so much to me."

"Please . . . please . . . five . . . five . . . ."

"Not even a *nikka* paisa less. I may even raise the rent."

Harbans had strong sturdy hands, he began beseeching and coaxing him as if he was in a delirium and tightened his grip. Gupta could not stand the pain in his calf muscles.

Finally, he agreed to reduce it by rupees three; it was done to free his leg.

They went home laughing and resolved not to drink any *beer-sheer*, but as they passed by near a wine shop, Vijay said, "Let's celebrate for the success of our new venture."

"Sure." Harbans replied.

They bought three bottles of beer and got food packed from a nearby *dhaba*.

They paid the rickshaw puller eight annas more than the agreed fare.

In the morning, they reached Gupta's house exactly at the appointed time for payment of the advance rent.

They gave him a fifty rupee note.

"Where are the other nineteen rupees?" Gupta asked.

"We will pay it after two days," Harbans replied meekly.

He threw the note on the floor.

"It has to be *fullum-full* and not in installments."

"You will get it in two hours time." Vijay said confidently.

"Who is going to lend you, ha?"

"I have a relation in Tarn Taran, he owes me some money."

"Then do it." Gupta shrieked.

"Do you know where Tarn Taran is?"

Harbans told him that going to the bus stop and then waiting for the bus and then to return to Amritsar and going to his house means consumption of lot of time. Gupta is going to suspect how we could make it in two hours.

"We will say that he just did not let us leave without having our lunch that is why it has taken us so much time."

"Correctly." Harbans agreed

They thought of another prank, they borrowed Kenny's cycle and reached his home just before 11 pm.

After much knocking, Gupta opened the door. He was wearing only a striped *kutcha* [long under wear]. Vijay took out the money from his pocket, counted it and gave it to him.

"You have come so late at night?"

"Actually, we went on the bicycle to save money on the bus fare."

"It must be about eighteen miles from this place, and you went on a bicycle!"

Harbans replied immediately, "Sometime I drove, some time he drove, sometime I drove, sometime he drove, sometime I drove . . ."

"Stop it," Phool Chand cried out, then in a confidential manner he whispered, *"Madar chodo*, leave my house, my wife is sitting ready . . ." He smiled and pushed them out of his house, it was a friendly push.

Next day in the evening, they were discussing the name of their shop. Suddenly, Harbans said, "We are going to make it a top-o-top general store, so let it be called, Top-o-top General Store."

The idea was liked by everybody especially the kids. Then Vijay gave the kids a five rupee note each to bring good omen. Before Kenny could protest, Harbans announced, "They are going to be our first customers . . . . who could be more lucky for us than our own younger brother and sister."

Kenny did not protest any further.

Kenny was given the assignment to make the sign board. It was decided to write the name on the top of the board in English and right below it in Urdu. One could rarely find a sign board written in Hindi or Punjabi. Urdu was the main language which people could read or write. It was also the court language. Punjabi in Gurumukhi script was mostly taught in the Gurudwaras; and it was of just elementary learning. Of course, it was taught in Khalsa schools run by the missionary Sikhs, mostly in urban areas, which were insufficient for this very expressive beautiful language. People, both Hindus, Sikhs and Muslims spoke in Punjabi, but wrote in Urdu or amongst educated classes in English, and a few in Hindi, in that case mostly females. In the whole of India, Punjab was the only state which never really cared to bring Punjabi, their mother tongue, to its literary heights. Even the court language of Maharaja Ranjit Singh was not Punjabi but Persian.

After the partition, the Shiromani Akali Dal took cudgels for the development of the Punjabi language. Whereas the Arya Samaj and the Bhartiya Jan Sangh worked hard for the development of the Hindi language, perhaps they wanted it to flourish at the cost of Punjabi. Some felt that their ultimate aim was to make it the first state language and Punjabi the second state language for the cause of national integration. The Indian National Congress in this respect had a could-not-care-less attitude. In the Arya Samaj schools run by the D.A.V. institute, hardly any school had a Punjabi teacher on their rolls, even in a school like, Arya high School in Ludhiana, known for its brilliant results for years and years, they did not have a single Punjabi language teacher for many years.

Now the Punjabi language has been made compulsory subject up to class 10th when the Akalis came to power. This time the Jan Sangh, renamed as the Bhartiya Janta Party did not oppose it. The Shiromani Akali Dal for years together fought hard to bring this language to its deserved exalted position.

Eighteen years after the independence of India, Punjab was divided into three states in the year 1966, namely Punjab, Haryana and Himachal Pradesh when Indira Gandhi was the Prime Minister of India, due to the continuous agitations and struggle of the Akali Dal. It gladdened the people of Haryana and Himachal Pradesh to have a state of their own without any struggle on their part. Punjabi Hindus vociferously opposed the further division of Punjab, but all their protests went down the drain, Punjab which was once called Panch Nad during the Vedic era because of its five rivers.

After the formation of Himachal Pradesh, which has a predominantly Hindu population, its government declared Hindi as the state language, though people mainly speak Punjabi. People in the villages cannot speak even two sentences in Hindi correctly. They also made Urdu as the second state language, but later on it was discontinued, because the state could not find enough Urdu teachers and students. Same was the fate of the third language Telugu, which people found much more difficult to learn than even Sanskrit.

Once, English had just about 800 words in its vocabulary. It sounds incredulous but it is true. At one time it was spoken by the down trodden and riff-raffs of its society. The nobles and aristocrats always conversed in French, even the court language of the Great Britain for a long time was French. It was considered vulgar to converse in English. Whereas, Punjabi is much more scientifically accurate in its grammar and pronunciation than English and French, the two most widely spoken languages in the world. Baba Farid wrote his sufinama verses in Punjabi, in the period when races like the English, the French, and the Swedes were considered to be uncouth and uncultured. The beauty of the Punjabi language is its earthiness, its verse, its effectiveness and passion, which was captured by Baba Farid, Waris Shah and Bulle Shah, and they were all Muslims, with full of human compassion. Of course, great writers of this language did emerge, like Bhai Veer Singh, Nanak Singh Bhaia Ishar Singh Ishar, Shiv Batalvi and Amrita Pritam; to name a few, but more was justifiably expected.

Of course with the impact of Punjabiat, even Bengalis and south Indians have started using some Punjabi words in their conversation in their day to day life. In Bollywood movies, hardly any movie is made which does not contain Punjabi or Punjabiat, in one form or the other. Punjabis are well known for their manly trait that they can laugh at themselves. They should be manly enough to accept the blame that they did little for the development of their own mother tongue. In Delhi which is dominated by the Punjabis, you will rarely, rather very rarely find a Punjabi newspaper or magazine in the homes of the Punjabis, say even the Sikhs. By the grace of God, they have not stopped speaking Punjabi, as a large number of them can neither read or write Punjabi in Gurumukhi script. Don't be surprised if some nouveau riche boasts that his kids don't know Punjabi, and they can speak English *furl-furl*, because he or she is studying in a reputed public school, where they paid a few lakhs to get them admitted. No one can imagine that a German or an Englishman or a Dutch or French or a Swede will say that their children are not conversant with their own language. Be it so, Shakespeare would have said, 'Fie on such people!'

They opened their shop in the first week of August, 1947, without any fanfare or *the hawan*, did not even consult any pundit to find out an auspicious day for the *mahurat,* which invariably all shop keepers do. As a matter of fact they had become pucca agnostics, for them God was still in his slumber and they did not want to wake him up, deep down in their hearts they could never forget about their tragedy of losing their entire family.

Kenny and Maria's kids were their first customers.

Kenny and Maria brought an English Vicar along with them, who blessed them and then prayed in Latin. They half listened but did not mind it, as they yearned for any opportunity to please them. The Vicar also sprinkled some holy water.

They tried to give him some money, but he gracefully refused it and blessed them again. They were amazed that a priest did not accept money for doing his priestly duties; perhaps being an English man he must be pretty rich.

In the evening, Phool Chand came to their shop out of curiosity and when he saw only a few items in the shop, he started having doubts whether these boys were capable of running a business.

"With very few items in the shop, I doubt whether you can even break even."

Vijay told him that they wanted to do their business in a unique way. "We will put the goods in our shop on our customers' demands," and he showed him a register with a list of fifteen customers along with their requirements.

Gupta still had his doubts whether these boys will be able to pay him the monthly rent, as he remembered the hullabaloo they created while paying him the advance.

Vijay could read it in Gupta's eyes.

"Actually, our house is full of goods, but we want to run the business in our own style. In case you doubt us, you can come to our house and can see with your own eyes."

"But you'll have to pay for the Rickshaw to and fro," added Harbans.

"Why should I?"

"Okay, pay for one side."

Gupta left without saying anything. He thought the boys are playful and gutsy. One day they are going to make it big.

Actually, they wanted to show to the people at large that because of the paucity of funds, they had started their business on a very small scale. Otherwise people may not start thinking from where these refugee boys got all that money to run a business, and this decision was taken because of the over cautious nature of Vijay.

Within days their business started picking up, because their prices were reasonable, besides they never over charged or under weighed. Their shop was mostly thronged by young girl and ladies, because they were very polite, cultured and above all both of them were very handsome. Soon their shop got nicknamed as, *'Soney mundia di dukan'* [a shop run by handsome boys]. Later on it got abbreviated to just *Sonia di dukan.*

Whenever somebody came along with small children, they gave them toffees for free, as they simply loved kids. Children also loved them and they always made a hue and cry to visit their shop. Some did feel embarrassed to get these free without paying for it.

Just after two months of opening their shop, when Phool Chand observed that they were doing pretty good business, he demanded the rent to be raised by fifty per cent.

"We will come to your house to discuss this matter, after we close the shop," said Vijay.

"It can be discussed right now."

"Not in the presence of the customers."

"Right now there is no customer."

"A customer can walk in any time."

Harbans then putting his hand on his shoulder said, "and we don't want them to know that we fight over *rent-shent* . . . we want to show others that we are of uncly and nephewly relations. And that is all in all." And to impress Phool Chand he spoke in an effective English accent.

Actually, Vijay was captivated by his young wife, which Harbans knew but kept it to himself. Even she seemed to take some interest in him. Though, they never took any liberties with their female customers. With them they were polite and somewhat reserved.

At 9 pm the two of them reached Gupta's house with plenty of eatables as they were feeling very hungry. Instead of Gupta, it was Harbans who went inside and instructed his wife to bring three plates and to prepare four cups of tea. When she brought only three plates and started going to her kitchen, Harbans said, *"Bharjai [sister-in-law]*, why don't you join us?"

Gupta through eye contact instructed her not to join them.

But she totally ignored him and came back with four cups of tea and an empty plate that made Gupta furious, but he checked himself. *I'll teach her a lesson later on,* he decided.

While eating and taking tea they started discussing about the rent.

"We have just started our business, we can't even think of raising the rent," said Vijay.

"Then start thinking about it. You underpaid me from the very beginning."

"No, we did not. Nobody raises the rent just after two months," said Harbans Lal firmly.

"But I do," replied Gupta sternly.

"You should not," said Harbans.

"Increase the rent by 50% or vacate my shop . . . . choice is yours," retorted Gupta

"Tell me *Bharjaai,* is he being fair?" Vijay asked his wife by deliberately touching her elbow. She felt a sensation.

"No, he is not," replied candidly Gupta's wife, and looked at Vijay with covetous eyes, which was observed by Phool Chand, and he started seething with anger and tried in vain not to show it. *I am going to turn you into pulp, once they leave my house.*

The discussion continued for another hour, and during their talks Gupta gave many hints to his wife to leave, but she did not budge. Finally, Gupta could not control himself and told her in a low but firm voice to go inside.

"No, she is not going.... she is sitting with her two *devars* [brothers-in-laws], she is your better half and she has every right to participate in your business affairs." Vijay said in mock politeness and once again affectionately touched her hand. Again she felt a sensation and finally an increase in the rent by Rs.7 Per month was settled between the two parties.

Gupta had relented, because he could wait no longer to thrash his wife for unashamedly flirting with another man in his very presence. It had badly hurt his male ego.

After they had left, Gupta roared, "You slut . . . . I will let you know what it means to disobey me."

He raised his hand, but she caught hold of it in a firm grip, and hissed, "Never dare to raise your hand on me; otherwise I will take out your balls." Gupta was stunned at her audacity, but wisely thought not to pursue the matter.

She tried to sleep, but could not. She cursed her alcoholic father for selling her to this wretched bania for some money. He, her so called husband, never allowed her to mix up with her neighbours, and never allowed any member of his family to visit her, as he did not want anybody to know that he was living with the daughter of a washer man, whom he actually had not married legally. He also rarely allowed her to visit her maternal family, with the clear instructions not to stay overnight. At night she was not a lady with a human soul, but an object of pleasure with whom he could play wantonly as it pleased him. She hated him from the core of her heart. She sobbed herself to sleep and dreamt of Vijay.

It took Gupta several days to make peace with her after much coaxing and with a gift of a gold necklace.

CHAPTER 9

Their business started having a roaring success and they even engaged a full time helper.

One day Kenny uncle came to their shop to make some purchases. He could smell that they were charging him much less than what they were charging the other customers, but he could not sense that they were over weighing also. When Kenny protested that they were charging him less than what they charged other customers, they replied that they were charging him at the wholesale rates. "Besides, the other customers don't happen to be our uncle." Kenny left quietly without carrying anything.

They made a bundle of the goods Kenny had chosen and after closing the shop they went to his house. On the way, they bought some non-vegetarian dishes also, as they knew that all of them relished it, but could not buy as they could not afford them.

They had exactly reached at dinner time. They put the dishes on the table and then squatted on the floor.

"Why are you squatting on the floor?" Maria asked.

"We are in a sit-in protest."

"What happened?" Asked Maria laughing.

"Kenny uncle is very cruel."

"Did he say something unpleasant to you?"

"He said nothing . . . . but today he was very cruel to us."

"Did he rebuke you?"

"No, we would have preferred that than his cruelty."

"Was he indifferent to you? Being an artist, sometimes he behaves like this for no rhyme or reason?"

"Not at all, but he was very cruel to us."

Kenny kept smiling, he knew why they were creating a drama.

"I can't understand anything," Maria said laughing.

"You can't because you don't know that at times he can be very cruel. Today he was very cruel to us." And they started sobbing dramatically, which immensely amused the kids.

"For God's sake stop all this. It is night time and the neighbours will start thinking that I have really beaten you," said Kenny with a smirk.

"Right now we are sobbing and soon we are going to cry loudly unless you promise not to be cruel to us."

"But why it is so, for Christ's sake!?"

"You have been cruel to us."

Then Kenny told her what had happened.

"But sons, your uncle was being fair to you."

"He is not our uncle, he is like our father . . . and sons are not supposed to earn any profit from their father . . . . AND THIS FATHER OF OURS IS VERY CRUEL TO US." And they started their sobbing again. This made the children laugh like hell.

"Okay, you rogues win and I lose . . . . now stop your slogan, *he is cruel to us.*"

"He Is No More Cruel To Us." And they started clapping, first the kids, and then Maria too joined them. Kenny could not as his belly was aching with laughter.

"Here is an *adha* [half a bottle of whisky] for you."

They had such a jolly time together. It was really a family get together.

When they were about to leave, Kenny took out his purse to make the payment for the goods they had brought. Both of them ran away.

Kenny off and on went to their shop, though not regularly, as he was scared that 'his rogues' would come out with some new prank.

A young girl often came to their shop, who loved to chatter and seemed to be inquisitive to know about them, especially about Vijay. She made a lot of inane inquiries, and it was Harbans who always replied. She was young, beautiful, vivacious and bubbly by nature. Vijay could sense that she had developed puppy-love for him. The way she dressed up and her elegant diamond jewellery bespoke that she belonged to a rich and well-connected family. Therefore, Vijay decided not to develop any intimacy with her, as it may create some trouble for them because of class distinction. Also they were new to this city with no connections and totally anchorless. Whereas, Harbans was unmindful of all that.

In those days mere friendship between a boy and girl was looked down upon and was unacceptable in the prevalent social milieu; funnily it was considered immoral. Good girls were supposed not to talk to men-folk to maintain their modesty. Even a friendly kiss on the cheek or on the forehead was a taboo. The first kiss was supposed to be performed on the first night and then also the girl was expected to show her reluctance, though outwardly. Most of the girls offered their cheeks rather than their lips to be kissed to show their bashfulness and modesty. They even pretended that they never knew that the lips are meant to be kissed. All this made her man think that his newlywed wife was pure and a virgin, which immensely satisfied his male ego. Virginity was considered as a great virtue and it was highly valued as a moral strength. In many parts of India, especially amongst the poor and uneducated classes, though the couples produce a number of children but they never interlock their lips, not even once. And breast sucking was not even thought of as boobs were meant for the infant to suck for their feeding. Nature abhors hypocrisy, but human race at times is inclined to pursue it.

Men, especially of higher class always avoided talking about their sexual life even with their friends, on the other hand women were much less inhibited.

One day that girl came to their shop fuming and complained that the bottle of coconut oil which she had bought from their shop, was giving a foul smell. Both of them turn by turn brought the bottle close to their nose and felt nothing wrong with it.

"No bad smell, it is first class," said Harbans Lal.

"It is giving bad smell and it is third class."

"No sister . . . . both of us have smelt it . . . . it is perfectly right-o-right."

"YOU better get your noses treated," said the girl haughtily.

"You seem to be in a bad mood, sister," said Harbans in a pleasing tone.

She liked the way he called her 'sister', but did not show it.

"It is you who has spoiled my mood," she replied to Harbans but looked at Vijay accusingly.

Vijay ignored her and that made her angrier.

"We are ready to replace the bottle," said Harbans.

"I don't want it to be replaced."

"We are ready to pay you back."

"I don't want the money back."

"Then what do you want?"

"Can you repay me for the time I have wasted?"

"I can," said Harbans.

"How come?"

"By running two miles at a stretch as a punishment."

This made her laugh.

"Why does not your friend speak . . . has he sewn his lips?" This time she spoke in English.

"Because you have come with the intention of picking up a spat," replied Vijay in English.

"So, I am quarrelsome?"

"No, I never said that."

"You meant it."

Vijay kept quiet and that further angered her.

"You sell spurious things . . . and then you have the temerity to belittle me . . . . you don't know who I am . . . I will teach you a lesson . . . . my father is Deputy Superintendent of Police."

"Then it is all the more important for you to behave properly . . . you are beautiful . . . indeed very beautiful, but beauty is only skin deep. Your father has not become a DSP by sheer good luck . . . but by his intelligence and hard work . . . and by your behaviour and by your demeanour, you should make him proud of yourself . . . and to my mind that is real beauty . . . . we are new to this city, hapless with no family . . . alone and anchorless . . . . without any base . . . . rootless . . . . with no connections . . . . nobody to soothe our pent up emotions. You are our regular customer . . . instead of offering us any protection . . . You are threatening us because your father is a DSP . . . ."

Vijay's eyes were wet but he managed to control his tears.

Nobody spoke for a while and then the girl blurted out, "Two days back, I wore a new dress . . . . does it cost anything to give a compliment?"

"I did notice that . . . you were looking becoming in that . . . . we are young . . . we also have a human heart . . . . but we avoid talking to girls . . . Especially pretty girls like you, as it may be taken in a wrong manner . . . I admit we are very insecure and some times we feel very scared, for no rhyme or reason."

He said I am beautiful . . . . very beautiful . . . pretty . . . . liked my dress also . . . . I will never be bitchy again, with anybody.

She patted his shoulder sympathetically, "Don't feel insecure, handsome. Please slap me for my bad manners and I won't report it to my father. Henceforth, never feel insecure because your friend's father is a DSP . . . . There is nothing wrong with the bottle."

She took the bottle, gave Vijay a meaningful smile and left.

CHAPTER 10

Just before going to sleep, Harbans asked, "Vijay, in which class you studying when you left from Pakistan?"

"M.A.[previous]."

Harbans could not sleep; he was thinking, such a brilliant student should not be running a shop. The way he spoke to that girl in English . . . . his accent was that of an English man . . . his persuasive power . . . his logic . . . No . . . . he should continue his studies.

He remembered when some unknown persons came to their home and urged them to join them in their venture to kill the Muslims. He was tempted to join them, but not Vijay. He argued with them that hardly one to two percent had participated in killing innocent people from both sides; Muslims from one side and Hindus and Sikhs from the other side. The actual killers are roaming scot free. What is the fault of those people who shunned from such activities that they should pay the price of the heinous crimes committed by those who are their co-religionist, but whom they don't even know? One wrong does not justify another wrong, never. Our religion does not teach us to kill innocent people and neither does Islam.

Look at Taimur Lang, who considered himself a devout Muslim, a true believer of God. In Delhi, he killed lakhs of people who were his prisoners of war. Elsewhere, he buried thousands of people who were alive at the time of their capture and built pyramids over their bodies. He captured a fort in Turkey with four thousand Christians in it, kept them hungry for days together and then buried them alive. And God must be clapping in his praise! After killing lakhs of people in Delhi, this so called devout son of God, went to the tomb of Sheikh Bakhtiar Kaki, the patron saint of Delhi, to pay his homage and to offer his obeisance.

This tyrant killed more Muslims than non-Muslims.

More people have been killed in the name of religion than due to devastation of some epidemic, a tsunami, a typhoon, a cyclone and an eruption of lava from a volcano, all put together. We murder defenseless women and even infants, who can't even pronounce the word Sikh, Hindu or Muslim. I am of the opinion that Deism is better, which pronounces that God created this world and then altogether forgot about it, yes it is far better than the religion which teaches us senseless killing of a man who does not belong to our own religion, for no rhyme or reason.

Every one pretended to have understood Deism, of which they have not even heard of and even appreciated it. Then a man who seemed to be the leader of their gang and who had in between called Vijay 'a eunuch' announced, "We won't kill a female or a child and old men but only those who are capable to sire another Muslim. And we have tolerated enough of your lecture. Keep it in your pocket. TIT FOR TAT AND THAT IS THAT." And they went on their killing spree.

When Harbans said that he was surprised that Vijay had so much sympathy for the Muslims, he replied that his father's Muslim friends had tried their best to dissuade him from catching the train and had even offered that their entire family should stay with them and they would provide them all the protection and he should leave for India with his family at the appropriate time, when it is altogether safe to travel and they also agreed with him that this part of Pakistan was not suitable for him to opt for. But his mother had just this single minded opinion, 'no Muslim can be trusted, otherwise why don't they speak against the creation of Pakistan' . . . . it was on her insistence that we boarded the train . . . . and her womanly obstinacy caused four deaths in the family and a lifelong torture for him.

Harbans brought up this topic again and told him that he strongly feels that he should complete his M.A.

On second thoughts, Vijay said, "It is the last week of October, admission time is over long time ago . . . . seems to be impossible."

"You had once tolded me that uncle Napoleon said that the word impossible is in the dictionary of fools," Harbans replied jocularly. Vijay was quite reluctant to pursue his studies, he had lost zest for it, but ultimately Harbans was able to make him agree.

They met the principal and narrated their predicament in a nut shell.

The principal was sympathetic, but categorically told them that it was beyond his powers to admit Vijay so late and also when the session was in full swing. However, they could meet the President of the College Governing Body, Mr. Sham Lal Bhandari to try their luck. If convinced, he can go out of the way to help them. He was very impulsive and daring enough to flout the rules and nobody had the guts to defy him.

They went to Mr. Bhandari's house and were told by his servant that he had gone out and won't be back before six in the evening. They again went to his house around 6 pm. They were told that the sahib was expected to come at 8 pm. Again when he was not available even at that hour, they decided to wait for him at a distance from his bungalow. At about 9 pm they saw a car entering his house, but did not know whether it was Mr. Bhandari's car.

The servant told Mr. Bhandari that since morning two boys had come thrice to meet him but he was not sure at what time he would come. Perhaps, they were still waiting for him outside the bungalow.

"Why did you not ask them to come inside . . . and did you offer them some *tea-shee?*"

The servant put down his head in shame.

Mr. Bhandari abused him and said, "This is not your Garhwal . . . . it is Punjab . . . you damn fool, bring them in."

The servant approached them and told them that Mr. Bhandari was waiting to meet them.

Harbans touched his feet and said, "We have come for seeking your blessings."

"You have waited so much just for my blessings!" Mr. Bhandari said with a smile, "come on, in case you need some job, I can help you." In those days there was a great dearth of jobs.

"Sir, we have not comer any job for . . . . it's for his admission in M. A.," Harbans pointed his index finger towards Vijay.

"Have you tried for it in some other college?"

"No sir. He studied in college of prestige in his home town in Pakistan . . . so he studies in college of most prestige in Amritsar."

"Why have you not come along with your parents?"

"We are mother, brother . . . father to each other."

It deeply touched his emotions and he admired their guts and tenacity.

"To which place do you belong?" He asked Vijay.

"Sir, I am from Sialkot."

"I have a friend in Sialkot, Professor Puri . . . what a scholar! What a littérateur!"

"I am his son."

"You are Professor Puri's son?? And he is . . . . he is . . ."

"He is no more, sir."

The three of them had tears in their eyes.

"Join the college tomorrow itself . . . . Waste no more time. Come let's have our meals."

Both of them apologized and said some other time.

"Sons, you want your uncle to keep you hungry. You can't leave my place until I want, I am a well known goonda [ruffian] of Amritsar," he said laughingly.

After the admission formalities were over, the principal gave him a bag. It contained all the books Vijay needed along with a pen and an inkpot.

In the evening they went to Mr. Bhandari's house to show their gratitude, especially for the books. After they had profusely thanked Mr. Bhandari, he said, "Would you have thanked your father?"

"Yes sir," replied Vijay with a smile.

"But don't thank this goonda . . . . and don't keep me hungry, otherwise I am going to thrash both of you. Let's have our meals."

CHAPTER 11

Surprisingly, Gupta did not turn up to their shop for almost two months, whereas they were expecting him to ask for an increase in the rental charges with immediate effect and they had decided to agree, as their business had flourished beyond their expectations. Actually Gupta desperately searched for his mistress, she had left without informing anybody and had taken all the jewelry and some cash. When her father Ghasi Ram came to know about it, he started crying for his darling daughter and accused him of killing her and wanted to be compensated for the same. Gupta started abusing him and he abused him back. Then, he asked him for twenty rupees for the time being, Gupta gave him two rupees which he grabbed.

Ghasi Ram went to the police station to report the matter in a drunken state and told *the Munshi* that one Gupta had killed his daughter and when the Munshi asked for the bribe to register the report, he started shouting at him. The Munshi dragged him out of his room and slapped him and then kicked him on his ass, and he fell on the ground and started yelling. No one bothered about him, as these are common sights at a police station.

When all his efforts to find her went in vain, Gupta decided to leave for his village in district Jalandhar, before people begin to set their tongues to wag. Moreover, he could not even report the matter to the police as there was every chance of getting it published in the newspaper and he never wanted his wife to know that he was keeping a mistress.

In the meantime that girl continued to come to their shop off and on and gradually developed sisterly relations with Harbans.

She observed that Vijay was too shy, insecure and unsure of himself to open up, and for that she admired him all the more. A woman in love keeps logic in her purse.

Vijay did talk to her but only sparingly and even that was satisfying to her. Her attraction for him was ingrained deeply in her heart.

Life for Vijay became very tough, he had to study a lot and then daily had to be in the shop for three hours in the evening. In the half yearly exams he just managed to pass in third division. He was much saddened with this result, but his teachers told him that it was more than they expected of him, and he was going to outshine many of his class fellows in the final exams, as his expression was unique and he had commendable originality. This gave him pep and he was resolved to put even more efforts. The best part was that the atmosphere in the college was very congenial for studies.

Harbans Lal was very happy that Vijay did not fail. To his rustic sensibilities there were only two things, you pass or you fail, the rest does not matter. He even wanted to celebrate but Vijay flatly refused as there was nothing to rejoice about.

One day at about four in the morning, Harbans got up to go to the loo and when he found that Vijay was no where to be found, he got really worried and went down to search for him and found him deeply involved in his studies under the street lights. Obviously, he did not want to disturb his sleep. He was unmindful of the fact that Harbans was watching him.

When Vijay was getting ready for college, Harbans told him that henceforth he need not come to the shop at all and he would be able to manage it all alone. He refused because he did not want to be a parasite. When Harbans told him that he would engage another full time helper, Vijay was still unrelenting.

When Vijay went to the shop as per his schedule, he found it closed. Harbans was watching him from a distance. He opened the shop only when Vijay had left.

During the night they had quite a spat accusing each other of unfriendly and unbrotherly behavior.

"I always treated you like a younger brother, and you want me to exploit you," cried out Vijay.

"And I treat you like an elder brother . . . and I am supposed to serve you."

"I should enjoy college life . . . and let you work like an Ox, this can never happen."

"With a full time helper hand . . . this going to happen . . . . and fully possible."

"Be reasonable . . . you want me to be dependent on you, that will simply kill me."

"I am being reasonable . . . The shop was opened with your money."

"It was stolen money."

"It was not."

"It was! It was! It was!"

Vijay raised his hand.

"You can hit me but you can't change mine mind."

"You are a damn fool, and damn swollen-head."

"Thanks."

"You are an idiot . . . impractical . . . self-ruinous."

"Thanks . . . thanks and many the thanks."

CHAPTER 12

That girl Pinki continued coming to their shop but rarely found Vijay. She and Harbans became very close to each other, they had an easy communication. No appellation could be given to their relationship. They had their friendly quarrels too where mostly Pinki had the upper hand. Harbans always teased her that as she was the daughter of a DSP, he had no option but to surrender. Quite often she brought home-cooked food for him and surreptitiously for Vijay also. And when Harbans tried to give her something in return, she put her foot down. She often teased him to get married 'and you will find how much I would eat and my sister-in-law would get tired of me', and this always amused him. In a way, she reminded him of his sister Durga, as such he became very protective about her.

On one such meeting, she found Harbans listless and pensive. He hardly had any appetite for food she had brought for him and talked to her only in syllables.

"What is wrong with you?" She enquired.

"Hun . . ."

"Now what is this Hun?"

"Nooh."

"Nooh! What does that mean?"

He did not reply.

"Something is eating you!?"

"We had already been eaten *fullum-full* . . . . we will have to close this shop."

"But why so?"

Harbans told her in nut shell, how they managed to get this shop on rent from one Phool Chand Gupta, how he always forced them to increase the rent after a short period of time, and now when the shop is doing good business, he wants his shop back. Moreover, he never gave them any receipt for the rent, as such they have no legal basis to continue even for a single day. In reality, this shop belonged to one Musalman who fled to Pakistan. Other shopkeepers in the market said that he was having some fake ownership papers. In their opinion he was a charlatan and a congenital liar. Harbans added that he had threatened them that in case we do not vacate the shop within two days, he would make our life hell as he was a well connected local man.

"*Wahe guru* will help you . . . . the true Lord cares for his fellows." She left without committing any thing.

She went straight to her father's office. Luckily he was there at that time. He was surprised to find her there as she had never before visited his office. From her looks, she appeared to be furious and frightened at the same time. Before he could ask her anything, she narrated the whole story to her father, as was told to her by Harbans Lal.

"How do you know him?" he asked her sternly.

"I often go to his shop."

"Since how long is this going on?"

"He is a boy, but not my boy friend . . . there is no relationship . . . well in a way, he is like a brother to me . . . yes, from this time onwards, and he will always remain my brother. And don't you look at me with suspicious eyes. If my papa is dear to me, his honour is even dearer to me. Never dare you doubt me. I am proud of you and you know it, but for me it is more important that you should feel proud of your daughter. This Pinki would never do a thing that her father has to bow his head, she would instead prefer death. Sorry, I bothered you."

She got up to leave.

He caught her by her wrist, "Sorry, I was suspicious. I am a father; a typical Indian father." And he laughed.

"Papa, he is a refugee from Pakistan . . . . he is running the shop along with a friend of his . . . both of them lost their parents, their entire family . . . no family . . . . friendless . . . anchorless." Tears began flowing from her eyes.

"But you are their friend. Aren't you?"

"Yes, I am Papa."

"Then I am proud of you. Ask them to file an F.I.R."

"What for?"

"Without that we cannot move forward with the case. Try to understand."

"By that time, it will be too late. You in the police force have strange rules, totally out dated and outmoded. You want first crime to happen and only then you will take action. You think your only job is to catch thieves, robbers and the murderers . . . . and then to get the murderers hanged . . . . and win your medals!! Why don't you work for the preventive measures? Why can't you help common, innocent people who even shudder to approach the police force, indeed, there should be police reforms. It is high time!!"

"Okay grandma, I promise to solve this problem within 24 hours . . . and now better go home and let me work on that."

She kissed her father on the forehead and left.

Today for the first time Bakshi Sahib thought that Pinky was both a son and a daughter to him. He felt blessed. She was born after six years of their marriage, after paying their obeisance at various Gurudwaras, Mandirs and Dargahs. His wife was incapable of giving birth to another child because of some gynae problems. Today he did not feel the remorse that God had not blessed him with a male child.

Later on, he called the incharge of the area police and instructed them that they should take extra care that nobody harasses or takes advantage of the helpless and unfortunate refugees from Pakistan, rather police should go out of the way to help them and assuage their feelings.

He then apprised the Station House Officer of Hall Bazaar how to handle one Gupta, who was bent upon exploiting two refugee boys in this holy city of Amritsar, and then he acquainted him with all the details Pinky had told him. His parting words were 'don't you spare him.' It was a sufficient hint for the SHO that he was supposed to tackle it immediately and with firmness.

That very day a constable went to Phool Chand Gupta's house, and asked him to report to the police station along with the papers of ownership of his shop near Hall Bazaar.

Phool Chand thought that he had to give some more hush money to these police personnel. He started planning how to give them much less money than what they were going to expect from him. So he went to police station wearing crumpled ordinary clothes. When he went to meet the SHO, he told him to report to Sub-Inspector Dayal Singh.

When he approached Dayal Singh, he kept him waiting pretending that he was busy enough to take any notice of him. Once or twice he tried to draw his attention but Dayal Singh ignored him and kept him standing for about two hours.

Having his patience exhausted, Gupta said meekly, "Sir . . . . you called me. I am at your service."

"Are you blind, don't you see I am busy in my work?"

After another half an hour he called his Assistant Sub-Inspector and asked him to check the Registration Papers of his shop and in case he does not have the relevant papers, then bestow on him some 'Extended service', befitting for a guest in the police station.

Sher Singh, the ASI, took him to a remote cell and asked him to show the relevant papers.

Gupta gave him a note written in Urdu and said that everything had been very clearly mentioned in the letter.

"Is this a Registry?"

"More than that . . . nevertheless, I am here to please you in any manner your honour desires."

"But first let me please you."

Sher Singh threw him on the ground, took out his rubber-leather [which leaves no sign of police torture], and then bared his buttocks and started striking him and with each stroke he started reciting *Sa re ga,* the basic notes of Hindustani Music. On the fifth note when he recited *pa,* Gupta begged him not to beat him, as he was ready to confess everything. He admitted that it was a fake letter and he had illegally and forcibly occupied the shop, but Sher Singh gave him two strokes more to complete the seven surs reciting the last two *nee saa.*

Sher Singh was an unsuccessful classical singer, who could not pursue his musical career because of lack of encouragement and financial help, and he instead joined the police force for a living, but his love for music never abandoned him.

Phool Chand was presented to the SHO and was told that he had confessed about his crime. The SHO ordered his ASI to put him behind the bars.

After much begging, crying, cajoling and touching of his feet, Gupta quietly placed a hundred rupee-note on his table. And promised he won't ever harass those boys. He was finally released.

As he was going to leave the police station, the ASI caught him by the collar and said, "You paid him hundred rupees for doing nothing and I who served you so nicely, should remain empty-handed. This is injustice."

Phool Chand gave him a twenty rupee note.

"For my services only this much?" He threw the note on the ground.

He gave him another ten rupees, the ASI again threw it away. "I am not a beggar."

He gave him ten rupees more; he felt disgusted and kicked him on his leg.

Phool Chand gave him another ten rupees and put his forehead on his feet.

The ASI collected the money and asked a constable to fetch a Rickshaw for the *Sahib.*

A Rickshaw was duly brought for him. When he reached his home, the Rickshaw puller did not ask for the fare thinking that he was a policeman. Gupta also didn't offer to pay.

The very next day Pinky told Harbans that his problem had been entirely solved. This Gupta of his dare not ask them to vacate the shop. As a matter of fact he had admitted in the police station that he was not the owner of the shop and was carrying fake papers for the ownership of the shop.

Harbans Lal felt greatly relieved and he was on cloud nine and he profusely thanked Pinky. In his excitement he was almost going to hug her but checked himself at the right moment. People did not embrace their sisters if they had developed chests. It was a taboo.

When Gupta did not come to visit them for seven days, Harbans became doubly assured that their days of uncertainty and insecurity and what-is-going-to-happen-next were over. He immediately engaged another helper as he was determined to expand his business.

Next day he went to Bakshi Sahib's house to thank him. When Bakshi Sahib saw that he was carrying a box of sweets and a costly suit-length for Pinky, he chided him, "You should not have brought all this. Honestly I have done you no favour. It is the duty of us in the police force to come to the aid of people like you who in spite of all their miseries are still determined to brave it out, and are making efforts to stand on their own legs. Kid, I am proud of people like you."

"Sir, this Harbans Lal of Montgomery comes at his sister's house and come empty hands, the whole village of mine will laugh at me and condemning me. I will get myself dig in earth."

If somebody spoke to him in English or using English words, he always replied in English.

Bakshi Sahib felt amused with his style of speaking in English language. And with his astute mind, he was sure that there was no hanky-panky of relationship between two of them.

"You consider Pinky as your sister, but call me Sir, Very Strange."

Harbans touched his feet out of respect and said, "Never again after, *Chacha ji* [uncle, ji connotes respect]."

Bakshi Sahib instantly liked him immensely, hugged him and said, "You are always welcome to your chacha's house."

CHAPTER 13

One day Inspector Dayal Singh's wife told him that her neighbour Taro had bought a new necklace, weighing two tolas and she was pompously showing it to everybody and she had decided to buy a necklace worth three tolas *to break her mouth* [to belittle her]. Dayal Singh told her to forget about it as he simply did not have money to buy it. When she consistently continued insisting for it all day, he blurted out, "Tomorrow if she buys an elephant, would you force me to buy one of a bigger size, just to break her mouth, out of sheer jealousy?"

"I am talking of a necklace and not an elephant."

"I just gave you a befitting example."

"All ladies like necklaces and I am no exception."

"It costs lot of money."

"She did not get it free."

"You have many things which she does not have."

"Name one."

"Go, open your cupboard and see for yourself."

"All old and outdated things."

"One day this necklace will also become old and outdated."

"That means we are going to buy it."

"No, we are not going to buy it."

"Then who is going to buy it?"

"Your wretched two-penny father."

She left in a huff and straightway went to the kitchen and the utensils started making an incongruous music.

Dayal Singh was used to such an orchestra, he paid no heed to it.

He had come home in a despondent mood and to soothe his pent up emotions, he opened the bottle and started drinking. Punjabis start drinking in case they are in a good mood, or to assuage their feelings when they are in a bad mood and when they feel bored they drink to kill the ennui. They can always find an excuse to start drinking which is never liked by their wives and female family members.

At night, he felt the urge for copulation and as he tried to take her in his arms, she jumped out of the bed like a cat, went to another room and bolted it from inside.

For full seven days his wife, Banto did not allow him to come near her. Earlier, he was able to set her right by occasionally beating her. He could do it no more, could not even think of it.

He still remembered the day when he tried to beat his wife, his eighteen year old son, Gurdit Singh tried to intervene and caught hold of his hand. This made him very furious and he gave him a hard slap. The boy was stunned but said nothing. The atmosphere in the home became very tense. Nobody had their meals that night.

In the morning his son was found missing. He had left home without leaving a note. The very next day, he was to appear for his intermediate examination. Life became hell for him. His wife cursed herself for making noise during their fight which attracted her son to intervene. Dayal Singh felt like a culprit. His son was obedient, gentle, and studious and never gave a reason for any complaint and was a role model for other boys in the locality. He was well aware of the fact that his son was hyper-sensitive. He could not pardon himself the way he had behaved with his beloved son. He lost his appetite, started speaking to himself as if he was of an unsound mind. His wife had two-fold tragedy, she was worried for her son and also for her husband who had been a pillar of strength to her and the family. They searched for him, here, there, and everywhere, but all in vain.

Ultimately, after ten days they were able to find him roaming around Dera Baba Jaimal Singh near the holy river of Beas. He looked dazed, forelone and despondent. For quite some time none of them could utter a word.

"I cannot live with this man," Gurdit at last broke the ice.

"You call him 'this man', he is your father!" yelled Banto and slapped him and then hugged him tightly.

"You know after you left, how miserable he has been . . . . lost his appetite . . . . hardly slept . . . . started searching for you in the streets and the adjoining villages to find his dearest son . . . . he has always fulfilled your every demand . . . . never denied . . . . never delayed anything . . . . had become almost insane without you . . . I deserve it when he beats me, yes I do . . . . I get on his nerves . . . . I exasperate him. In case you try to insult him, I will jump into the river Beas and I mean it. Now touch his feet and seek his pardon."

Gurdit had never defied his mother. He touched his feet, "I apologize, *Daar ji* [Papa]."

His father hugged him and tears started flowing from his eyes and then the sturdy Sikh started crying like a baby.

"Daar ji [father], please promise never to beat *bebey* [mother] again. When you beat her, I feel very miserable."

Dayal Singh nodded in affirmative. He was finding it hard even to speak and then in a choked voice he said, "I am ready to promise you anything in this world."

The rift with his wife was killing him. He went to a jeweler known to him, he bought the necklace and paid him twenty percent of its price and promised him to pay him the rest of the amount in monthly installments. The jeweler was too ready to oblige and to befriend a police officer was always advantageous to a business man. In the evening, he presented the necklace to his wife. He looked sullen and lost.

Her sixth sense worked. "You got it on loan."

"I did not have the money."

"I am surprised you could not manage the money, which is not difficult for a police officer of your stature."

"After I found Gurdit in Dera Baba Jaimal Singh, I vowed in the name of Gurus that I would never take bribe again. At times I can't avoid it, then I donate the entire amount to Pingal Wada."

"But you never told me."

"I wanted to pursue my vow humbly, never to feel proud of it."

"We are going to return this bitchy necklace right now."

"Now when I have purchased it . . . . it's okay . . . I will manage to pay . . . . I am going to cut down my expenses."

"If you don't return it, then I am going to cut down my throat. I am the greatest bitchy woman in this town!"

And she started pushing and banging him tenderly, which excited him.

"Gurdit did grave injustice to you by asking you to stop beating me."

"A little slowly, otherwise my bones will crack." He laughed. She started dragging him out. And then she began beating her own face. Dayal Singh caught her hands and kissed them.

"I will burn myself to death or eat *Sankhya* [poison] if you don't return the necklace this very moment."

She pushed him out of the house with necklace case in her hand.

Peace prevailed in their house after seven days. When at night, he tried to denude her, she said huskily, "Let this slave please her lord."

He was amazed at her enthusiasm.

After their love making, when she was going to sleep on her cot, he asked, "What about another trip?"

"Look at the watch, it is so late. I've to get up early to prepare breakfast for our daughters. I don't like it if they are late for the school."

They kissed each other and he gently stroked her breasts and slept peacefully.

In the morning, Basant Kaur [Banto was her pet name] was resolved to sever all her relations with her mother who was her philosopher guide in her coquettish behaviour.

The great Gurus have their own ways to teach their followers, as they themselves lived by example.

A week later when they were all having their evening tea, Gurdit said, "I find lot of change in you daar ji, you have mellowed down but I feel uncomfortable when you abuse, which you do a lot."

"Then I have to leave my job. If we in the police force stop abusing, then there will be more criminals than law abiding people in the city . . . Our job is a very tough one. We have to deal with convicts and criminals and not with gentlemen. Do you think a criminal will confess if I recite *Gurubani* to him? Of course it can be effective if a criminal intends to reform himself."

She giggled and then added, "I always know when he is upset or tense, because then your daar ji starts abusing."

After a pause Gurdit said, "I am lucky to have parents like you."

"We are luckier *laal ji* [darling]."

CHAPTER 14

Two days after Gupta was beaten in the police station, he fled from Amritsar in the middle of the night and went to stay in his village near Jalandhar; luckily he had never talked to anyone about his village. He was shit scared that he may not get exposed about his other nefarious activities.

He was often surprised why his wife never insisted that he should stay with her permanently in the village or take her with him to Amritsar. She always gave him money which she earned by managing his lands. He always pretended that he needed money for further investment in his business. Money was the be-all and the-end all of his life. His wife, Sunaina never knew that he was having a mistress with whom he was living in Amritsar. He made it a point to come to his village after every two months. He never stayed there for more than two to three days. He never found a hint of sadness or remorse on her part when he left for Amritsar. She was open-minded, kind hearted and was free from womanly guiles. She had agreeable features, though did not look much attractive because she lacked femininity and had a husky manly voice, but God had endowed her with buxom seemliness. She was an inch taller than Gupta, so after her marriage she discarded her high heeled sandals, and never put them on even during his absence. She was born and brought up in Kenya, had studied in a prominent convent school and spoke immaculate English, at times she found it difficult to express herself in Punjabi. Her family had a flourishing business in Kenya and she was a silent partner in one of their concerns, who regularly sent her money and gifts on important festivals, which are too many in Hindu religion. Gupta knew about it but preferred not to talk about it.

The only thing she hid from her husband was that she was a practicing dyke, who had always managed to have a young docile girl as her lover, but never more than one at a time. She had well thought of it, never to disappoint her husband in the bed. She was always cooperative, keen and enthusiastic during their love making, that is why her husband could not know that she was a lesbian, though heterorsexual. She was initiated into this practice by an English gyaenecologist, a spinster in her early forties, who had a great genital urge, and despised men. She even avoided to be wished or to wish a man. She was only fourteen when she first husbanded her. Of course, she looked older than her age. She was tall, well-built with fully developed bosom. She remembered all the details of their first sojourn, and cherished its memory.

Margaret Ellison, the gyaenecologist had very bitter memories of her family life. Her father was a brute and a terror in the house, when angered he would become extremely vulgar. Her mother was meek and very submissive and was always in awe of her husband. His father was too indulgent for her brother and never reprimanded him, no matter what he did. With his tacit encouragement, he became wayward and immoralist, which surprisingly pleased her father. Once his brother tried to be fresh with her and she complained to her father, but he said nothing to him and advised her not to wear miniskirts and 'B' line showing blouses. 'Keep your skirts a little down and your top up. The way you dress up, even I get excited. I am your father, so I check myself.' Her mother died at the age of forty eight due to low blood pressure, aneamia and her hemoglobin was much below the required level. She had left her home four years before her death, the day she saw her father sodomising her mother. She totally cut off all her relations with her family, including her mother for tolerating so much. She equally blamed her mother for her pitiable condition. If she had the will to fight for her rights, the family atmosphere would have been much different, much better. Once, she got a telegram from her brother that their father had died. She immediately replied, 'not coming. Do piss on his grave on my behalf.' She had not attended the funeral of even her mother, but she did cry on that day because in her own way she was a loving mother.

Sunaina had three affairs with her young maids from the hilly area, till she met Neelam in the local mandir, which changed her life altogether and made it meaningful.

Neelam was a young beautiful widow, who was working as a teacher in the local school, not because she needed money, she belonged to an affluent Khatri family, but to have some purpose in her life. She had high moral values, and was straight forward and never told a lie. In her college life, she was both a brilliant student as well as a class athlete. She was a dotting mother to her only son, but never pampered him. She strongly believed that a child should be treated like the strings of a *Veena* [an Indian musical instrument], if you tighten it too much the strings will break and if you loosen it and then the instrument will produce no music.

Once Sunaina asked her why she did not remarry. She replied that it was not because she was against the remarriage of the widows, and also amongst the Khatri families of Punjab the remarriage of a widow was unacceptable. It was simply for the reason that the memory of her late husband was very precious to her and she won't be able to adjust with any other man.

That night lying awake in her bed, Sunaina was thinking that she was a lesbian, but those poor maids whom she was able to woo were not, rather far from it. She was able to lure them in her trap because of her money power and tact, initially all of them were very uncomfortable by her amatory advances but she cryptically silenced their resentment by showering them with expensive gifts, which they could not afford to buy even in their dreams and she treated them royally just to satisfy her sexual urge. Later on, when they left they must have lamented doing all this, as they never wrote to her and also must have destroyed her letters. *Henceforth, I am not going to pursue innocent, vulnerable poor girls for my physical compulsions. I am going to befriend only bona fide lesbians, though they are difficult to find in this part of the world. Lesbians have their peculiar physical urges, they are different from other female genres, far . . . far different. They may become heterosexual because of social compulsions or by choice. But their predominant attraction is always for the one belonging to their own sex. Their sense of devotion is much more than that of a girl for a boy or a boy for a girl. They might be able to suppress their libidinous cravings, but they cannot backpedal from their physical compulsions.*

One of the reasons that Sunaina and Neelam became close friends was that they could converse in English fluently. One day, Neelam happened to tell her that she wished that English was taught to the girls in her school. English, at that time, was taught from class 5th class onwards in government and government aided schools. Vast percentage of students who failed in Matriculation exam was those, who conked out in their English paper. The reason was that they started too late to learn this language. Education system was at a standstill with no new ideas, with no zeal to improve the system, and those in authority in the education department were fully content with obsolete ideas. There were no innovators to think of improving the education system. The law makers were too busy in their political in fights.

Sunaina suggested that they should have a talk in this matter with the school headmistress.

Neelam replied, "Of course, we must, there is a Punjabi saying, *Baba gur nahin davega, ghar taa aan davega* [if the ascetic won't give the treacle, he will at least let us come home]."

It was Sunday and they decided there and then to go to her home.

The idea of teaching English to the young girls from the very beginning appealed to her, but she showed her helplessness to take a decision in this matter of her own, at the same time she told them that she would talk about it favourably to the Chairman of the School Advisory Committee. The head-mistress, Mrs. Kanta Khanna straight way went to the house of the Chairman, Mr. Yash Pal Khosla, and told him about this brilliant idea emerging from two enthusiastic ladies. He decided to call immediately an emergency meeting of the Advisory Board.

The school peon came to Sunaina's house with a letter inviting her to attend a meeting to be held in the room of the headmistress. She went along with Neelam and when they reached there, they found that Mr. Khosla was speaking on the importance of education for the girl child. On such occasions, he always spoke for only twenty minutes, never a minute less or a minute more. In between he always looked at his watch. After his speech there was loud clapping, because there was the chance of his treating them lavishly at his home, moreover he had two beautiful daughters. If there was no clapping, there was no party, never. In his speech, whenever he used bombastic words, he looked at his audience proudly and felt elevated that they did not understand the meanings of the words he had used. On such parties, he sometimes offered them drinks depending on the volume of the applause.

On one such occasion when drinks were served, raising his glass, he toasted, "A votre sante."

Seth Jetha Mal, who was as usual half listening, got up and said, "I am not going to drink *santra*, as this country liquor does not suit me."

Mr. Khosla got up and said with a self satisfying pride, "Damn it . . . it does not mean santra . . . it means, to your health."

All of them shouted in unison, Santre . . . . Santre [which in Punjabi means oranges]. And they started drinking. For a change, he did not correct them that it was not santre but sante.

After the clapping subsided, he asked Sunaina what were her views on this subject. Sunaina gave her views in immaculate British accent. Nobody was listening to what she was saying, but all their attention was how she was speaking . . . . *what an accent*, every one thought.

Mr. Khosla felt a bit awkward, he realized that he speaks in Punjabi accent.

Later on, he switched over to Punjabi and and said, "I don't think there is any need for an interview. We request her to join our school as an English teacher."

All ten members agreed by waving their hands.

For a school run for the girls, there was not a single lady member in the Advisory committee.

They started discussing her salary in whispers, Sunaina heard it. A Punjabi whisper can be heard ten feet away. She got up and said, "Please listen . . . . your attention please . . . . I will be happy with just one rupee as token money."

Santokh Singh who on this appointment was joyous of all, took out his kirpan [sword] from the scabbard and started half jumping to and fro and saying, "You bring laurels on our village . . . and pay we just you one rupee, it is better to drown inside a river . . . . no . . . big no . . . . we pay you finely, rather very finely."

Everybody agreed and clapped and after a few more to and fro half jumps, and waiving of his sword which twice struck the ceiling fan, which luckily was motionless due to power break down, he finally took his seat.

Through out this display, all the members including the three ladies who were sitting on their haunches on the floor took back to their seats. Barring the three ladies, the antics of Sardar Santokh Singh were of no surprise to anyone, at times they waited for it. Sometimes, others also joined him in these antics. Today, he was the lone performer because of the lack of space.

After everybody had calmed down, Mr. Khosla uttered, "Santokh Singh, when you speak in English, it appears that English is the mother tongue of we Punjabis, you speak it so naturally."

All of them laughed including Santokh Singh. Jetha Mal who was asleep thought a joke had been narrated, started laughing belatedly, this made others laugh. He further increased his volume, and this time others matched his volume with their volume. Afterwards, tea and *pakoras* were served and when it was all over, Santokh announced.

"Bill this Santokh Singh pay from his own pocket and no from school money." And he did pay the bill.

Sunaina received a hand written appointment letter within fifteen minutes. There was no mention of the salary, as the committee members felt it can be decided later on, any time.

Sunaina joined the school the very next day, and it was decided to allot one period for every class, i.e. from class I to class IV.

Like her friend Neelam, she was resolved to teach her students in an innovative way and not in a dull and drudgery manner. She was of the opinion that studies should be fun for the young students and not a pain in the neck.

Whenever a student gave the right answer or did her home work in a neat and proper manner, she rewarded her with a toffee. Her purse was always full of toffees. Soon, she was being called *toffee wali madam* [madam with the toffees] and no student ever liked to miss her class. After Neelam, she became the most popular teacher. The headmistress never felt jealous of them, because she was going to retire within six months.

With the passage of time, students were now speaking to each other in English, in short sentences as instructed by Neelam and Sunaina. It was also being picked up by their elders in their homes. Within no time, the ambience of speaking in English prevailed in the entire village. Even the local cobbler, washer man and the barber started using some English words. Their village got the nickname of *Angreza da pind* [village of the English] by the adjoining villagers. They felt honoured and decide to have a grand party with drinks and lavish dinner, this time they did not let Khosla Sahib spend. Being Punjabis, they just need an excuse to celebrate with drinks, it is their weakness.

During the party, Mr. Khosla took Santokh aside, as he wanted to discuss with him the salient features of his article on corruption, on which he was working presently and which he was going to send to the Tribune. He continued telling him about his article till they had finished three pegs. Santokh did not feel bored listening to his long discourse, as he felt that he found him erudite enough to discuss it only with him. Actually, he wanted to know the reaction of a not so educated man and Santokh could comprehend it here and there but most of it went over his head.

Whenever his article was published in the Tribune, he always threw a lavish party, where his close friends were invited and that also included three members of the School Advisory Committee, Santokh for his emotional but burlesque reactions, which immensely amused him and Seth Jetha Mal because his 'Wah Wah' in appreciation was the loudest and Pundit Sunder Lal Sharma a book lover like him, who was invariably a good guest, who rarely invited anybody to his house. Whenever his friends came to his house, he immediately asked his wife to prepare tea for them, but she continued sitting on her *peeri* [a kind of small stool], and participated in their parleys and when there was nothing more to discuss, she languidly walked towards her kitchen and by that time his friends decided to leave. Then she would come out with her pet sentence, *ey chuthi gal ey* [this is not the done thing], you are leaving without having tea. His friends often used to say, 'it is easier to milk a bull than to make Sunder Lal spend.' The Sharma family was quite well off, but fate eluded them to spend even on themselves. They were sickly stingy.

Jetha Mal was replaced by a young brilliant student, Dushyant Bakshi, as he was once found snoring during one of his intellectual discourses, where he expected to be appreciated the most. He discussed his article on corruption with Dushyant Bakshi, a young student, and appreciated his reaction and suggestions. Then Bakshi suddenly asked, "Uncle, what is your aim, to be admired or you want your article to have impact on the people and if it is so, then please don't use unheard of words." Actually, he meant not to use bombastic words. Mr. Khosla agreed and he rewrote his article that way.

They often had their stag parties which were held in the lawns of Mr. Khosla's house, which was abhorred by their women. But nobody dared to speak against him as he had done so much for the village with his generosity. He always saw to it that no one got over drunk, lest they were not able to go back to their home. If he had not taken this step, after the party was over, some would have been just able to stagger back home, others would have slept on the lawns itself. When they tried to drink more at home to make up for their quota, often there was a big fight between the husband and wife, as she urged him not to drink more, which was a source of enjoyment for their neighboours and when taunted by them in the morning, the wife always defended her husband, 'all men are like that, my man is no different. Try to mend the ways of your own husband', and it most of the time led to a short quarrel between them.

Punjabis often try to out drink each other to show their manliness and to repent it in the morning because of the hang over, vowing never to do it again. Within a few days, they altogether forget about this vow. The taking of vow and forgetting about it after a few days continues all their life.

During the drinking sessions, suddenly drinks were stopped from being served. Then commenced the session of jokes and poetry recitation, which was mostly recitation of Urdu poetry of which people of North India including Punjabis are very fond of, although at times they are unable to understand the Persian and Arabic words used in Urdu poetry. Well, people in India so often appreciate the most what they understand the least, although they can't conceal their boredom.

The very next Sunday, his article was published in the Tribune, and this time he had decided to frustrate the sub-editor by not using any foreign word or phrase, so that his pen remains idle. There was hardly any editing, however, the sub-title in the news paper was changed from, 'The Corruption – the Leviathan Menace' to 'Corruption, a Gigantic Menace.' Khosla was not happy over this change of title, but he tolerated it.

He decided to give a lavish party where Scotch whisky was going to be served. Not only there was no editing of his article but also for the fact that he got a letter of appreciation from the Editor, that too hand written, and it was for the first time in his writing career.

He decided that he himself won't read his own article, but assign this job to someone and will watch the reactions of others with eagle's eyes. He thought of two to three names, including that of Pt. Sunder Lal Sharma, but finally selected young Dushyant Bakshi for this job.

People were amazed at such immaculate and tasteful arrangements, as was least expected by them. His friends were always punctual for these parties, because if somebody came late and the article was being read, Khosla always started reading it from the very beginning, the late comers always received curses from others in abundance.

When Jetha Mal came to know that Khosla had altogether stopped inviting him to his parties, he complained to him, "This you have done on the instigation of that *Sharanarthi* (refugees) boy Dushyant Bakshi from West Punjab."

Mr. Khosla retorted, "He is above these petty matters and these people from West Punjab are not Sharanarthis but *Purusharthis* (Action Oriented).

Have you seen anyone of them begging? Note it in your diary, one day these very people whom third rate people like you look down upon will make their mark in every walk of life by their sheer hard work and tenacious determination."

Later on these Purusharthis called Sharanarthis could boast of two Prime Ministers who belonged to West Punjab, namely Inder Kumar Gujral from district Jhelum and Dr.Manmohan Singh belonged to a village called Gah in district Chakwal. Har Gobind Khorana, the Nobel Prize winner in physiology and medicine belonged to village Raipur in Khanewal district. The noted actor producer Sunil Dutt, who later on became the sports minister of India, lived in village Khurd in Jhelum district. The greatest cricket all rounder of India, Kapil Dev's father, Ram Lal Nikhanj was a timber merchant in Montgomery (renamed Sahiwal). Many of them made a name in the field of art, literature and industry. Financially they are better-off than many Indians belonging to other regions.

Mr. Khosla further added that many of the people who made a name in the history of Pakistan were outsiders, they belonged to places which are now a part of India. The first Governor General, Mohd. Ali Jinnah was a practicing lawyer of Bombay, and their first prime minister, Liaqat Ali Khn belonged to district Karnal. General Parvez Musharaf, and the President of Pakistan was from the walled city of Delhi. The prime minister, Nawaz Sharif's father lived in village Jati Umra near Amritsar. His father migrated to Pakistan in 1947. When the whole world was aghast about the imminent execution of Nawaz Sharif, under the regime of Parvez Musharaf, Hindus and the Sikhs of his ancestral village held a congregation and had night long prayers for his long life. It speaks volumes about the cultural, social and emotional ties between the Hindus, Sikhs and the Muslims. Then why was this Qatal-e-aam [genocide] during the partition of India?

Jetha Mal listened to him very attentively and praised him highly for his knowledge, and became sure that henceforth, he would be invited to his parties, but it was not to be.

Before the meeting, Khosla gave Dushyant Bakshi the letter from the editor to read and he told him that he was not going to tell others about this letter, as it would sound boastful. Dushyant Bakshi got the hint.

At the very start, Dushyant told the audience about this letter, there was a huge applause and when he said, the entire village should feel proud of Mr. Khosla, their applause was thunderous. Just then, Santokh Singh's hand automatically went to the hilt of his scabbard, which someone stealthily removed without letting him realize it. Mr. Khosla had deputed two people for this job.

And then he straightway started reading the letter. He was a real good debater, so he had already marked the paper with a read pen, where to pause and where to stress.

'Corruption, a Gigantic Menace'

By Y.P. Khosla

"In its march towards progress, any nation has to face many obstacles and hurdles to achieve its goal. Be it lack of certain natural resources, geographical barriers, paucity of capital and financial backing, lack of growth of flora and fauna over population. A nation in its growth faces numerous impediments. But corruption stands tall against all these stumbling blocks. Even the occurrence of a typhoon, a cyclone or some epidemic cannot be that far reaching than the appalling menace of corruption – It may be said that the former don't create havoc too often and extensively as corruption does. The roots of corruption are stronger and more wide-spread than that of a *Peepal* tree."

Hearing the name of the holy *peepal* tree, people applauded and bowed their heads in reverence.

"Surprisingly, in most corrupt countries like Indonesia, India, Pakistan and some African and Latin American countries, a vast majority of people are theists and Gnostics. They know and behave that it is a sin to be corrupt, yet they do not disengage themselves from corruption, because they do not have fear of God's wrath. Rather the corrupts have found means by being ostentatiously religious, by observing fasts, organizing religious congregations and other religious rites prevalent in their respective religions to appease God. So, they can compensate for their sins by doing religious prayers. It is surprising that amongst atheists and agnostics, very few are corrupt."

Dushyant Bakshi took a pause for people to applaud. And they did. They had seen bottles of Scotch whisky.

"The old dictum that corruption starts at the top and masses are blamed for it is now just a hackneyed phrase. What goads us to break the queues at religious places, bribe the priest, get out of turn *darshan* of idols and be bestowed with *prasadam* much before our turn? The answer is, none."

The audience duly applauded.

"It is because we have become mentally corrupt and corruption is the in thing."
This time, there was some genuine applause.
"It's true, sometimes a man leans toward corruption due to dire needs, but once one plunges in to it, the greed becomes insatiable."

"It may seem ridiculous, but it is a hard fact that many traders, contractors and industrialists prefer to deal with corrupt officials than to face an honest one, because they can manage to get their work done smoothly and without any delay. This way, they hardly face procedural hassles."

The audience could hardly understand anything and started wishing that soon the lecture was over.

"The poet Akbar Allahabadi, who was a magistrate in the British India said long back, perhaps a hundred years ago."

> 'Lekey Rishwat phas gaya hai
> Dekey Rishwat chhoot ja'
> (Took bribe, got entangled
> Give bribe, be free)

Now the audience was out of their slumber, and started shouting, "Wah Wah, Muqerer Muqerer (Once more, once more)."

"We are not having a poetic symposium," smiled Dushyant Bakshi.

Santokh's hand started towards his scabbard, but it was quietly removed again.

And he continued, "In the realm of corruption scenario, there are some who are not corrupt being moralists. They find themselves misfit, weak and unwanted. They lack guts to expose those around them who are corrupt, because the latter are clever and can go to any level to entrap them in some false case. They may get finally absolved of their charges and reinstated, but this takes many years to happen in India. Often one finds an honest man in shackles and those who are corrupt and unscrupulous moving around scot-free. At times, these idealists are not liked by their own families who consider them naïve and impractical, when they see their colleagues having much better life styles. Comparisons never get ignored."

The audience clapped with fake enthusiasm, thinking when will this *Siapa* [mourning] stop.

Dushyant Bakshi realized that it has not stirred the audience and this applause was just a show off. He finished the rest of the article without taking any pause and at a fast pace and at the end of it there was uproar of applause and clapping. Actually people felt much relieved when it got finished.

They surrounded Mr. Khosla in a melee, everybody wanted to be the first to embrace and congratulate him. They then decided to form a queue and Santokh Singh was the first in the line. Nobody tried to take his place because of his height and strong built. Actually, he was very soft spoken and never fought with anyone verbally or physically but because of his awe-aspiring physique, nobody ever dared to take any *'panga'* with him. They did it profusely one by one.

Mr. Khosla thoroughly enjoyed this fan-fare. Of course, they had their intellectual discourse every Sunday in the evening, in which Pundit Sunder Lal, Santokh Singh, one Kundal Lal and Dushyant Bakshi participated. Bottle was opened only when Sunder Lal left and in case he lingered on, they went to Santokh Singh's house and he dared not enter his house, because once Santokh Singh's wife rebuked him, "I can't understand why you drink, what sort of a Brahmin you are!!"

Once Dushyant Bakshi just happened to ask uncle Khosla if he had read Munshi Prem Chand and he replied in the negative. He got 'Nirmala' and 'Godan' issued, two of Prem Chand's well known novels from his college library and urged him to read them.

He was immensely impressed by Prem Chand's simple and effective style, and he learnt much from him. He started adopting simple and easy to communicate style and he became one of the most eminent columnists.

Once Dushyant Bakshi and Khosla were discussing Shakespeare's tragedies and Dushyant just asked him, "Uncle, I guess the way you love Sardar Santokh Singh ji, that way you love none. Am I right?"

After some moments, Khosla said, "Do me a favor, go to Santokh's house and tell him that I need him. There is an emergency."

Dushyant Bakshi was surprised at this command, but could not disobey and he went to Santokh Singh's house. It was 11 pm, people in the village used to go to bed between 8 to 9 pm.

Soon, Santokh Singh came rushing to his house bare-footed, bewilderment was written large on his face.

"What's the matter?" he asked.

"I was just missing you and wanted to have a peg with you before going to sleep."

And they had a peg each and after that Santokh Singh left. He did not complain even once why he was disturbed when he was sleeping.

"You got your answer?"

"I did, sir."

CHAPTER 15

Dushyant's father, Uttam Chand Bakshi was working as a station master in the Indian Railways. Just during the outset of riots, he was transferred from Ambala Cantt to Multan. His wife asked him to quit his job which he could not as he had a large family to support, with three sons and four daughters. He had some income from his ancestral property but that was not enough to support a large family. His wife suggested that he should go on long leave, but he quietened her by saying that one day he would have to join, then why to go on leave.

Just one and a half month before his matriculation exams, Dushyant Bakshi had typhoid, which got relapsed. He was an exceptionally brilliant student, but he wrote his papers with trembling hands, sometimes darkness was cast on his eyes. He passed with a poor third class and he could not get admission in an agreeable college in Multan. With local influence, he was able to get admission in DAV College, Jalandhar.

In the meantime, riots made their headway by leaps and bounds, he could never go to Multan to meet his family though he was entitled to travel free, being the son of a railway employee. Though he missed them immensely, he continued studying diligently because he wanted to avenge his third class in matriculation. He was informed by his elder sister through a letter that their mother was once again pregnant. He felt disgusted, became a loner and stopped mixing up with others. Apart from studies, his only interest was to participate in debates, and he won many prizes in inter-college debating competitions. He always shunned the company of girls, no girl ever attracted him.

When the Independence Day was being celebrated on 15th August, 1947, it was not a day of rejoicing for him. He had not received a letter from home for the last twenty days, otherwise religiously he got a letter once a week. It was always a post card with a printed three paisa stamp on it. Days passed, his disorientation increased. He could never know what happened to his entire family. He drowned his despair in his studies.

Then he met Khosla Sahib and his sorrow found some solace.

He developed an aversion to religious chartings, practices, congregations and political processions. He lost all faith in God and never prayed.

He cleared the Civil Services examination in the very first attempt and fared very well in the interview. His Professor, Mehta Vashisht whom he idolized, had advised him to 'be yourself', and it paid. He had no coaching, though Khosla uncle was too ready to finance it, but the advice of Professor Vashisht was supreme for him.

At the age of thirty nine, he was Deputy Commissioner of district Gurdaspur. He was an honest and diligent officer, though somewhat unconventional, and was known for his quick decisions, made no friends, never smoked or drank and was a strict vegetarian. He worked with missionary zeal, after office work the books were his only companion. He never invited anybody to his palatial bungalow and never accepted any invitations. Of course, he kept in touch with Khosla uncle.

The only one with whom he talked intimately was his gardner, Shankar Prasad. His interest in gardening was that of a curious enthusiastic child.

A fare was organized in Batala, a tehsil of district Gurdaspur by the Red Cross Society of India which he was to inaugurate. After the inaugural, he started taking rounds of the stalls, asked a question or two and then moved to the next one. In one of these stalls, he met a lady and asked her how the sale was going on and if she needed any help. She started talking to him as if she knew him since long. She had a melodious voice and a bewitching smile. For the first time in his life Dushyant Bakshi felt attracted to a woman. Actually, it was her coquetry and few could escape her trap.

The very next day, she came to his office and told him that she was a widow with a one year old child and desperately needed a reasonably good job to make both ends meet and she had come to seek his help.

He noticed that she had very expressive hazel-coloured eyes. He assured her that he would do his best. She left and he started day dreaming about her. He started inviting her to his house and found her companionable, a good listener and very feminine. One day, he proposed to her, which to his relief she accepted.

After ten days they got married in a very simple ceremony, the only invitees were Mr. Khosla and his family and Sardar Santokh Singh.

After one month of their marriage, Dushyant Bakshi resigned from his job as deputy commissioner as he had got fed up with political interference in his work, day in and day out. He joined Larson and Tubro as Deputy General Manager, with the assurance that he would be promoted to the rank of the General Manager with in one year. He got his posting in Bombay and was provided an accommodation in the suburban area of Khar. He was also given a chauffeur driven car and he got a better pay scale than what he was getting from government of India. The company paid the salary of its officers in such a manner that they were to pay much less income tax than a government officer has to pay.

His wife was excited to go to Bombay, a metropolitan city with life full of hustle and bustle, compared with the dull and drudgery life of Gurdaspur, with no charm of night life, besides there were monetary gains. Above all she could have a look at film stars, she was simply crazy about them.

When she found that they were allotted a three bed room accommodation on the second floor, she was really disappointed. They had a sprawling bungalow with full of amenities provided by the government of India, but other things far outscored this dejection.

Within days, with his intelligence, diligence and on the spot quick decisions, he made his presence felt in the company. He got his next promotion after just six months.

After just three months of his stay in Bombay, his wife started showing her true colours. She dressed up vulgarly, which according to her was the fashion of the day and her make up gave the impression of a street walker. She always preferred the company of men than that of the ladies. What surprised him the most was that she never talked about the custody of her son, who was living with the parents of her first husband, which he would have readily agreed to live with them and would have given the child all his love and care.

Once he got an invitation to attend a party organized by some of his colleagues, he refused politely saying he was not a partygoer and he said it in such a manner that they would not invite him in future. When his wife came to know about it, she created quite a scene and even called him 'a dull pig'.

He started losing interest in her and gradually developed aversion for her and almost became asexual.

Once he had to go to such a party to avoid her bickering. When they reached the venue of the party, it was in full swing. He was offered drinks which he refused, but Shobha promptly took the glass, as she had seen some ladies drinking, she had always craved to appear modern. Dushyant Bakshi just managed to keep his cool. She started drinking as if it was not a new thing for her and she was sipping with sham sophistication. After two pegs, she began flirting with his colleagues.

When they reached home, she was so drunk that he had to drag her to the bed and she said trying to open her eyes, "Darling, come jump over me." He did not respond, soon, she was snoring.

The very next day, he got a letter that Mr. Khosla had left for his heavenly abode. He did not go to his village but promptly sent a letter of condolence showing his great grief. Mr. Khosla was only sixty two at the time of his death. After the loss of his family during the riots, it was the greatest shock of his life. *The citadel has crumbled, what is the use of looking at the debris.* So he did not go to attend even the Kirya ceremony.

Her wayward avocations extremely upset him, he tried to counsel her but it had little effect on her. He started losing interest in sex. She always dressed up and applied the make up in such a manner which was unbecoming for a lady from a respectable family, but still he did not lose his composure and did not let his office work suffer, although he felt anguished all the time and even lost his appetite.

She even found a lover, a rich Gujrati jeweler. Initially, she met him on the sly, then cared two hoots for anybody. Dushyant had kept his eyes closed, and this had emboldened her and she started meeting him openly. Later on, sometimes she did not come home during the night. He reconciled with all this stoically. *It is her body, let her use it the way she wants.* Now nothing affected him, he had become a man without any aim, zeal, hope and emotions. And with no love for life, with no sense of belongingness with anybody, anything in this cruel world, he started suffering from insomnia.

One Sunday evening, she was all sweet and honey with him. There was going to be a grand party organized by his office in which he was invited along with his wife. She implored him to attend this party but he refused. She continued with her pleadings but he was a sort of a man who once takes a decision does not budge from it. She started shouting to scare him with the contention 'what will the neighbours think', and it will make him change his mind. When even this had no effect on him, she cursed him with choicest Punjabi abuses, he just kept mum. Finally, she called for a taxi on the phone and left for the party in a huff.

She came home quite late at night and was quite drunk. He was working on an important project which he was to present in his office the next day. She pushed away his papers and took off her top.

"Look at my boobies . . . aren't they beautiful . . . . very very sexy . . . come on . . . enjoy me."

He felt disgusted, but just said calmly, "Better go to your bed," and resumed his work.

She flew in a rage. She felt like a woman defiled and laughed in a sarcastic manner. "You are not a man but a eunuch . . . . you son of a eunuch . . . . yes, so was your father, now say something."

"I will do," He squeezed her tits till she started writhing in pain and then gave her a hard slap.

"And your mother was a five rupee whore." She shouted at the top of her voice.

He gave her another blow with the back of his hand, it was even more severe. She grabbed a chair to hit him, and he easily managed to snatch it from her and hit her belly with his right knee. She fell on the ground with unbearable pain.

She wailed loudly, and with her roof-shattering cries wanted the neihbours to come to her rescue, but it was Bombay and not Punjab. No one came to save her.

Then she began abusing him like a slut and when her quota of abuses got exhausted, to shatter his pride she yelled, "When those Musalmans were raping your sisters, they were really enjoying it . . . . and were asking for more and more."

He took a shoe and started beating her left and right with all his strength. The more she cried, the more severely he beat her. She began pleading with him with folded hands to pardon her only this time and she would behave henceforth, and be a good wife. But he continued beating her, as if some lunacy had prevailed on him, and stopped only till he had no strength left in his hands and then he kicked her with his foot and left for his room.

In the morning, she packed her clothes and a few other essential items, and told him before leaving, rather meekly [she remembered last night's thrashing] "I am leaving."

"Thanks." He said mildly and closed the door.

In the morning he went to his office, as usual he was punctual and immaculately dressed as he was resolved that his personal life should have no impact on his work. His project report was really liked by the managing director. He was feeling giddy as last night he did not have a wink of sleep and had not eaten anything both in the evening and in the morning. He just had bed tea in the morning and another cup of tea in the office. He took half day's leave.

He started walking aimlessly on the road and wherever he found a chemist shop he bought a few sleeping pills, as he had realized that only sleeping pills can induce him to sleep so he should collect enough quotas as to last at least for a fortnight. He continued walking where his feet dragged him. *There is no hurry to reach home. No one is waiting for me.* He continued walking for about four hours. *What is the hurry to go home . . . I have no home . . . . it is a house, not a home . . . not at all.*

He continued buying sleeping pills. He had such a personality which bespoke of nobility, no chemist could think of doubting his intentions. In India, in day to day practice, you don't need a doctor's prescription to buy any kind of medicines.

He had completely lost his sense of proportion.

He reached near a railway station, he did not even care to read the name of the station and bought a first class ticket for Khar and when the train arrived, he was so absent minded that he got into the third class compartment. From Khar, he walked towards his house and on the way bought a bottle of whisky . . . . *others say that they feel highly spirited when they drink whisky, let me try at least once . . . . I am craving to feel spirited.* He reached his home and opened the bottle, but did not like the smell. *I will give it to someone. There are many, who will love to take it . . . . let me not waste the money by throwing it.* He corked it back. He brought a jar of water and a glass tumbler from the kitchen. He was feeling very thirsty. *Better I sleep. I have hardly slept for the last three months and for that I need the pills . . . . one is enough, no better I take two . . . . I want to sleep for long hours . . . . why I can't mix up with any one apart from my family whom I have lost for ever . . . . and of course, there was Khosla uncle . . . very generous . . . . erudite . . . a wonderful man with a child like ego.* He took one more pill and then laughed. *I had to use my tact to make him read Munshi Prem Chand to stop him from using bombastic words and he started writing much better. He was like a wall which supported me, but the gusty winds of the nature have thrown away the wall . . . . Far, faraway . . . .* He took another pill. *Then there was Sardar Santokh Singh . . . such a wonderful man . . . . simple minded, I liked him yet could not communicate with him . . . .*

there is definitely something wrong with me . . . . decidedly, I am insipid. He took another pill. *That woman, my so called wife, said that my sisters were raped . . . . how she knew it . . . . perhaps it was her guess . . . . it can be true, because the world at that time was ruled by a powerless God . . . . or were they abducted and got forcibly married or made concubines . . . who knows or they paid the price for the two nation theory and got murdered, the wretched villains were unmindful of the fact that their mother is also a Woman, The Creator of the Human Race . . . . Pak means, the pure and the Hindustan was named, 'Bharat' after the great son of India who could tame the lions . . . . but women were meant to be raped, defiled, disgraced and if they were spared for their life, they were ravished . . . mauled . . . . battered . . . . on both sides . . . . for the glorification of their nation . . . for the cause of their revered religion, so that they have a sound foundation.* He took another pill. *Men were killing each other, not women . . . there were less murders of the female sex in comparison only this way, they were lucky, ha, because they were commodities for great entertainment . . . . They justified their killings, otherwise how could they show their manliness . . . . and it was for the glorification of their august religion . . . . to show that their religion was better and more exalted.* He took two more pills, unaware of what he was doing. *I must sleep . . . . we had our quarrels, but we were a very happy family . . . . I should not have left Multan or should have visited them at least once . . . . I did not, because I lacked guts . . . . I should have died along with my family . . . . now, I have to live alone, a joyless life, can't even enjoy a joke . . . always feel lonely, even sometimes in the company of Khosla Sahib I felt so . . . .* and he took two more pills. *I should not take these pills any more, it may not turn into a habit . . . it has bad side effects . . . . today is going to be the last time. Only one more is enough . . . . how many were killed from the both sides . . . it was never counted, only estimated, of course . . . . I should have been there at Multan . . . . should have tried to save them . . . . Hate myself from the core f my heart for being away from them . . . . I am cowardly . . . . indeed, I am. What is God . . . . who is God . . . . when . . . . where . . . . why . . . and we feel proud, when we pray to him.* He took one more pill. *Your role models are Guru Gobind Singh . . . . Sardar Bhagat Singh . . . . Lincoln . . . . why are you here? Damn it, go to Multan . . . then this woman will be out of your life . . . . Rush.* In his delirium, thinking that he was going to Multan, took two to three steps and fell like a log on the floor and slept.

Even when on the second day, there was no information about his absence, and no one was picking up the phone at his home, two officials were deputed to go there. There was no response to the ringing of the call bell. They felt the stench but could not know from where it was coming. They knocked at the door, still there was no response. One of them pushed the door; it got opened, as he had forgotten to bolt it from inside. They saw him sprawled on the floor and a foul smell was emanating from his body. They immediately informed the office and their PRO informed the police who along with them went to his house.

The post mortem report revealed that he died due to an overdose of sleeping pills taken on an empty stomach. The doctors were of the opinion that his life could have been saved with timely treatment. When his body was brought to his home, his wife was already there waiting for its arrival.

On seeing his dead body wrapped in a coffin, she began wailing loudly and continued beating her breasts and thighs and it became very difficult for them to console her. Two ladies from the office were asked to stay with her during the night. They were concerned that because of this extreme tragedy, she might not take some wrong step.

During the night, some cops came and asked Shobha to report to the police station, but the two ladies were smart enough to refuse and asked them if they had any warrants. They left immediately. In the morning, the PRO, Dilip Manekar, along with the company lawyer, P.C.Ghawre went to the police station. The SHO told them that under the promise of anonymity, some of her neighbours had informed him that they heard some noises from their house a day before, may be because of that Mr. Dushyant Bakshi committed suicide, so there was a liable case of abetment to suicide and it was a good enough case to take her into police custody. Mr. Ghavre snubbed him that he was going to file a case against him for defaming a helpless widow. He further told him that no case worth the name can be framed as there was no suicide note. The PRO quietly gave the SHO a bottle of scotch, the matter got hushed up there and then. Mr. Manekar was a kind hearted man who thought that there can be quarrels in any family, whatever has happened has happened and the poor widow should not suffer any more. He did not even inform his office about the presentation of a bottle of whisky. He was very loyal to his company and he never wanted the name of the company to be dragged in any unsavoury manner.

After the mourning period of thirteen days, Shobha was given a job in the company on compassionate grounds. Within fifteen days, she was transferred to another section as she was not able to pick up the work assigned to her. People in the company were smart, intelligent and really efficient and she could not match up with them. They were too fast to make her learn, and she was of a below average brain so far office culture was concerned. As she started making others do her work by her flirtatious and arousal bearings, it was noticed by other woman employees and tongues started wailing. One day, she happened to tell her two lady colleagues that her husband was getting a very handsome salary and in comparison she had been offered just peanuts. That was her undoing. Within fifteen minutes, the matter got reported to the bosses. The very next day she got a sack and was given pay packet for the number of days she had worked and one month's salary in lieu of one month's notice period. In a separate letter she was asked to vacate the company's accommodation as the same was allotted to her husband and never to her. She tried to win sympathy by throwing her tantrum, crying and pleading to retain her, but with no effect. When she found not a single backer, she began using foul language, but it fell on deaf ears. Ultimately, Dilip Manekar assured her that they would try to find another job befitting her qualifications and capability, it was just to assuage her pent up emotions. Ultimately she left the office with no hopes, no future and totally helpless.

After she had gone, everyone had the same opinion that she was the reason of Dushyant Bakshi's suicide. They considered her vulgar, uncouth and a shrew, whereas he was suave, cultured and very cooperative, though he was of reserved nature. It was a clear case of mismatch. Manekar agreed with them, yet thought differently. Perhaps she needed a man who could handle her. In his own way, he was sympathetic to her; by disposition he could see beauty where none could be. He had inherent sympathy for the downtrodden and the befallen people, he was a true reformist. Though he was a Hindu Brahmin by caste, yet he was an ardent admirer of Jesus Christ, although he had never been inside a church.

Within seven days of this happening, she got the job of a sales girl in one of the Bombay Dyeing show rooms. By sheer chance Manekar happened to meet the general manager of Bombay Dyeing, who was his college friend, who just casually mentioned that they needed a few sales girls for their show rooms. He told him that he knew a lady who was very needy and suitable for the job.

Next day, after some preliminary interview, Shobha was handed over the appointment letter. Things move very fast in Bombay in comparison to rest of India, the outlook of this metropolitan city is somewhat westernized, moreover people in the private sector are known for their quick decision, and there is very little red tapism, which is in abundance in the government departments and the general public suffers.

This time, she was determined to work hard and to make her presence felt and never to be flirtatious.

She was well liked by her customers as well as the manager. Some regular customers preferred to deal only with her; at times they were even ready to wait for her to be free from the other customers she was dealing with. The manager though was somewhat stern, but kind hearted and was her mentor and guide.

One day, Manekar just out of curiosity went to the show room to see how she was conducting herself. He told her that he wanted a pant and a shirt for some special occasion. He was amazed at her knack of colour choice and sense of matching.

Whereas people in his office had very bad opinion about her, she was considered a scattered brain.

Instead of one pant and one shirt, he bought three pants and three shirts and then to have some fun, he went to the manager and complained that he had come to buy one pant and a shirt only, but his sales girl manuevered to sell him three each. The manager replied that they take it as a big compliment. Manekar told him that he had come to examine whether she was doing a god job and then he told him that he was a friend of their general manager, Mr. Lele, and on whose recommendation she was given the job. The manager told him that she was an asset to the company. He forced him to have a cup of tea with him, saying 'please believe me it is not because you are a friend of Mr. Lele. I like people with your kind of approach, and I immensely enjoy your sense of humour.'

Over a cup of tea, they became friends for ever.

Before leaving, he met Shobha again and told her that she had made him feel proud of her and he was going to give her a nice treat and left without waiting for her reply.

They started meeting quite frequently. After their courtship of four months, one day he gave her a call and told her that his work got finished earlier than expected and he was coming to pick her up, and he was to discuss something very important with her.

"There is so much rush, I can't leave the customers unattended!!"

"Mention my name to your manager, he won't refuse."

"My job is very important to me . . . it has become the be-all and end-all of my life."

"Is it more important than even me?"

"That's true." She giggled.

"I appreciate that . . . okay after the closing hours . . . . I will be waiting for you in the corner," and he gently put down the receiver.

He took her to Juhu beach and took hold of her hand and kept quiet for a pretty long time. He was in deep thoughts of nostalgia.

"Here, I lost my wife to the waves, forever . . . . she was such a wonderful woman . . . beautiful . . . . very beautiful . . . and even more beautiful was her heart."

Tears started flowing from his eyes. She had the woman's intuition what was coming ahead. He proposed to her.

He was swaying in his own mood, what she said had no effect on him. He also told her that he had a one and a half year old son, who was well looked after by a Goanese ayah.

She said, "Look Dilip I adore you . . . . but please believe me I don't deserve you . . . my past . . . . the horrendous past . . . . if you know it, you are never going to like me . . . . at the same time I don't want to lose you as a very dear friend . . . . never . . . . never."

"Past is full of memories, happy, sad . . . . and full of agonies. Past is past. We should always think of the present . . . in case we still have time and energy, then we should think about a little bit of future," he laughed.

Shobha teased him, "You are such an emotional fool."

"Emotional fools are invariably honest people."

"You are just a kid."

"And this kid is going to marry you next Sunday . . . and in case you refuse, I am going to abduct you . . . . I am a Maratha . . . . belong to a warrior race . . . . hot blooded like the Sikhs of your beloved Punjab. Now choice is yours."

"On what day of the week will you allow me to say 'yes'?"

"Right now, and say it loudly . . . . I am a bit hard of hearing."

"Yes . . . . yes . . . . and yes," she said it in his ear.

He kissed her. It was a sublime kiss, which she was going to remember all her life.

At night, she was unable to sleep. Her past was haunting her. It was true that Dushyant Bakshi had died because of her obnoxious behaviour, but was she only to be blamed? Dushyant Bakshi was an idealist, a no-nonsense man, but with little zest for life and not social at all and she was an ordinary mortal, who wanted fun and hustle and bustle in her life, loved to meet people and have a tete-a tete with them, whereas he had least interest in all this, rather avoided it as far as it was possible for him to do so. He loved only his work and always got deeply involved in it and he was a work-alcoholic, and in spare time books were his only love and pastime. Even when she forced him to see a movie, he felt it as a burden and made it quite obvious, which always spoiled her mood. He hardly watched what was happening on the screen and mostly dozed off. He made no friends, called none to his home whereas she was very gregarious by nature. He was totally unromantic, even when he made love to her it was as if he was carrying out a duty assigned to him. But otherwise he was a very generous man, and as a bachelor most of his salary was spent on the needy and the destitute and he never talked about it. He derived great happiness when he could help a poor student. He always dressed immaculately, but never wore expensive clothes and never had too many. He was an exceptionally intelligent man, very tolerant. Before that eventful night, what to talk of raising his hand, he never even raised his voice, even when she nagged him. Of course, whenever there was some discussion with someone, he did argue and with his logic, knowledge and intelligence always had an upper hand. He never deserved a wife like her, who wanted a life full of excitement, which she had missed all her life and for which she yearned and he was a poor sport.

It was she who forced him to go sometimes to a restaurant. He was always reluctant to go as he always said that 'you prepare the food much better, then why to waste money and to waste time by going to a restaurant', but often he had to agree to avoid her tantrums. He always admired her cookery, which made her very happy, but women do like a change, and he could never understand a woman's psyche. He had never witnessed even once, when her mother defied her father.

I should not have left my home that morning. I was beaten during the night and I deserved it. I was being bitchy and proudly so. Perhaps it was the power of fate . . . . cruel fate. Life was miserable in her parental home, which turned into at times nightmarish for her, which was exactly reverse of what a young girl dreams. Her parents took hardly any interest in her as they had to take care of a very large family, nine in all. Actually her mother had given birth to eleven children and they were butts of jokes in their community, where people exaggerated in their jokes about their large family and often said that Lajwanti, her mother had a breed of fourteen litters, out of which to our good luck five went astray hither and thither and never to be found again, and nine had been left to make life complicated for us to give money for all of them on their marriage and they had to feed eleven people on any function held in their community. Their parents cared more for their three sons than their six daughters, whom they neglected unashamedly.

Once, some elderly ladies chided her for her frequent pregnancies, "When will you go on for your vacations?"

"I am his woman, I have to submit."

"Why doesn't he use the rubber?"

"It needles him . . . . he does not enjoy with the rubber on."

"Then go to hell and produce a dozen more."

She could not forget her first night. Her husband slapped her for not taking his shoes off, [His mother had guided him to make his wife take his shoes off, that way he will always dominate over her] and after having his sexual enjoyment made her sleep on the floor as a punishment. In the morning when she complained to his parents, they took their son's side and advised her to be careful in performing her duties as an obedient wife. She had asked for their sympathy, but instead they taunted her, "In the name of furniture, your wretched parents have not even given a stool . . . . even a peon gives better dowry." They continued with their taunts for full two hours.

During the night, her husband first thrashed her for misbehaving with his parents and then made love to her. He often beat her on one excuse or the other. He felt charged after beating her and often had kinky sex with her. Whenever he was ravishing her, she prayed to God to take her life away.

Once she went to her parent's house with bag and baggage and narrated to them her woes. Her father told her that her real place was in her husband's home, but he would try to settle the matter amicably. He had heard about the beatings and ill treatment, but he did not pay much attention to it, thinking that it often happens in marital relations, but by and by things get settled down. He did not want to aggravate the matter by his intervention.

Shoba's father was a sanitary inspector and it is such a job that everybody needs him at one time or the other. Only ten days back his services were required in the police station to find out two dead rats, which had created an untenable bad smell. He took two of his ablest men for this job, even they had to spend two hours to find out the dead rats. The SHO wanted to give him a big treat, but he pretended that he had an important assignment to perform. *I will use him as and when I need him.*

One day, a kind hearted neighbour of Shobha told him that his daughter was beaten very badly by her husband last night. His blood boiled, after all she was his daughter. Now enough was enough. He met the SHO and told him everything which was a clear case of dowry harassment. He sent two of his toughies who were known to first beat the accused before making their enquiries.

It was decided that he along with his daughter will go to his son-in-law's house on Sunday, and they will be there when they least expected them. As per the plan, he went there along with his daughter and started pleading with them to treat his daughter kindly and humanly. His son-in-law started abusing him and asked him to get lost. He again entreated even more humbly, but a bit loudly. His father said, "Your daughter is a bitch and she instigates our son against us; our own son. She is getting the treatment she deserves."

By that time, a few neighbours also gathered there.

His mother commenced beating her breasts rhythmically, and with force, and yelled, "We know that our son is a jewel, but we did not know that he is going to marry the daughter of a pauper . . . . in the name of furniture, they did not give even a stool." Then, addressing the gathering, she said, "Listen people, listen this rascal has the temerity to accuse us, the noblest family in this area."

At that very time, arrived the two cops, named Fauja Singh and Dayal Chand.

"The stool will be provided by us and a bigger one than even *Qutab Minar.*" Fauja Singh said with all humility and pulled the father-in-law by the hair, "If she is a bitch, then you are a dog. Aren't you?" And he gave him one after another slap. When his wife rushed to his rescue, Dayal Chand pushed her down by the blow of his elbow. In those days to handle such matters, they were rarely accompanied by lady constables. No one came to their rescue. None wanted to help this infamous family.

Fauja Singh asked him, "Do you agree that you are nothing but a dog."

He nodded his head in affirmative out of fear.

Fauja entreated him to say, 'yes'.

Again he just nodded his head.

He kicked him on the shin and humbly asked him, "This is not enough. Say, I am a dog."

"I am a dog."

He slapped him four-five times, "Even this is not enough, say I am a mongrel of a dirty drain."

"I am a mongrel of a dirty drain."

On the other hand, Dayal Chand had thrown the son on the floor and was beating him mercilessly.

Then an elderly Sardar ji asked them to stop as they had learnt their lesson. Others also seconded him. They stopped there and then, as they did not want the public to go against them. And they were shrewd enough not to leave a trace of their beatings which could be produced against them in a court of law, they were aces in that.

Their two daughters had hidden themselves in the toilet.

All three of them were taken into the police custody and they left the father after some more beating, as it suited their strategy. They did not let the mother and son sleep during the entire night.

The father rushed down to a better known lawyer, who told him that it was a case of dowry harassment and they could be jailed for at least seven years, but he can get it settled with the police, as he had the right connections with them. For this work, the lawyer charged him rupees two thousand.

He touched his knees and said, "Please do."

With the arbitration of the lawyer, he had to cough up another five thousand for the SHO, though initially, he had demanded rupees twenty thousand and gave rupees five hundred each to Dayal and Fauja, it was done on the behest of the SHO for putting up their human efforts beyond their duty hours.

Afterwards, Shobha broke off all marital relations with her husband, she loathed his very touch.

He continued giving her money for her personal needs, but never in the presence of his mother. It was obvious that his mother was very possessive about her son. He knew that the main culprit in their torment was his own mother but he blamed his father also, although he never talked about it openly. Out of sheer nonsensical jealousy, she never wanted him to belong to his wife. It was a clear case of circuitous sexual jealousy on her part. So far her father-in-law was concerned, he was a spineless hen-pecked husband who invariably endorsed his wife's actions right or wrong, mostly wrong. The son was unconsciously pleasing his mother by being fiendish to his wife. He was out and out a mama's boy.

Shoba's husband, Mangat Ram was born after his mother had two miscarriages. Every thing he did, good or bad, had the approval of his parents, especially his mother, who dotted on him. He was an extremely pampered child. In case he fought, he was considered brave, in case he avoided the fight, he was thought to be gentle. If he abused, he was being manly and in case he did not abuse back, he was kind hearted, in case he helped someone monetarily, he was considered generous and if he did not, he was wise and practical. All his actions were applauded in superlatives by his dotting parents. This made him a spoiled brat. And he idolized his parents, especially his mother. Their two daughters had no say in the family matters, and they were constantly in dread of their brother's wrath. Moreover, they were always too busy either in their studies or in house-hold work.

As a child, his mother never stopped breast feeding him till the age of four, it was he who put his mouth away from her ever eager boobs, as other kids had started teasing him.

The humiliations had a complete metamorphosis in his personality. He was a changed man. His day started with prayers and he daily went to the temple in the morning. He was now greatly influenced by the Bhagwad Gita and unflinchingly believed that it was his karmas which had made his life miserable. His wife became boorish, intolerant and foul-mouthed, and she had become lowly because of the atmosphere she got in their house. He knew that the root cause of all their misery was his mother, but he never openly accused her.

He badly wanted to patch up with his wife, but she was unrelenting. Once he almost begged her for sex and she said, "Better go to your mother." She left the room after banging the door. She knew that he had been torturing her on the instigation of his mother. Now she wanted him to sever all the relations with his mother, only then she would accept him.

His life became directionless; his evenings became melancholic; the torture and the indignity he faced in the police lock up never went out of his mind, particularly when he was made to draw lines on the floor by rubbing his nose in the police station, eleven times. It was worse than the physical torture.

He led a pious life during the day, and started hitting the bottle in the evenings.

One fine morning, his mother lamented, "Son, you have stopped talking to me, your own mother . . . . it pierces my heart. This wretched woman has done some voodoo on you."

"Let us not blame her, let us blame ourselves." And he left the house.

He came back after one hour. "Here is the stool for which you created life hell for all of us." Again he went out of the house.

His mother was now convinced that her daughter-in-law had created some magic spell on her son. She got even more scared of her. She consulted some astrologers who fleeced her by their illogical counseling and made her perform some weird rites, but nothing happened and peace and tranquility did not return to their home.

After a few months, Shobha gave birth to a son and even this did not make her happy, the son reminded her of rape after rape after rape. She was a beleaguered woman.

Six months later, her husband died in a road accident when he was drunk. It was a hit and run case. Some thought he was murdered, rumours need a slight chance to get spread.

After fifteen days of her husband's death, she left her in-laws house with bag and baggage to her father's house as her mother-in-law day in and day out shrieked by making weird sounds, particularly during the night. She already had managed a job as a sales girl in a DCM show room with her father's help.

As she was leaving, his sister-in-law almost snatched her son from her lap and pleaded, "This way you will come back to us."

She did not utter a single word but felt relieved, as the son reminded her of her late husband as he resembled his father, and she wanted to forget about him altogether. Moreover, she had never been unpleasant to her.

When in the morning she got up, her first thought was, '*I have got my nest, and I am going to guard and protect it. I will never let Dilip complain about anything . . . I adore him.*'

The next Sunday they got married in a simple ceremony by exchanging garlands in a remote temple without even the chanting of *the Vedic mantras*. The company advocate Mr. Ghavre had told them that such a marriage had legal sanction.

She became a doting mother to her step son who within days became closer to her than his own father. She even learnt to cook Marathi cuisine without even his asking her for the same. She quit her job to look after the child.

One day, Manekar received a registered letter in his office and after reading the letter he began clapping with a child's enthusiasm. Everybody felt aghast at his behavior, even he himself felt awkward and before anybody could ask any thing he announced, "My wife has written me a letter . . . . AND IT IS IN MARATHI. I don't know when and where did she learn it?"

Everybody insisted for a treat, but he slipped away to go home to make love to his darling wife.

CHAPTER 16

Harbans started going to Bakshi Sahib's house quite frequently and he always went there without Vijay accompanying him because of his nearing final exams.

Pinky always wanted that he should have brought Vijay along with him but could not express it explicitly, although off and on she gave subtle hints which went over the head of Harbans Lal. Whenever Harbans did not come to their house for more than ten or fifteen days, it was Bakshi sahib who sent a message to him through a constable, as in those days very few shopkeepers had a telephone.

Pinky and Harbans often had a spat over some petty matter which always amused the Bakshis. They watched with keen interest but never intervened. They always felt that Pinky needed a brother or sister as a companion and this void was amply fulfilled by him. Whenever he came to their house, he always brought something or the other, which Pinky resented as he had never let her spend on him. The way they mixed up, chatted, quarreled and then made up, none could guess that they were not real brother and sister. Their close knit bondage was beyond description.

On one such occasion Pinky gave him a bundle and asked him to unwrap it. It contained a matching pants and shirt, seemed to be quite expensive.

"*Chachaji* will look very smart wearing them." Harbans said.

"Damn it, it is not for him! It is for you, you fool."

"For me?"

"Of course, do you like my choice of colour?"

"Immensely, but I won't accept it."

"Why??"

"Because I can't stand my little sister spend so much money above me."

"I am not little!"

"You are."

"I am not!"

"I simply don't want you spend on me."

"Have you ever let me spend on you?"

"It can never happen . . . . what sort of a man I am if I let my little younger sister spend on me."

"I am the elder one."

"No, I am elder to you."

For another ten minutes they continued saying I am the elder one.

The two elders were enjoying the fun.

"Okay stop it," Pinky shrieked.

"Do, Did, and Done."

"You don't even know your date of birth."

"My mother used to say that I was born when it was the season of mangoes, and you born during the season of oranges, so I am elder from you."

The Bakshis let out a loud guffaw.

"Okay . . . okay, tell me do I earn?"

"You don't."

"That means when I don't earn, then I have no right to spend."

"But it is your pocket money involved in this purchase."

"How do you know?"

"I am intelligent enough."

"You are stupid enough . . . . out and out."

"But *Kakaji* [son], the money was given to her by her papa, so you should accept it," finally Mrs. Shanta Bakshi intervened.

"You have revealed every thing, now Pinky's case has become weak," said Mr. Bakshi.

"How does my case become weak, Paprey?"

Pinky called her father papa, papu, and paprey depending on her mood. Generally she called him papa. When she wanted some favour from him, she called him papu. When they were in a playful mood, she called him papey. And in case she was angry with him, then it turned to Paprey. He never felt annoyed when his doting daughter called him Paprey, it was a signal for him to relent.

"Okay, if I give my decision, will it be acceptable to everybody?"

They agreed as there was no other way out.

Mr. Bakshi coughed and spoke as if he was sitting on the chair of a judge, "It is a proven fact that the present was purchased by Miss Pinky Bakshi from her pocket money which is not acceptable to Mr. Harbans Lal because of his moral and traditional values, which are of course outmoded, but we have no right to change them. So I Dharam Pal Bakshi, son of Mr. Amrit Lal Bakshi, have decided to replenish her pocket money. That way her pocket money remains intact. That way the present must be acceptable to him."

"Papu, now I am not going to give it to him. He has misbehaved with me."

"I will snatch it."

"Try."

Harbans snatched it from her and she intentionally loosened her grip. Harbans stumbled but managed not to fall.

"I wish you had fallen . . . . Oh God! Never be it so."

One day Shanta told her husband that Pinky will be completing her twenty years after a few months and it was high time that they start looking for a suitable groom for her. Bakshi agreed with his wife, he heaved a sigh of agony thinking what would be their life without the bubbly presence of Pinky in the house. He felt miserable, *the daughters are paraya dhan* [someone else's bounty], *one day or the other they have to be sent to their home.*

"But Pinky is still too young . . . . immature . . . . we can wait for a year or two, when we find that she has acquired the ability to take the responsibility of household, then we will think about it," he argued weakly.

"This concept of one or two years often turns into more years than one can think of . . . often, it turns to many years . . . . then girls become over aged for marriage . . . and at that age even if they marry it is hard for them to adjust with their husband, as they develop minds of their own with strong inclinations, which appears whimsical to her man. Some become cranky spinsters."

Bakshi Sahib left the house without saying anything and with a heavy heart.

They started looking for a suitable *Munda* for their daughter. Munda in Punjabi means both a teenage boy and a son. It is also used for a groom.

Pinky sensed it that her parents were in a hurry to marry her off. One day she gathered the courage to tell her mother that she liked a boy named Vijay, though she hardly knew him.

"So you have been meeting him on the sly!"

"I have never dated him and please don't deduce any meaning out of it . . . . the final approval will be made by you and papa. Otherwise forget about it. Remember, Pinky will never take any step which displeases her parents."

Shanta could realize through her woman's instinct that it was normal for a young girl to fancy some boy. Even she had, when she was a young girl and girls normally never disclose it to anybody, not even to their close friends. Those who do it are thought to be to outspoken, extrovert and even shameless.

In the evening when Shanta told her husband about Pinky's fancy for a boy, it made him very pensive and thoughtful. He could never think that his darling daughter was having an affair with some unknown boy. Affairs between a boy and a girl were looked down upon in their society. It was considered as a sin against the family honour. The Punjabi literature and folk songs are all for love and full of admiration for the lovers, but in reality it is just the opposite. Nobody really voices against this attitude of double standards.

When a girl in love is caught with her lover and confronted, she merely begs for pardon or entreats for the approval of the elders to let her marry the one of her choice. Those who cannot endure a life without their lover, they either try to elope or attempt suicide. In literature love is extolled, but in day to day life it is considered to be a sinful disgrace.

Bakshi Sahib could not digest that his very own daughter was secretly having a liaison with a boy. He was furious and determined to teach that boy a lesson, which he won't be able to forget all his life. He thought his daughter was gullible and he should take every step very cautiously, in order not to duress his daughter, lest she took some extreme step. Through his police network, he collected all the information about that boy named Vijay. When he came to know that the well known philanthropist Mr. Bhandari had helped him in getting the admission in the college, he decided to have a teat-a-teat with him. The same very evening he fixed an appointment with him.

Mr. Bhandari poured a glass of whisky for him and said, "I am already down with two pegs. I can guess you have come with some purpose. Come out with it straight away."

"You remember last year you got admitted a boy named Vijay in your college."

"Has he done something wrong?"

Mr. Bakshi kept quiet.

"Remember, he is under my patronage. First of all, he cannot do anything wrong, he is such a sweet boy and even if he has done some thing wrong which your tone shows, I will protect him and go to any length to save him. I will engage one of the best lawyers for him, you know money is no problem for me."

Bakshi decided to keep quiet.

"As long as I am alive . . . nobody can touch him . . . . young boys, because of their youth, sometimes take some wrong step, we have to tolerate it and act judiciously and not harshly. Of course, when we were young we did a few things which we should not have done and which were not to the liking of our elders and that includes you and me."

He unnecessarily laughed and finished the rest of his glass in one gulp. This was to show him his power and resolve.

"Oh, it is not that . . . please try to understand, I have a marriageable daughter," Mr. Bakshi blurted it out without realizing it.

"Oh my, my . . . . and I thought . . . hell, I am sorry." And he slapped his own face. "But I don't know, if he is ready for that he once told me that after clearing his M.A., he is going to sit for I.A.S."

When Mr. Bakshi came out of his house, he was in a real dilemma. If a man of Mr. Bhandari's stature liked and loved him immensely, there must be something in the boy. And Pinki is no fool, she also likes him, although Shanta had told him that Pinki said that 'the final approval rests on her parents, and under no circumstances she can ever contemplate to defy them.' Moreover, I have not got a single unsavoury report about this boy. *Perhaps, I am too conservative and full of outdated ideas, when it concerns my daughter.* The entire matter became a quiz for him. He decided to meet the boy.

The very next day, a constable went to Vijay's house and told him that the DSP Sahib wanted to meet him regarding some important matter. Vijay was both surprised and scared why a police officer wanted to meet him, there must be something . . . 'like a bad omen.'

"Please let me know his address, I will be there after some time."

"She is waiting for you to take you there," the constable spoke in English.

"Who?"

"The jeep."

When the constable reached his home along with Vijay, Mr. Bakshi waved him off with the gesture of his hand.

Bakshi Sahib sitting in his lawn was busy with some paper work and he continued doing it and kept Vijay standing. It was an intentional police style move on his part. Vijay kept mum but now he was really scared, his legs started shaking and his stomach became taut.

After a while Bakshi Sahib spoke, "Have a seat." And he continued with his paper work. Vijay felt mentally tortured.

At long last Mr. Bakshi broke the ice. "My daughter is a student of B.A.[Final], she is weak in English. I want you to be her tutor."

"Sir, I feel honoured that you thought me to be fit for this job, but with due apologies, I think it's better for a young girl of her age to be taught by a lady tutor."

"Since you and Pinki know each other, it does not matter."

"Sir, I don't think I have ever met any girl with this name. There must be some other gentle man whom you wanted to be her tutor."

This boy is trying to be smart. I will evaporate his smartness in thin air.

"No, it is no one else but you. By the way, what is your name?"

"Vijay."

"When some elder asks to know your name, always tell your full name."

"Vijay Kumar . . . . Vijay Kumar Puri, Sir." Vijay now started trembling. It had the desirable effect, which Mr. Bakshi wanted.

"You are from . . . . ?"

"Sial . . . . Sialkot, Sir," stammered Vijay.

The word 'Sialkot' made Mr. Bakshi somewhat nostalgic.

"I studied there . . . you are Puri . . . There was a Professor Puri . . . he taught us English literature . . . . what a teacher . . . a great man . . . . even the English men in Sialkot bowed before his knowledge of English literature . . . . today what I am, it is because of him, otherwise I was quite a rogue. He made a man out of me."

Mr. Bakshi forgot about his plan to be rough with the boy.

"Thank you, Sir."

"Why the Dickens are you thanking me?"

"He is my father."

Mr. Bakshi almost jumped from his seat. "Where is he . . . . I want to seek his blessings. Life must be very hard for him in these critical times . . . . I am ready to do anything for him . . . . let's go this very moment to meet him and seek his blessings."

Vijay could not reply. He felt choked.

"Why the hell are you quiet?"

"I am the only surviving member in the . . . ." Vijay could not complete his sentence. Tears started rolling from his eyes.

This was the third time he wept after landing in India, the Free India.

"Oh my God!" Mr. Bakshi felt miserable. *And I was bent upon creating life hell for this unfortunate boy. Oh God, why was I thinking to do so. Thank God you have saved me from the sin of being nasty to an innocent boy.*

Now he was genuinely affectionate towards this boy and he started consoling him but it had the opposite effect. Vijay could not control his pent up emotions and started sobbing. Mr. Bakshi cuddled him and Vijay's sobbing became uncontrollable and louder.

Sitting in her room, Pinky was all ears for what was going on between the two of them though she could hardly hear anything. But when she heard him weeping, she rushed to her mother, "Paprey has beaten him and I am not going to speak to him all my life, and I mean it."

Both mother and daughter rushed out to save him from further beatings. They felt aghast when they saw him in his clasp and Bakshi Sahib was very tenderly consoling him and when he saw them, he shouted, "Bring a glass of water . . . . and fast."

Pinki rushed inside, brought a glass of water, gave it to her mother, who gave it to Vijay. When they went inside, Vijay narrated his story in nut shell. He was composed now. When the family insisted that he should have his dinner with them, he replied, "Please, some other time, my friend Harbans will be waiting for me."

"Papu, he means our Harbans."

"You two are friends . . . . what a pleasant surprise!"

Mr. Bakshi ordered his driver to bring Harbans along with him.

During their chit chat Vijay told him that he knew his daughter but did not know her name. "Of course, once she threatened us, I will teach you a lesson. My papa is a D.S.P."

All of them laughed, except Pinki.

"And he gave me such a big lecture. I can never forget when he said, 'instead of threatening helpless people like us, you should by your demeanour make your papa proud of you.' When I came home, the first thing I did was to find its meanings in the dictionary."

Everybody laughed including Pinki. This made the atmosphere light and congenial.

A noble father's noble son and I thought my daughter is having an affair with him. Hell to me!

Together, they had a swell time.

By the time Vijay and Harbans left, it was 11 pm.

After their departure, Bakshi Sahib addressed his daughter; "I have liked the boy, are you now happy?"

There were tears of big relief in Shanta's eyes.

"But there is one condition . . . you will never fight with our Vijay like you do with me, because during our quarrels I am always the loser . . . so he should never have any complaint against you in your spats, I am always going to take his side. I like him more than I like you, I am going to be biased and take his side."

She kissed her father and ran inside. Her happiness had no bounds. In her ecstasy, she jumped . . . . *Oh, papa likes him more than me. Always do that papu!*

It was a memorable day for Mr. Bakshi. After the self inflicted torture of a few days, he was out of his mental captivity. What a relief!

From then onwards Bakshi Sahib regularly went to a Gurudwara. He rarely missed it.

He also stopped to force anyone for bribe.

CHAPTER 17

Vijay not only secured first division in his M.A. [final] but also stood second in the Punjab University.

It was Harbans who was more ostentatious on his fabulous success than Vijay himself. He closed the shop earlier so that they could celebrate in grand style in Kenny uncle's house. Vijay suggested that first of all they should go to Mr. Bhandari's house with a packet of sweets and seek his blessings. Harbans admired his friend's sense of gratitude.

"We buy two packets, one from me and one from you."

"That's a good idea."

They bought sweets from the best shop of the city and went to Mr. Bhandari's house. They sensed that some party was going on inside his house. Vijay was reluctant to go inside as he felt awkward because he was sure that Mr. Bhandari would ask them to join the party and he won't be able to say no and he would feel like an intruder. Harbans said that they had come all the way to his house and Mr. Bhandari would understand that they had no knowledge of this party. He literally pushed Vijay to enter his house.

They gave the sweets to him and touched his feet.

"I have thrown this party in honour of your grand success. I was hundred per cent sure that you would be coming that is why I did not inform you. I love to give a surprise."

He had invited the entire college staff and a few of his close friends. Mr. Bakshi was standing in a corner talking to someone.

Mr. Bhandari gave a short speech in praise of Vijay, followed by a much longer speech by the principal. Mr. Bhandari did not mention at all how he had helped Vijay.

Then everybody asked Vijay to say a few words, as they were very keen to listen to this brilliant boy.

"It was first week of October when my dear friend Harbans persuaded me to pursue my studies further. We approached the principal and then Bhandari Sahib went out of the way to get my admission possible. When I reached the college the next day, I found that he had paid my admission fee from his own pocket."

Vijay's voice got choked. He controlled himself and then continued, "There were books, pens . . . everything a student needs . . . . since then he has been my godfather."

There was a loud applause for Mr. Bhandari. Now Mr. Bakshi understood why he had challenged him on that day. In a way now he liked it, immensely.

"It was never my idea to complete my M.A . . . . it was simply my friend Harbans Lal's persuasion . . . . he is like my brother . . . . HE IS MY BROTHER. He is younger to me . . . but this rogue always behaves like an elder brother . . . . I can't even take my revenge on him as he is too smart for me."

There was a big laughter.

"We were running *a kiryana shop,* on seeing my poor result in the half yearly exams in M.A., he forced me not to come to the shop at all. I felt miserable. My conscience pricked me, the elder brother goes to college for a better future and the younger one runs the shop to make both ends meet. It maddened me. So one day, I put my foot down and in a compromising mood I decided that I will work in the shop for only two to three hours daily, but he is a very steely character and flatly refused and tried to push me out of the shop . . . . and then I slapped him . . ."

"That slap was my biggest reward," shouted Harbans by waving his fists in the air.

"After a few days, I tried again and do you know what this rascal did? He sent away the two helpers on some pretext and when I was least aware of what he was going to do, he went out and put the shutters down and locked the shop from outside. I yelled at him, even cursed him which I normally don't. He opened the door after almost after one hour when I promised him that I won't even come to our bazaar, as it may not entice me to come to the shop . . . and worst of all, he made me swear by my father."

Tears started flowing from his eyes. Everybody had wet eyes.

"See, he is laughing . . . he is my friend, my brother. Please don't clap for me but do it for my angelic father Bhandari Sahib and my dearest rascal Harbans."

Everybody stood up and clapped vigorously and reddened their hands.

Then people started shaking hands with three of them and hugged three of them tightly. They did it with such warmth and strength that their hands and backs started aching. But they had no qualms about it.

When the party was in full swing, Mr. Bhandari quietly took Mr. Bakshi, Harbans and Vijay to his study room.

"Vijay I have a request to make . . ."

"Sir, I am your son . . . . please order . . . even in my dreams, I can't think of disobeying you."

"Bakshi happens to be a very close friend of mine . . . he has approached me . . . . Pinki is a good match for you. If you have some other ideas, please let me know."

Vijay touched Mr. Bhandari's and then Mr. Bakshi's feet.

It took less than a minute for this match making.

Mr. Bhandari also gave him a letter and asked him to read it when he reaches home.

It was an appointment letter for the post of a lecturer in the same very college.

When they reached home, it was 12 o' clock. So they decided to go to Kenny uncle's house next evening to celebrate.

After a week, their betrothal ceremony was performed in Mr. Bhandari's house. Apart from the clothes and money given by the Bakshis to Vijay, everybody from the girl's side gave money to Vijay. After the ring ceremony, money and gifts were given to Mr. Bhandari and Mr. and Mrs. Kenny and of course Harbans.

Some of the invitees gave money to Pinki also. To offer any money or presents to people from the girl's side is against the custom and unheard of. Mr.Bhandari presented Pinki with a beautiful Banarsi sari, which he had especially purchased for her from the market.

Later on a lavish dinner was served. Before the dinner was served, Mr. Bakshi told Vijay and Harbans that he knew that they drank beer and asked them to go to the other room to have beer. Both of them refused politely, which was immensely liked by Mr. Bhandari and his chest expanded with pride, he had started feeling that he must have been their father in his previous birth and treated them like his sons, and he was very protective about them and both of them gave him the respect which a father deserves and desires. Bakshi sahib and especially Mrs. Bakshi felt that now they don't have to worry at all about their only daughter, about her life after marriage and she blessed them profusely. As a mark of respect, youngsters avoid drinking in the presence of the elders. Both Mr. Bhandari and Mr. Bakshi took less than their normal quota as they had to take care of the guests.

Mr. Bhandari badly missed his wife who had left him for her heavenly abode a few years ago. His two sons were settled in England, married to English women. They kept just formal relations with their father, otherwise they were least bothered about him. He cursed his own self for sending his sons to England for higher studies. That is why Vijay and Harbans had become cynosure of his eyes. Even in this hustle and bustle, he felt lonely. With their love, devotion, and respect for him, these two boys had filled the gap, yet the pangs of the indifference of his two sons could never forsake him.

Only on the day of the ring ceremony, he came to know that his fiancée's name is Indu. Pinki was her pet name.

Late in the night when they went home, they drank six bottles of beer and slept till late in the morning.

A few days later, Bakshi Sahib asked Vijay to search for a suitable accommodation as he would not be able to help him in this matter. People are usually reluctant to give *police wallas* and even their close relatives their house on rent, as it is not easy to get it vacated for year's altogether, when they need the same for their own use.

Vijay and Harbans searched for a house, but they could not find any suitable one. Either the rent was too high or they did not like the accommodation. Someone in the college told Vijay that a house on rent was available on Lawrence Road. It was an outer house in a big bungalow and when he entered the house, he met a young girl who seemed to be very excited to see him and when he was talking to the landlord, the girl ejaculated, "*Bauji* [Papa], he is the one who stood second in the University in M.A. English." It surprised him but he did not ask how she knew it.

"The accommodation is yours . . . . I would not have agreed to a paisa less than 100 rupees but for you it is Rs. 80 per month."

When they were having tea, the landlord asked him, "But why you want such a big accommodation?"

"I am getting married."

The girl sulked.

"Any advance, Sir?"

"*Oh ji*, no *advance-shadvance* from you."

"But why, sir?"

"I have a college going son, studying in B.A. [First Year] . . . . he has gone a little wayward . . . in your company he will mend his ways . . . . and you will help him in the English subject, and for that I am ready to pay you any money," he said it with folded hands.

A month later, their marriage was performed with great pomp and show. Anyone who mattered in the city was present on this occasion.

The *milni ceremony* [formal meeting] of the father of the groom and the bride was performed by Mr. Bhandari and Mr. Bakshi. And that of maternal uncle and brother by Kenny and Harbans with the maternal uncle of Pinki and one of her first cousins.

Milni is a ceremony which is performed between very close relatives of the bride and the groom, when the groom riding on a mare with a sword in sheath hanging on one side of his body, arrives at the venue of the marriage ceremony. Important male members from the brides side are already there with garlands in their hands to receive and honour their counter parts from the groom's side. They embrace them and give them money and other gifts. Nothing is given to those from the bride's side. Often they are not even thanked, because these offerings are taken for granted.

The ceremonial seven *pheras* [Rounds] before the holy fire were performed with the recitations of Sanskrit shlokas. Vijay put *sindoor* [vermilion] in the *maang* [hair-parting] of his bride. And amongst much shouting and *halla gulla*, they were declared husband and wife.

The entire ceremony is performed by a pundit reciting Sanskrit shlokas, which hardly anybody can understand. The pundit took three hours to perform it. The pundit is given money and clothes both by the fathers of the bride and the groom. The donation by the bride's father is usually more than that of the groom's father, exceptions are there if the groom's father happens to be very well off. A truck full of dowry items, containing boxes for the boy and girl's dresses, furniture, utensils, crockery, bed sheets, quilts, blankets and what not, so that boy does not have to buy anything from the market to start his married life, was dispatched to the groom's house. Clothes were given to Mr. Bhandari and Kenny and his family members. A big trunk containing clothes and other gift items was presented to Harbans.

When the couple reached their new abode, it was 4 am. They were tired, yet did not feel drowsy or knackered. A beautifully decked bed with beautiful seasonal flowers was waiting for them.

They started chatting and then Vijay said, "The first time I saw you, I was fascinated by your beauty, it was a case of love at first sight."

"I can't believe it, because you always avoided me."

"I thought you are a rich girl . . . . somewhat snooty . . . there is no scope, no chance. Whereas I was a down-trodden man belonging to riff-raff of society."

"Never say that again. You are my lord . . . do you know I performed *chalisa* . . . . I mean, I went to Gurudwara daily for forty days and prayed for your hand."

"It still feels like a dream that I have married a girl of my dreams. Do you know I did not reveal my feelings for you even to Harbans, when we are so close to each other?"

Then he told her how he started his life with Harbans, whom he both loved and admired, and he continued talking about Harbans's generosity to bring him to this position and he could eventually marry her.

Pinki realized that what to talk of kissing her, he had not so far even touched her. She started giggling.

"What makes you laugh?"

"It's just that . . ."

"Please tell me."

"It just happened."

"You are hiding something."

"No."

"Your 'No' is not convincing . . . . Please tell me."

"I can't."

"You must, if you love me."

"Please . . . . please don't force me."

"It has made me all the more inquisitive."

"For God's sake, don't compell me."

"I am requesting you."

"By telling you, I will feel very awkward and uneasy."

"Is it something bawdy?"

"It is."

"Then do tell me . . . today we are going to be two bodies with one soul . . . . we should not conceal anything from each other."

She giggled again and then said, "You will think I am shameless."

"Never."

"Then listen . . . . but I can't . . . . please forgive me . . . I should not have laughed."

After much cajoling, Indu agreed. "My cousin Roopa said . . . . the boy is sooooo handsome, but very shy . . . . please I can't, and don't insist . . . . I am ready to touch your feet."

"I know it is something lascivious, but between a husband and wife it becomes pure romance . . . . come on . . . . I'm very eager to listen to it."

Priya lowered her eyes and said, "She said . . . . she said . . . . he is so shy, that on your first night, you will have to make the first move . . . . otherwise . . . otherwise . . . . the rest I can't tell you."

"I can fill in the blank."

Vijay took her in his arms and started kissing her passionately. And he got over excited and their first night turned into a fiasco.

On the second night, thanks to Priya's subtle moves and implicit guidance, their marriage was consummated.

CHAPTER 18

When Vijay and he were staying together, life was a bed of roses for Harbans. Now it became a burden for him, especially during nights he felt lonely and bored and found it difficult to sleep. Beer did help him but he checked himself from becoming an addict. Both Pinki and Vijay did ask him to shift to their new home, but he wisely declined this offer. He would have felt very awkward staying with a young newly married couple. He often went to their home and together they had a marvelous time, but he never stayed overnight. Sometimes Vijay and Pinki came to visit him, and then Pinki never allowed him to bring any eatables from the market because she loved to cook for her husband and Harbans. She also did not allow them to bring more than three bottles of beer and they never defied her. She was never even offered any beer because in the prevailing social milieu, it was unthinkable to offer a woman drinks and it was worse than a sin for a woman to drink. Privately sometimes some women did take a sip or two on the persistent coaxing of their husbands, but later on they made a long face. The very bitter taste of alcohol was awful for them they felt surprised why men folk loved to drink.

Harbans found that Vijay's landlord's daughter had started eyeing him and he also looked at her from the corner of his eyes with passion and desire. This girl at first envied Pinki and even hated her, but with the passage of time and moreover Pinki by her friendly, extrovert and jovial nature was able to befriend her and the latter's animosity for her went to the winds.

After only a few visits, when nobody was to be seen around, both Harbans and that girl started looking at each other with passion and libido, but they did not utter a formal word to each other. They did not even know each other's name, it was silent, pure and impetus love between the two of them.

It did not remain unrevealed to Pinki and Vijay, but they decided to keep mum on this issue. They knew heart to heart that her father would never agree to marry his daughter to Harbans, he being a very rich transporter would marry his daughter into a rich family of some status. Moreover, they were *Khatri* and Harbans was an *Arora*. In those days because of the strong caste system, Khatris always avoided marriage alliance with Aroras. They felt sorry for Harbans but were helpless in this matter. They strongly thought that he should at least be a matriculate otherwise he will never find a suitable match for himself. They did not have to persuade him as he readily agreed and it was decided that he would study privately and the shop would be run entirely by the helpers. Even if they cheated, it hardly mattered as they had enough money. Then they had the consolation of being related to Bakshi Sahib, and it would dissuade them from any temptation to dupe them.

Harbans Lal increased the salary of the two helpers to further discourage them from doing any flim-flam.

Harbans Lal joined a private coaching institute and was thoroughly engrossed in his studies. Vijay offered his help to teach him English language, but he declined saying, 'English is my left hand's play.' It did not amuse Vijay, because he knew that Harbans was very poor in this subject, but he did not say anything lest it discouraged him. Even Pinky wanted to help him in his studies, but he paid no heed to it as he felt too shy to be taught by a girl. He almost stopped going to their house as he did not want to be distracted. That girl was also the reason as he did not want to be distracted.

Having not seen Harbans for days together, that girl named Priya felt shattered. Her figure improved as she lost weight, because she had lost her appetite to a great extent.

His first paper was that of English language and when Vijay went to him to know how he had fared in that paper, he told him that he filled seven pages to write the essay. Vijay was sure that he must have made numerous grammatical mistakes. As he had done well in singular and plural, in genders and active and passive, he may get through with just passing marks.

Whereas Harbans thought that he was going to get distinction, but did not go gaga about it.

For his next Maths paper, Vijay advised him to first try to solve those questions which appear easy to him and the difficult ones, he must solve in the end. He listened to him with rapt attention.

Again for the History paper, Vijay advised him that he should give appropriate time to each question keeping in view the marks allotted to that question. And in case he knew much about some question, then he should not keep on writng about it, otherwise he would not be able to complete his entire paper. This advice proved very useful to him.

Harbans passed his Matriculation examination in second division, securing 52%. He secured just pass marks in English, 35%, whereas he got a distinction in History. Vijay just told him that he should improve in grammar and increase his word power. And thanked his stars that he had been able to persuade him to opt for Urdu medium, although with great difficulty.

"Now you understand why I begged, cajoled and insisted to opt for Urdu medium . . . and you were insisting on English medium . . . . I almost wanted to thrash you . . . . otherwise you would not have been a matriculate, but an . . . . M.A.B.F."

"And what is that?" Asked Pinki.

"Matric appeared but failed."

All three of them laughed.

They celebrated the occasion quietly, because they did not want anybody to know that Harbans was not even a matriculate.

When after many months Harbans came to their house, Priya felt jittery to meet him. She even thought of entering their house on some pretext, but could not gather the courage. Passing every minute became heavy for her. When after two hours he left, he found her waiting for him in a corner outside their bungalow.

"I want to say hello. I am Priya."

"I am Harbans. Hello from me also."

"You came after many months . . . . after November 7th to be exact."

"I was busy."

"Someone missed you."

"Who?"

"I am not going to talk to you," she tried not to sob. And she started for home.

This conveyed everything to him. He earnestly wanted to stop her, but could not because boy-meet-a girl was full of problems and it was considered immoral by the society.

The next time he came to their house, she was resolved to meet him in Vijay's abode. As she thought shyness would lead her nowhere.

She came with a big bowl of *halwa* [a dessert made of carrots].

"Today is *sankrant* [first day of the month as per the Hindu calendar], I have cooked it with my own hands, hope you like it."

"What is in it . . . . some pebbles?" Harbans said with a smile.

"Silly, these are almonds and cashew nuts."

Soon both of them opened up. Vijay and Priya remained straight-faced. They neither encouraged nor discouraged them to have a chat.

When she left after an hour, Pinky could not help uttering, "She stuck like glue, she hardly let us talk. I am going to stop her from coming here."

Harbans made a long face but did not say anything, which was at once noticed by her.

"Actually your visits are a few and far between . . . and we don't want an outsider . . . ."

She could read that Harbans was upset with the word 'outsider' for Priya, she changed her stance, "Otherwise, she is a lovable girl, friendly and helpful."

Vijay was thinking . . . . only the other day, her father had asked him if a suitable boy was in his sight . . . . 'Please let me know, as I am very anxious to *yellow her hands*' [a ceremony performed before the wedding of a girl by applying myrtle on her hands] and he had added, 'the boy should be from a well to do family, educated and definitely from a Punjabi Khatri family.'

Vijay eased the tension by changing the subject. He told him that they were of the opinion that he should straight away start preparing for Intermediate. Whereas, Harbans had himself come to discuss it with them, particularly about the subjects to be chosen. Vijay told him that he had already thought of it. Besides English which was a compulsory subject, he suggested for History, Economics and Urdu, with Punjabi as optional subject. He told him that he would be able to learn Punjabi within a few days, as it was their mother tongue. Harbans wanted to opt for Maths.

"It will be very tough for you. There won't be simple Maths like in Matric. There would be Calculus and Trigonometry, which I am sure that you have not even heard of."

"You are right . . . . what next?"

"You are going to have English medium this time."

"English medium! Are you joking?"

"No, I am not. Only it would be initially tough. You have to learn the basics of English grammar. And this time if you refuse to be taught by me I am going to break your knees."

"My knees are very precious to me. So I agree, big brother."

"You are going to study for 2 to 3 hours in the morning, you will go late to the shop and it will be opened by our helpers. Moreover there are not many customers in the early hours. You will revise in the evening what ever you have read in the morning. Pinki will teach you Economics."

"What about History and Urdu?" Pinki asked.

"He has flair for Urdu and History and for that he needs no tutor."

Vijay himself was apt in Urdu, and loved Urdu poetry and was a big fan of Mirza Ghalib and Mir Taqi Mir.

When he took their leave, it was 11 pm. He was surprised to find Priya waiting outside the gate. In the corner of the street, she gestured him to stop. She gave him a pink rose, looked deeply into his eyes, smiled and rushed towards her home.

Harbans was on cloud nine.

Time passed rapidly.

Harbans Lal once visited their house and could not find Priya around, he felt really surprised. Vijay and Pinki never talked about her. He was dying to know about her but could not find a way out. On one such visit, he casually asked Pinky, "Don't find your friend around, what is her name . . . . I think it is Priya, if I am not wrong."

"She has flown to her nest . . . . gone forever to Delhi after her marriage."

The entire castle of his dreams crumbled. It became extremely difficult for him to behave normally. He couldn't even concentrate on what was being talked about.

Meals were served and he had to force himself to eat. He wanted to show that the news of Priya's marriage had no effect on him, but failed miserably. Both Pinki and Vijay could understand his plight. Harbans had never bared his mind to them about his feelings for Priya, so they could not even console him.

He did not stay for long.

He was lying on his bed thinking why he could not have got a hint about her marriage, sleep had totally abandoned him. He was smoking and thinking longingly for her, he had never ever smoked before. After the first cigarette he immediately lit another one and after a few puffs threw it away.

Smoking won't heal my broken heart. He decided never to smoke again. *Priya never told me about her marriage. She did not even invite me. Why should she?* They had hardly ever talked to each other. *I had never promised her to have a life together with me . . . . had never made any commitment to her. No, she has not betrayed me, she is such a good girl . . . So sweet. It is fate which has forsaken me.*

He wanted to throw away the petals of the rose she had given him which he had kept safe in a book.

No, I would not do it. She had given me the rose with sublime love. No, throwing it away will go against her wishes. It will always remind me of her.

He wanted to remember her fondly till his last breath. He continued gazing at the ceiling, did not know at what time he slept.

CHAPTER 19

Harbans just managed to clear his Intermediate. Vijay had changed his mind and had asked him to change from English medium to Urdu medium, because of the state of mind in which he was. It would have been really hard on him to devote so much time and energy to improve his English.

Pinki was very keen that he should complete his graduation but Vijay felt that he won't have the zeal to study further.

"How have you come to this conclusion?"

"Just my intuition."

"He is crazy about studies. You will see that one day he will be an M.A."

"I don't think so."

"Then you have gone nuts!!"

They went to Harbans' house in Model Town. He had lately shifted over there. It was an apartment with one large bed room and one living room. He had liked this locality, mostly confided to himself and made no new friends.

"First of all you must take one month's well deserved rest from studies. Then you should start studying for B.A, clearing B.A. is much easier than Intermediate," said Pinki.

"I have no interest for any further studies," said Harbans flatly, "I already feel too exhausted."

They kept silent for a few minutes.

"When I left my village I was studying in Class 8th . . . . I admit that deep down, I had this complex that I am not educated . . . . I am a bumpkin. No more now, and this is quite satisfying to me. I can never be an erudite scholar like Vijay. Yes, Vijay is my role model but I don't want to be Vijay. I am what I am."

"You seem to be distressed."

"No I am not distressed but I feel listless. I want to do something new, but even that is not clear in my mind."

"You feel lonely."

"Yes, I do."

"Then why don't you stay with us."

"That we have discussed a number of times. I will simply feel very uneasy."

"You want to keep your distance from us," this time Vijay spoke.

"No."

"It seems to be so."

"Pinky even you think so?"

"Yes."

"If like Lord Hanuman, I rip my chest, you will know the answer. Pinki, I am very close to your parents, Uncle Kenny and his entire family, and of course Bhandari Sahib. In this free India all of you are my only people whom I can call as my family. All of you are very dear to me. You are all very important to me. The way I got attachment to Vijay, I did not have it that way with my own family members, although I can never forget them."

"Stop your melodramatic discourse. I have brought bottles of beer. Let's drink."

"Why did you take so much time to tell me," laughed Harbans. It was a weak laughter. He used to laugh with free abandon, but not any more.

After they had beer, Harbans suggested, "Let's go to some nice restaurant. I feel suffocated sitting in this room."

In the restaurant they talked shop. The usual easy communication between them was missing.

While changing his clothes for the night, Vijay said, "I think Harbans needs a change of scene, let's go to Kulu Manali for a week."

"That's a great idea."

They were able to persuade Harbans to go to Kulu Manali with them for a short holiday. He could not say no to them as he knew he was getting on their nerves.

The scenic beauty of these hill stations had little effect on him. Inwardly, he remained passive and gloomy, though outwardly he showed that he was enjoying every moment of this escapade. It was just pretension which did not remain hidden from them. They were at a loss how to cheer him up. Throughout this sojourn, he remained simply obedient, never argued, always accepted whatever they said, where to go, what to eat and when to take rest. He plainly became a 'yes man', which further exasperated and saddened them. In their conversation, Priya was not mentioned at all.

Harbans liked and loved them intensely, still he was drifting away from them. His newly acquired friendship with Kishan Lal was more satisfying to him, it gave him some solace. With him he felt like birds of a flock together. It was a chance meeting which turned into friendship. He had gone to Rialto Talkies to see a movie but the house was full, as such no ticket was available. He asked a few people if a spare ticket was available with them, this practice was in vogue asking strangers if they had any spare ticket. Then a boy who was almost of his age told him that he was waiting for a friend and in case he did not turn up, 'the ticket is yours.'

During the interval Harbans treated him with cold drinks and snacks and they started chatting and instantly became friends.

Kishan Lal was a student of B.A. [Final] in DAV College. He was the wicket keeper of his college cricket team and a dashing middle order batsman. He all the time talked about girls, movies and of course cricket, which was all Greek to him. He once took Harbans to a cricket match in which he was playing. As one member of their club did not turn up, so he asked him to play as a replacement. Their team batted first and Harbans batted at number ten. Kishan Lal's agility and smartness behind the stumps fascinated him.

After the match was over Kishan told him, "You play with a cross bat."

"No, I did not cross my bat."

"Then better do it." Every body laughed.

Harbans was at sea what made them laugh. It angered him.

"But you were great in the field. Any team will love to have you in their side, of course as a twelfth man."

This pleased him, though he did not understand what the term 'the twelfth man' means.

Harbans was very annoyed with himself because he knew that he was getting on the nerves of both Vijay and Pinki. They loved him and were very caring, and this caring business was the root cause of all his discomfort. They often took him to their high society parties where he felt like a fish out of water. He had to wear a suit and tie in order not to displease them. In a suit he felt as if his shoulders and armpits were imprisoned. He felt too wrapped up and felt very uncomfortable. And the worst part to this discomfort was the tie, he felt strangulated. He had to put on shoes with laces and wanted to kick them out and free his feet. He walked clumsily wearing these shoes.

And the socks . . . . the very idea to put them on made him sick. He wore socks only when it was bitter cold. He admired Einstein because he never wore socks, which he had read in an article in an Urdu Paper. He always felt comfortable in his *Gurgabi* which has no laces. The worst of all was the buffet system which was appalling to him, putting all the food items in one plate. He was not supposed to eat using his fingers and eating with a spoon was not easy-eating for him. He could never learn to use the fork, he hated its very sight. He never opted for a food item, where he had to use the fork. He wanted to butcher the man like a tyrant who had introduced the buffet system. He could never talk about his discomfort to them, as they were so well-meaning and concerned about him. They were bent upon turning him into a genteel. He had no desire to appear urbane. There lied the whole problem.

He never used to tuck his shirt in his pants, which they asked him to do. When Vijay found that all his pleas had fallen on deaf ears, he took him to a barber's shop and asked him to look at himself in the big mirror. And then he asked him to tuck his shirt in the pants and when he saw himself dressed like that. Vijay spoke up, 'see the difference'. He agreed, yet felt bemused that why one should put himself to discomfort just to look better dressed. He did what Vijay advised him, but always took his shirt out when he was not around, he never wanted to displease his dearest Vijay. Yes, when he was besotted by Priya, his shirt was never hanging around his waist, life is such a paradox to reason it out.

After the papers, Kishan left for Delhi where his father was posted now at New Delhi Railway Station. He really missed him as he was such a jolly-good company. He felt very lonely but did not let his interest in the business dwindle, as he did not want Vijay to get less than his usual share. He adored both Vijay and Pinky but felt at peace when he could avoid their company.

Kishan Lal kept in touch through letters, always boasting of having one or the other girl friend he was able to hook. It was always 'the girl has fallen in love with me' or 'she is madly in love with me.' It was never 'I have fallen in love with her.' Girls were meant to fall flat for him. Although the fact was contrary to what he wrote, the way he looked it often offended them. They felt denuded by his leering looks.

He wrote to him that he had passed securing 54% marks. It had proved a bane for him, a curse in disguise. He had aimed to clear his graduation by securing just pass marks, that was why he most of the time neglected his studies. Being a wicket keeper his focus and concentration was intense,

besides he had photographic memory. His domineering father left him with
two choices, either to pursue his master's degree or to do a job. He had
already managed the job of an upper division clerk for him in the Municipal
Corporation of Delhi, where chances for bribes were immense. To him both
the options were not appealing.

He confronted his father that he had planned something altogether
different. His father took out a cane to beat him, and he ran away from
his home with just a rupee in his pocket. He traveled to Amritsar without
ticket, it was the accepted convention that the family members of a railways
employee rarely bought the ticket. If caught, the ticket examiner ignored it.
It was a part of the unwritten perk for them. Harbans was both surprised and
pleased to find him at his door.

When he did not turn up for seven days, his mother wrote him a touching
letter asking him to return home, telling him that his father had agreed to let
him pursue the career of his choice. He never received the letter because of
the incomplete address.

He started persuading Harbans to wind up his business in Amritsar and
suggested that they should jointly start some business in Delhi, as it is the city
of big opportunities.

"First of all find some shop in Delhi."

"No shop, we will have an office."

"What kind of an office?"

"Railway cargo, remember my father works for the Indian Railways.
Later on, we will go for air cargo also."

This occurred to him on the spur of the moment.

When he told Vijay and Pinky that he wanted to settle in Delhi and
suggested to sell the shop, they were taken aback.

A meeting was held in Mr. Bhandari's house, where Mr. and Mrs. Bakshi
were also present. Harbans wanted to bring Kishan along with him, but it
was over ruled.

All of them tried their best to persuade him from not going to Delhi, but
he was adamant and continued arguing in favour of his decision. They smelled
the rat that it was Kishan Lal who had trapped and mesmerized him.

"Brother, you are going to cut your feet by your own axe," said Pinky
agitatedly.

"It's not so."

"Why do you want to go to Delhi?" Mr. Bhandari asked rather plainly.

"To make more money."

Vijay stood up in a huff, "Okay . . . okay . . . . henceforth, I will stop taking my share . . . not even a paisa . . . . I swear by my mother that I would stick to it."

"It can never be acceptable to me."

"Then what do you want?" Mr. Bakshi asked.

"I want to go to Delhi."

"Damn it! Stop this crap of going to Delhi," cried out Vijay in desperation.

"Try to understand Vijay. I am sick of running a kiryana [grocery] shop, I want a change."

Mr. Bakshi intervened, "Fine, you can start some new business. We will . . . . myself and Mr. Bhandari will lend you as much money as you want . . . . sorry Bhandari Sahib, I have committed even without seeking your consent."

"You have snatched the words from my very mouth, my dear Bakshi."

Mr. Bakshi added, "It will be interest free and you pay us back as and when you can."

"I don't think I will need it, as I already have a partner and I guess he is quite well off."

"Well, have your way, but there is one condition . . . ," said Mr. Bhandari.

Harbans was all ears and he chose to keep quiet.

"If you fall on bad days, it will be killing for you to ask for any monetary help from any one of us, I know you too well. Am I right?" Mr. Bhandari asked.

"You are right, sir."

"In that case, forget about selling the shop . . . it will be kept running by your helpers. A separate account in a bank will be opened in your name and your share of profit will be regularly deposited in this account. No money will be sent to you. This will remain for your security." Mr. Bhandari gave his final judgment.

Harbans beamed with joy and relief. And he started dreaming of a rosy life in Delhi.

After Harbans Lal left, every body was after Bhandari's skin for yielding to his juvenile audacity.

"He would have cooled down after a few days . . . He has been brainwashed by that rascal, Kishan Lal," lamented Mr. Bakshi.

After what seemed to be a long pause, Mr. Bhandari spoke, "This lad has the knack to catch a fish from the sand . . . mark my words, he is not going to look back, because he has the innate talent to be a winner under all circumstances and Vijay knows this more than me."

Vijay could not disagree.

Kishan Lal was a dreamer, an incorrigible one, yet somewhat pragmatic but he did not have a penny of his own to invest.

CHAPTER 20

When Harbans Lal alighted from the train at New Delhi Railway station, he found Kishan along with his friends to welcome him. They were his team mates. Some of them garlanded him.

"He is going to be our permanent twelfth man," announced Kishan.

"If I am going to be always the twelfth man, then I am going back."

"So, you understand."

"I do. Now I can play with a straight bat."

"That's great."

"Have you found some accommodation for me?"

"You will be staying with me."

"No, I won't feel easy."

"Remember, when my father was transferred I stayed with you for three months and you never charged me any rent."

"True, but I am too used to live independently . . . . I won't feel comfortable staying with your family. Till then I will stay in a hotel."

"What sort of a business are we going to start?"

"Railways cargo."

"That's fine."

"There is a lot of money in this business . . . but it will take time to pick up."

"We should be prepared for it."

"Fantastic."

He had found an accommodation for him in Tilak Street, Pahar Gunj, as Harbans had told him that he would decidedly prefer to live of his own. It was a corner room in a big old-style house. At first, the landlord Mr. Chaggan Lal Aggarwal was reluctant to give it to a bachelor, but when he told him that his father was the Station Master of New Delhi Railway Station, he immediately gave his consent. He was a well known timber merchant and had his shop near St. Anthony School in Pahar Gunj. He thought that now he won't find any problems with the Railways Goods Staff and won't have to give them bribe of their asking.

"What is the rent, sir?"

"Rs. 5 plus Rs. 2 for the electricity," he asked for less than the expected rent, lest they change their mind. "But first I have to ask my wife. If she says yes it is yes. If she says no it is no."

He called his wife from inside, when she came both of them touched her feet.

"This boy, his name is Harbans Lal and he is from Amritsar. He wants a room on rent."

Looking at Harbans, she wished if God had blessed her with a son like him. Instantly she felt motherly feelings for him.

"Give him and don't charge any rent. God has given us enough."

"*Mataji* [mother], I seek your blessings . . . with all due respect, I don't want free accommodation, please."

"You called me Mataji . . . and a mother is supposed to be generous toward her son."

"Then I will seek plenty of it."

Everybody laughed.

Harbans touched her feet. "But allow me to pay the rent, please, please."

"Then we should charge you double."

"I am ready for triple."

Again they laughed.

Mr. Aggarwal had three daughters, all married into well-to-do families and the couple adored all the three sons-in-law. They were loving and caring husbands and never demanded anything from their in-laws. When they came to know that they had given one of their rooms on rent to a young Punjabi bachelor, they became apprehensive. They knew that their mother-in-law, Kesar Devi, when on her emotional waves, was quite generous and vulnerable. They decided to pay a visit to their house the very next Sunday.

When they came along with their wives, Harbans Lal was incidentally at home. "This is our Harbans Lal," the old lady said, and then pointing towards her daughters, as she was going to introduce them by saying, "And they are . . . ."

"My sisters."

These two words pleased all of them. And gradually they mixed up. In between, the second daughter said, "Isn't our brother very handsome?"

"Not very, but very much handsome," said the eldest daughter.

Harbans said by lowering his head, "A brother always appears very handsome to his sisters."

On their way home, the youngest daughter said, "It is very good for the security of our old parents that someone like Harbans stays with them."

None differed. They felt very satisfied with this arrangement.

Mr. Aggarwal, who was called Lalaji in the market, was their first customer. He always preferred to do his own work but lately he had started feeling that his physical strength was waning. He decided to engage them as his cargo agents. He also got them some assignments from his fellow traders. Their work started picking up but the pace was rather slow. They found it even difficult to break even.

Their office was on the first floor in the main bazaar of Pahar Gunj. Harbans did not like the stairs leading to their office, they were uneven and needed repairs.

The railings were rusty and gave the appearance that they had not been painted for years. They approached their land lord, Shadi Lal Jingan for the needful to be done. He flatly refused to carry out any work in this connection. He was a much moneyed man, but pathetically stingy. Harbans suggested for spending their own money for the work to be done as he felt appearances are very important in any trade. Kishan opined to postpone it till they have enough money for this purpose. Harbans decided to do it with his own money and did not even consult Kishan.

When the landlord got the wind of it, he came rushing and ordered the work to be stopped.

"Continue doing it," Harbans said calmly.

"I won't let you deduct the money from the rent."

"Who has asked for it?" Snapped Harbans Lal.

"Then you are most welcome to do it. I have decided to allow you."

Harbans did not answer him back, as he felt that it was important to have cordial relations with the land lord.

"Will you have tea?"

"And samosas also, I don't take empty tea."

Kishan Lal didn't like it that Harbans did not even care to consult him. He had no money to share this avoidable expenditure, and when the latter did not even mention it, he felt relieved. After that there business started flourishing with leaps and bounds. He decided that with regard to their business, he was never going to object to any step taken by Harbans. He felt that he had the will but Harbans had the real knack, he was in the habit of having his way but he was always well-meaning. Besides, he had no source for any further investment. His mother had given all the money she had been saving over the years plus she had sold her gold necklace to help her dear son. He never asked his father for any financial help, neither had he offered any.

He was still deeply annoyed with him. They hardly talked to each other. He despised him, but he still outwardly respected his father. The root cause of their animosity was the generation gap.

One day when Chaggan Lal was brushing his teeth, Harbans noticed that he was spitting blood and was in pain. He felt really worried for his health. Mataji was in the prayer room oblivious of the ailment her husband was suffering from.

"Are you feeling alright, *pitaji* [father]?"

"Why are you asking?"

"Just . . . ."

Lalaji always felt wary of the doctors. *They aggravate the disease to make more money by trapping the patient.* He had little faith in the allopathic treatment. He went to a *Hakim* [a doctor who treated with traditional Indian medicines] only when it became too necessary and he always avoided confiding with his wife about his ailment, because she always created a great fuss over his health. Even in their old age, they were like two love birds who adored each other. They did have their occasional quarrels, but if one burst out in anger, the other kept quiet. Thus, there was always peace at their home.

The same very day he was surprised to see Harbans waiting for him in his shop.

"What is the matter, any problem?"

"Yes, there is."

"What is that, I will be too glad to help you out," he said affectionately.

"You are not well and I am taking you to a doctor."

"I am alright," Lalaji half laughed.

"No, you are not. You bluffed to me in the morning. I have already enquired about the best doctor, he is in Karol Bagh."

"Turn out my mad son out of the shop . . . . I'm not well, huh." He ordered his *Munshi* [accountant].

"Your son is from Mintgummery. When he takes a decision, IT IS THE DECISION."

"Look at him, look at him! I am not going to any bloody doctor and that is my last word."

His workers told him that they felt the same way as he did.

He lifted the old man on his shoulders and asked one of the workers to bring a Rickshaw. Lalaji strongly protested, yet loved it. There were tears in his eyes. *God has blessed me with a real son in my old age, otherwise in these days, some sons do not care a fig for their parents.*

After examining him thoroughly, the doctor took Harbans aside and told him that it seemed that the patient was suffering from tuberculosis, he recommended some tests and prescribed the medicine.

After leaving him at home, Harbans went straight to meet his eldest son-in-law. And he made him aware of Lalaji's illness.

In the morning, the son-in-law came and they took him to a lab where all the tests were taken.

What they feared proved to be true. The treating doctor told them that diagnosis could be known too late for effective treatment, only God could save him at this juncture.

The very next day Lalaji wanted to go to the shop, but everybody in the family prevented him from doing so. And within a week he was totally bed-ridden. And he started losing his strength day by day.

One day he called all his daughters and son-in-laws and told them, when Harbans Lal was not present, "I know my days are numbered . . . . I want Harbans to run my shop after my death . . . . I treat him as my own son . . . . indeed, he is a son to me. And very dear to me . . . . I want him to light my pyre. Be always kind to him without being explicit about it. You don't know his past . . . his parents and sister were killed during the riots in Pakistan . . . . this he told me after much cajoling. His younger sister escaped and he does not know whether she is dead or alive. You must treat him like a family member, luckily your mother simply adores him."

Kesar Devi went inside and sobbed by putting her hand on the mouth because she did not want her husband to know that she was crying, as it would have added to his agony.

After three days he breathed his last. All the rites which are to be performed by a son as per the age old Hindu tradition were performed by Harbans. He had lost all faith in religious rituals, yet he devotedly performed all the rights, as he could not betray his old man after his death. He was a father to him and he revered him.

After the Kirya ceremony, a family meeting was held in the house of Mahesh Chand Mittal, the eldest son-in-law, where all the family members were present and that included Harbans Lal.

Mahesh, the eldest son-in-law coughed and then started, "I won't discuss preliminaries. Pitaji desired that after him, Harbans should run the shop . . . . it was his last wish, as a matter of fact, he told us this thing three days before his death . . . . even Mataji also so desires." Addressing Harbans he added, "We know you already have some cargo business and it will be hard on you, but please . . . ."

"Pitaji's word is law for me."

"What salary do you expect?"

"I've always wanted to be my own master . . . to be a salaried employee will be hard on me."

"You want it on some percentage?"

"Yes."

"How much do you want?"

"Being the eldest member of the family, it is for you to decide."

"Is 40% okay?"

"It should be much less."

"What do you suggest, Mataji?"

"I want it to be more than 50%, your father and I discussed it . . . ."

"40% is okay."

They then started to chat about Lalaji. Everybody had something lovable to talk about him, they really missed him, and very fondly. They had their meals and just when Harbans Lal was going to leave, Kesar Devi said excitedly, "Mahesh son, you have not told him about that."

"Oh, yes. Listen, Harbans, so far you're staying in the house is concerned . . . ."

"I should not pay any rent."

"You are right there."

"Often I eat meals cooked by Mataji . . . . oh! Really delicious . . . . but whenever I bring some vegetables or fruits, she starts fighting with me, she does not want me to spend any money and I feel miserable, because I can't fight back with her, she being so lovable. Brother Mahesh, ask mother to mend her ways."

Kesar Devi kissed his forehead, patted his head and said, "I won't . . . promise . . . . I am not going to . . . ."

"I bet." He smiled, touched her feet and left.

Every body felt relieved, especially Mataji.

Harbans went to the shop and told the workers that he was going to learn from them, only for a few days and afterwards they would work as per his diktats. After that he went to meet Kishan Lal in their office.

He told Kishan that after the death of his landlord, his family wanted him to run the shop, as a result of that they were going to part their ways. He also told him to pay back his investment as and when he can.

He watched his workers diligently, particularly the way they dealt with the customers. They resented his very presence and tried hard not to show it, but it did not escape Harbans Lal's notice. He had expected it. He made small notes in his diary.

Just after seven days, after the closing of the shop, he took all of them to a nearby restaurant and treated them lavishly. After they had their meals he told them, "You charge different rates to different customers by mentally judging their status and mentality. It is not going to happen anymore. Same rates shall prevail for every customer and without any discrimination. If somebody buys in bulk, what concession is to be given to him shall be decided by me, ONLY BY ME. And in my absence by Munshiji and his decision will be implemented, whether it is to my liking or not. And now listen very carefully, if somebody buys goods worth only one rupee, we will still be courteous to him."

Everybody felt appalled. *This chit of a boy has started behaving like Hitler . . . . we will show him.*

When they were having their tea, Harbans Lal addressed them again. "I have an important announcement to make."

What fucking more, they thought.

"After one month of my personal observation of your work, I am going to raise everyone's salary. How much raise am I going to make that will depend on your performance? It will be done in consultation with Munshiji. Mark my word whether we make any profit or not, the salaries shall be raised."

"So, from now onwards try to be in the good books of," he deliberately took a pause and then added, "IT IS Munshiji."

Everybody laughed.

He paid the bill and left.

"I am ready to shed my blood for him." Yasin yelled.

"So am I," others shouted in one voice.

Munshiji really felt elevated. He was known for his sincerity, hard work and loyalty. After the death of Lalaji, he had some nice offers and was thinking of joining one of them. He felt ashamed of himself and cursed himself silently. *'Pitamber Sharma, you are a madarchod [mother fucker]. You have entirely forgotten how Lala Chaggan Lal treated you when you were a lad of sixteen who came from Pauri Gharwal in search of a job and was nearly penniless and he treated you like his own.'*

The very next day, Munshiji went to meet Mahesh Chand Mittal early in the morning and as desired by him told him everything, almost verbatim as he was gifted with a sharp memory. As he was going to leave, Mahesh called him back and said, "I don't want any more reports about Harbans. I am fully satisfied." Then he forcibly put a ten rupee note in his pocket. Pitamber felt as if a heavy burden has been taken off his head. He had decided to treat Harbans as his master and he felt treacherous to report on his master, but he was duty-bound to the family also. Indeed, it was a big relief for him.

Later on Mahesh told his wife Radha Rani, "Your brother, Harbans has the knack to run business. He will go places. He is like an American, really dashing."

"Really, you mean it?"

"Mark my words, he is not going to stick to the shop only."

"How could you guess it?"

"It is just my hunch."

"Who knows?"

"One day, may be, he is going to be richest in the family. And we may borrow money from him." He laughed at his own joke.

"He will never refuse, I bet."

"I am sure of that. He is such a lovable character. He is bold and shy at the same time. When he talks to me, he never looks straight at my eyes."

"That is out of respect, you being the eldest brother-in-law."

"I know."

"I love to hear something good about him." And she kissed her husband. Soon they were in bed, took off their clothes and made love.

One day, the husband of middle sister, Ayodhia Prasad Garg came to meet Mahesh. He was very ambitious, a man with big dreams, but was basically a man of mean mentality, with not much care for ethics and morality. He was basically a dim-wit, who had very high opinion of his own intelligence. He seemed to be excited.

"Do you know Harbans has opened counters for hardware needed for wooden work?"

"No."

"He should have taken your permission. Why?"

"Does not matter."

"Especially yours. Why?"

"The man has ideas. He has a creative mind vis-à-vis business."

"He should have at least talked to us. Why?"

Mahesh let him continue.

"Especially as you being the eldest. I don't think it was right on his part. Why?"

Mahesh did not reply. He wanted to know what was in his mind.

"I see something fishy. Why?"

"I don't think so."

"This surprises me. I am of the opinion that we should not have fully trusted him right from the beginning."

"It was our father-in-law who trusted him. It is our mother-in-law who dotes over him. And he is not playing with our money. Why?"

"But it is high time that we check him, and stop him from having a free will. Why?"

"No, the shop belongs to Mataji and not to any one of us and there ends this matter," he took a deliberately pause to amuse himself by saying, "WHY?"

Ayodhia Prasad always used 'why' for 'isn't it', especially when he wanted the other person to agree to his point of view, and Mahesh always enjoyed counter attacking his 'why' with his own 'why' and by putting emphasis on it.

After that, he went to the house of Shankar Behari Lal, the husband of the youngest sister-in-law. Shankar was a happy-go-lucky fellow, content and devoted to his wife Usha Wanti and his two sons. He was a born hedonist, least cared for morality but was generous and kind hearted. Although he took his business seriously, yet he was not very ambitious. He liked to work but hated hard work; which was to him at the cost of enjoying life. His biggest pass time was to tell jokes and he had a great passion for it. Before Ayodhia was to take his seat, Shankar uttered, "Here is the latest one for you . . . it is a little bawdy. Two girls went out to buy bananas . . ."

"Later. I've come to discuss . . . . . something very important."

And then he told him about Harbans Lal's misadventures and high-headedness.

"Don't you have enough of your own business?"

"I do."

"Then why the hell you are losing your sleep over it? Let him do the way he wants . . . . Believe me he is a real good chap."

"You will never take any matter seriously, why?"

"Now listen, the girls went to a vendor and asked for two bananas . . . . the vendor said, I will give you three for four annas. But they said we need only two . . . ."

"Hell to your jokes!"

"You are a killjoy!" Shankar said teasingly.

Ayodhia Prasad felt miffed and left the place immediately.

He went straight to his astrologer, Pundit Jagdamba Prasad Chaurasia and told him about his predicament. After listening to his quandary, the pundit continued looking at him, but said nothing. When Ayodhia placed 21 rupees on his desk, the pundit started consulting his holy books. In between he was muttering . . ."Venus in sixth house . . . *Rahu* in 8h . . . . overpowering *shani* . . . *Maha dasha* in the sixth house . . . . *Ketu* is inimical . . . ." and some blah blah about the position of the stars. And a few hard to pronounce and understand Sanskrit words and he kept quiet, it was a hint to him for the offering of money to proceed further. Ayodhya put a five rupee note on his desk. The pundit frowned, he had expected more. After about twenty minutes with a unique glow on his face, the pundit said, "Your problem can be solved", and then kept mum until Ayodhia placed another five on his desk. The pundit felt disappointed, he expected much more.

"I was cock sure that you would be able to solve my problem. Why?"

"Go son, feed a cat with the milk of a polar bear."

"But, where will I find it?"

"Befriend an Eskimo."

Mahesh by using his business acumen expected that the shop will run at a loss for the first three months, and it will just break even for another two to three months, only then there would be the flow of profit. When in the very first month, there was some profit though not as much as in Lalaji's times and in the very next month there was so much profit which he could not even think of even in his dreams. Only then Harbans told him that he had increased the salaries of all the workers keeping in view their performance. As they were making profit, the workers had every right to have their share.

"I appreciate that . . . . you have human angle even in business . . . . never leave it from your system . . . . It always pays."

This was not appreciated by Ayodhia but he failed to impress the other two and to bring them to follow his point of view. He could not have even the support of his wife who out rightly reproved him for his base mentality.

He went to his mother-in-law with a well prepared speech with the emphasis on that Harbans would bring the shop to its doom. She told him that at times her husband discussed business with her which she could not understand the A B C of it, now what ever he was telling her was beyond her comprehension. She advised him to go to Mahesh and Shankar and whatever they say it would be acceptable to her.

Kesar Devi was a shrewd woman from business men's family and was married to a business man, she understood everything that ultimately Ayodhia wanted to grab the shop for himself, as her other two sons-in-law had no interest in running the shop, besides she had unflinching faith in her Harbans. *By the grace of God he can do no wrong.* She just tolerated him, lest he made life difficult for her daughter.

There lived a girl called Babli two blocks away from their house who always looked at Harbans with covetous eyes, but he always ignored her. One day when nobody was around she confronted him.

"Do you know my real name?"

"I don't even know your unreal name."

"I am Suprita, but my nick name is Babli."

"It does not make any difference to me."

"You never talk to me, but your friend Kishan talks to me on the sly. And you don't even know it."

And then she showed him her cleavage. It was in her hands when to show it and when to make it revealed. She was an expert in this art, a near genius. She had worked hard on this expertise. Harbans did feel turned on, but considered it unethical to have an affair with a girl staying next door. All girls residing in the surrounding area must be considered as sisters, was the social dictum of that time. So he averted his eyes and walked away.

The girl felt jilted, but it made her all the more determined to have him. Her stairs remained always dark, thanks to her maneuvers. It was easiet for the boys to fondle and kiss her over there. She was promiscuous by nature, so far cuddling and kissing was concerned she was SOCIALIST by disposition, she was ready to oblige anybody, of course he should not be ugly and she totally debarred those who were pot-bellied. She decided that in case she was able to empower Harbans, she won't even look at any other boy. *He is so different . . . . And so handsome.*

When he reached home, Mataji was waiting for him. "Why were you talking to that girl?"

"I did not, she did."

"What did she say?"

"She told me her name without my asking for it."

"And you?"

"I said that it was of no interest to me, and if you were watching, you must have seen that I left soon after."

"She is not a good girl."

"I guess so."

"I am going to find a suitable wife for you."

"I am too young for that. Don't you think so, ma?"

"I must marry you before I breathe my last."

"Never say that again, please."

"One cannot fight against nature. I must do my duty towards my jewel."

Harbans embraced her and cried out, "I have lost my mother once . . . . I am not going to lose her again . . . . you will live long . . . . for my sake."

"What a son!" She could not control her emotions. Silent tears flew from her weathered eyes.

One evening, when it was an off day for Harbans, Kishan asked him to accompany him to the nearby Railways Park as he wanted to talk something important with him.

They sat on a bench, but Kishan kept quiet. He seemed to be worried and fuming inwardly.

Finally, Harbans said, "You are quiet . . . . come out with it, whatever you have to say."

Harbans intuitively felt that everything was not alright.

"Why are you taking interest in her, she is my girl?"

"I take interest in her!? My girl!? What the hell are you talking about! Have you gone mad?" Harbans became really edgy.

"You are meeting her surreptitiously. Lately, she is all the time talking about you."

"Nonsense."

"Of course, you have been meeting her on the sly so that I should not know it."

"I am not meeting any damn girl on the sly or fly."

"Don't be clever."

"I am not being so."

"You are pretending."

"I AM NOT."

"I am talking about Babli."

"Oh, you are talking about that cheap girl!" Harbans laughed.

This infuriated him and he slapped him. Harbans slapped him back and it was a real hard one.

They started fighting and soon their bodies joined in tight embrace, in sheer hatred for each other. Harbans by putting his right leg diametrically into Krishna's left leg, what is called *tangri* in local lingo, threw him on the ground and gave him a few quick blows on his stomach and chest. Kishan Lal cried in pain.

I should have known his strength, he is such a great fielder.

Harbans wiped his hands with his shirt and said, "Now get up. Even *Mataji* does not approve of her. And you know it well that I never defy her."

After what seemed to be a long pause, Harbans said, "I am sorry . . . . I hit you rather badly."

"It is my fault. I should not have come to this conclusion without even trying to know your version."

They went to a pub and had beer.

"Let's forget it as a bad dream."

"I am never going to take any interest in that slut. She told me that you are a great kisser."

That made Harbans laugh, "I have not even kissed a doll in my life."

They were friends again and became even more devoted to each other.

A month later, Babli eloped with the son of her mother's second cousin.

Within days, Kishan was able to hook another girl and fell much in love with her. She had lovely black eyes, full lips and her shinning black tresses fell on her hips. She was both sensuous and very feminine. She was originally from a northeastern state, but had studied up to Senior Cambridge in Calcutta and had developed a great love for Bengali language and its culture. Her swarthy complexion added to her sexuality. She loved to sing and sang very well, but she always sang Bengali songs, which to a crude Punjabi like Kishan was a torture for his ears, especially when she sang Rabindra Sangeet with great fervour. He was full of carnal hunger but had no sense of culture. He felt that his friend, Ammongla, whom he always called Ammo, could sing a song while being laid, and she was a great lay.

She was very good in studies, but naïve in worldly affairs. She was simple minded, undemanding, credulous, very sentimental and vulnerable. Kishan had to make no efforts to exploit her, she herself was too ready for it.

Kishan Lal found that whenever he went to his friend Jagdish Kumar Khanna's house, his sister Mona looked at him desirously from the corner of her eyes and stealthily gave him a lovely smile. He felt bewitched by her and instantly fell in love with her. She had beautiful dark brown eyes and was quite tall as per Indian standards, of fair complexion, had pouted lips and a terrific figure. She had an inviting smile. He decided to hook her and then have great fun with her.

One day, he went to her college, Daulat Ram in the north campus of Delhi University. He waited for her for more than two hours and when she came out, she knew why he was there.

"Surprised to see you here," she said demurely.

"Really?"

"Yes."

They went to a restaurant, where Kishan Lal, without any preliminaries declared his undying love for her. He was well-rehearsed for it, but made it sound genuine and natural.

"Have you ever played cricket," he asked.

"No, never."

"But you love watching it."

"Not at all, it's so boring."

"But often you come to watch us playing."

"Damn it, I come only for you".

He put his hand on her hand and she did not take it away and smiled at him.

Their relationship immediately got cemented.

They dated quite frequently, but their rendezvous remained confined to the university area, so that their families could not know about their ongoing affair.

In between he continued meeting Ammo also, though less frequently and she never complained, thinking it was because of the business pressure. The poor girl had unwavering faith in her lover.

And Mona could never imagine that he was two-timing her, otherwise she would have kicked him on his ass, as she was a no-nonsense strong willed girl.

One day Ammo came to his office and when no one was around, said with a sullen face.

"There is very sad news."

"And what is that?"

"I am fixed."

"Fixed?"

"My parents are going to marry me off next month."

"Oh, no!" He showed false gloom.

"I will abide by whatever you say."

"You love your parents."

"Very much."

"I am ready to make any sacrifice for the happiness of your parents, for their honour."

"You have sublime feelings. My would-be-husband will have only my body, not my soul."

"I know that."

"I thought that by listening to this news you would start weeping."

"I will weep-o-weep . . . . but later on . . . . as some customer may not turn up."

"Weep-o-weep!? What does it mean?"

"It is Punjabi style of saying that I will weep . . . . weep, and weep till I fall asleep."

"Oh, I understand. I am also checking myself for the same very reason."

"Let's decide to weep together . . . . though separately . . . at the same time . . . . it's our joint tragedy . . . . let's say at 10 pm, when everybody is asleep."

"I've always obeyed you, my love."

"And there should be no sound."

"No sound."

"And only for one hour."

"I thought . . . . for the whole night."

"Our swollen eyes will tell the entire story in the morning."

"How right you are!"

"Before you leave, we must have *jhumbak-jhumba* [sex] once for the last time."

"What does it mean in Punjabi?"

"No, it is a Haryanvi expression. It means vigorous sex by doing tit for tat."

As she was going to leave, he called her back and spread his arms, she came running to him and he started kissing her. In between the kisses, he said, "Before you leave me for ever, you've to make me a promise." She waited for him to finish. "On your first night, you must imagine that I am on top of you."

"I promise."

Again they embraced and kissed each other and then he quickly made love to her.

At 10 pm he was having beer in a pub with Harbans. He was feeling both sad and relieved. For the first time in his life, his conscience pricked him. He was thinking that she was a paradigm of love, beauty and loyalty and he was nothing but a scum. *You are a fairy who never deserved a man like me. You're lucky to be away from this haram ka tukham [son of a bastard] . . . . I wish you a very happy married life from the core of my heart. I'll always remember you very fondly, you were such a pleasure.* Then he resolved to be true to Mona, although he himself was aware of the fact that old habits die hard.

He had already started dating Mona quite frequently. One day he took her to Ritz Cinema to see a movie. During a love scene he started fondling her breasts. She murmured "Stop it!!"

Her no means yes, he thought. His experience with Ammo had emboldened him. He felt when a girl was in love, she was an easy prey. He continued doing it.

She felt uneasy and he felt that she felt stirred. And then he pinched her nipple. She hit him with her elbow and left the cinema hall.

He came out of the hall to apologize and make amends, but she was nowhere to be seen. He cursed his luck and thought that he had lost her forever, but he was a cricketer who believed in fighting till the last ball. He decided to let the things cool down and then he would meet her and try to pacify her.

At night, when Mona was lying on her bed, she was annoyed with his dishonourable behaviour, yet deep down in her heart there was some satisfaction and enchantment. *I was so desirable, so appealing to him that he could not resist and control himself. Boys are boys and will always remain so. He should have first aroused me decently, before being daring and audacious. Big fool!*

After seven days he went to her college, when the weather was very fine on that day. When he met her, she refused to talk to him. He followed her and continued walking along with her. *Every girl is not embodiment of innocence like Ammo. I should not have gone that fast.*

"Stop chasing me, otherwise I am going to call the cops."

"I will say I am in love with her . . . . I am her slave . . . if she wants to get me arrested I am ready for it. I will consider jail as my father-in-law's house."

"You think I am a commodity meant for to play the way you want. You have no respect for the female gender."

"That is why I have come to apologize. I have spent seven miserable days. I want to confess that that scene in the movie was very exciting which goaded me to behave cheaply and then you are so exciting."

"You find me exciting, my foot! Now leave me alone."

And then he stood on one leg and apologized again.

"Don't behave like an idiot on the road side." His antic made her laugh.

They went to the same restaurant.

"Promise that you will behave like a gentleman in a public place."

And they patched up.

"I am going to kiss you."

"Again, you are up to mischief!"

"I'll do it at night, in my dreams."

"Do as much as you want . . . but not in a public place."

"I've already promised you."

In their next cricket match, Kishan promoted Jagdish from number seven to one down, after all he was his girl's brother. Jagdish felt delighted and was all concentration and did not let his team down and they won the match.

Kishan decided not to be flirtatious with her. He wanted to make her his own for ever. He told his mother that there was a girl he really liked. His parents met Mona's parents. Her parents always liked him and had even half-thought for this alliance. Both sides were Punjabis and belonged to Khatri caste, so what objection could be there? They agreed and congratulated each other.

After their engagement, her parents allowed them to see a movie together, but on one condition that Jagdish would always accompany them, otherwise people would talk. *After all, we are Indians, not westernized.*

It was a popular romantic movie they went together to see. Kishan managed to buy one ticket for a separate seat, about which he informed them and when she had gone to buy pop corn, Kishan said, "Better the two of you sit together."

"No, there are certain scenes in this movie that I will feel awkward watching sitting next to my sister."

"As you wish," he concealed his excitement.

During the movie Kishan tried to be fresh with her.

"Damn you, save your excitement for the wedding night," she kissed him on his cheek and he kissed her lips, this time she responded. And then said, "Beyond that no further misadventure," she said firmly and giggled.

Kishan had confided in his friend and team mate, Kasturi Lal Sharma that he and Mona had been dating, who confided in his friend Jawahar Lal Singhal and who confided in his bosom friend Naresh Chand Kalra and Kalra spilled the beans to Jagdish and by doing so he felt that only he was a true friend of Jagdish. This made him sullen and bugged . . . . *How could my sister do it, she had no concern for the family honour.*

He decided to divulge it to his mother. Both mother and son were very open and friendly with each other, a rare phenomenon in an Indian household in those days.

"They are just friendly and there is nothing wrong in that . . . . the world is changing . . . live with the times . . . . I am a woman . . . . every girls fancies for some man when she is young, but she keeps quiet because of our hypocritical society and anachronistic social morals."

"You mean . . . ."

"Yes, even I did."

"Even you mom!?"

"Of course . . . and the man was your father."

"Yours was a love marriage."

"In a way it was not."

"And you were meeting?"

"Big no . . . . we looked at each other with love and passed smiles."

"And then you dated."

"We never did." And then she told him that once his father went to the market to buy vegetables, when she was already there. His father coughed thrice before meekly saying, 'Hello' to her. She could not even greet him back, as her voice got choked and her stomach got taut with nervousness.

Both of them laughed.

She still cherished that sweet, intoxicating 'Hello', as if it happened yesterday. She confided in her mother and they got married.

"How did your father react?"

"My mother never told my father that I was in love, otherwise he would have beaten me to pulp. And till this day he does not know anything about it."

She sighed and then said that only our gods and goddesses are allowed to fall in love and have love marriages, it is forbidden for we mortals by our sanctimonious society, and the days of romance remain barren for us.

Her daughter had not betrayed the family, as she had confided in her mother.

"What you are saying makes sense . . . . and I had such stupid ideas and I thought so badly about my own sister."

"I guess you never told father what Mona confided in you."

"I am pained to say that you are right. Men happen to be more conservative than we women. They have different rules for themselves, and altogether different for their sisters and daughters."

He felt proud of his mother and felt relieved.

His mother added, "In future, if you find a girl . . . . have romance with her but be within limits and do confide in me. For us Indians, family ties are very important and there we out beat the western society."

One day they were sitting in the same restaurant, whenever they went to some other restaurant nothing came to their mind to talk about. Perhaps, sitting there they felt romantically charged. While sipping tea, Mona suggested not having lavish arrangements on their marriage and they should spend frugally and to invite only close relatives and very close friends and let the marriage be performed like the Sikh marriages, during day time and that way lot of money would be saved on lights and decoration. Money thus saved by both the sides should be invested in their business.

"The idea appeals to me."

"I am going to talk to my father and you must talk to your father."

"Not my father, I'll talk to my mother. For their sons, Punjabi mothers are the best to make them agree to their son's proposal."

"We must bring our business to new heights."

"You are hinting that you are going to join me in my business."

"I'm not doing B.A. [honours] in Economics to crack peanuts."

Mona talked to her mother who consulted her husband on this issue. They finally decided that first of all they must have the consent of the boy's parents in this matter.

Kishan talked to her mother, who promised him that she would be able to make his father agreeable to this proposal.

A woman has her own ways. She was still desirable in the bed, and her husband even in his middle age was a man of loose underwear.

When she talked to her husband about it, he felt for first time in his life that his son was serious about his career, otherwise he thought him to be wayward who took everything rather too casually. When she told him that it was his fiancée's idea, he felt all the more gratified.

"Kunti, you will see that our daughter-in-law is coming to this house in the form of goddess Lakshmi. Our son is going to go places in his business." He boasted in sentimental enthusiasm.

After two months they got married and about the arrangements, and the way marriage was performed, was condemned by most of their kith and kin, but friends refrained from commenting anything.

'Misers, mammonists, muck-worms, penny-pinchers, save-alls' were some of the titles used for them, but behind their backs only.

CHAPTER 21

Harbans Lal received a post card with vermilion sprinkled on it, a sign of some auspicious good news. It was written in Urdu by Bakshi Sahib conveying that God has blessed Vijay and Pinki with a son. He felt great and wanted to rush to Amritsar immediately, but before that he had to do some shopping and for this his youngest sister helped him.

Actually, he and Shankar had become very close to each other. Occasionally, they went to a pub to drink together, whisky for Shankar and beer for Harbans. They ate non-veg food secretly, as in Lala ji's entire clan eating meat was considered a great sin.

As such Shankar had cautioned him that Mataji should never come to know that they take non-veg food, it would be a big shock to her as she was a strict vegetarian who did not use even onions and garlic as these were considered *tamsik; bad for the body, bad for the soul.* And then she would refuse to have any food in his house and his wife would create a big scene. Harbans agreed on one condition that Shankar won't narrate more than two jokes in their sittings. Shankar agreed to it reluctantly, as it was hard on him and also against his constitutional right of freedom of speech.

Usha Wanti, the youngest sister realized that he was over spending on shopping and tried to check him, but he was indifferent to her advice and simply said, "My dear sister, you just don't know what I owe them."

When he reached Amritsar Railway Station, Mr. Bhandari, Mr. and Mrs. Bakshi, Vijay, Kenny uncle and his wife had come to receive him. With great difficulty, they were able to persuade Pinki not to come because of her a few days old baby.

When they reached home, Pinki was there with her small baby waiting at the gate. When she saw him, she turned her back and walked to go inside.

"Hello Pinki. How are you?"

Addressing her son, she said, "Gulu, we are not going to talk to him."

Gulu was the pet name of the child.

"What crime have I done?"

"Have you not listened, Gulu?"

"Okay, if you are not going to talk to me, I'm going back."

"Just try it and I'll break your legs. For a long time you have never cared to visit us. Only when Gulu was born you thought of us . . . . rarely wrote to us, you cruel rascal. And we missed you so much, always."

"Sorry sister cum sister-in-law . . . I won't do it again . . . I promise."

They hugged each other and laughed. Looking at his luggage, Vijay and Bakshi thought that he had come to Amritsar for good, but not Bhandari Sahib.

Looking at his thick chain in the neck, they presumed that he was doing well in his business. Actually, he had borrowed it from Shankar Behari Lal, not to show off, but to make them feel that he was well established in his business and this trick had the desired result.

When others left, he showed Vijay and Pinki the presents he had brought for all of them and that included their two helpers. And then he showed them the gift items for the baby.

"Nine baby frocks! Have you gone mad!?" Pinki yelled.

"Yes mad in happiness over the birth of my nephew, the first one in the family."

"My my, so many toys. Have you burgled some shop?"

"No, I begged and borrowed, from here and there," and he laughed heartily, that way he had never laughed during his entire stay in Delhi. Suddenly, Vijay chuckled.

"What happened?"

"You have started wearing socks. I noticed at the station."

Harbans admitted that it was Delhi's air which had its effect on him.

They chatted till 4 o' clock in the morning. Harbans told them everything about his stay in Delhi . . . how an old couple treated him like their own son . . . about the timber shop, about his three sisters and brothers-in-law, but he avoided that the middle one was not so amicable with him. Vijay also told him that the shop was running well and they had been depositing his share of profit every month in the bank.

After three days, he told them that he would be leaving for Delhi because of exigencies of work. Pinki hid his trunk which was nowhere to be found. He had to stay for another two days.

The best news Harbans could know was that Kenny was having enough work due to the connections of Bhandari Sahib and Mr. Bakshi and with their help he had purchased a plot of land measuring 125 square yards and the construction work was going on. The George family had become part of their inner circle and just to please them, they went to his church on special occasions, although Mr. Bhandari had no interest in religion at all.

Vijay suggested that they should not take their share of profit from the shop at least for four months and spend this money on furniture and decoration of his house. "Do you permit it?"

"You have no right to insult me by asking for my permission. DO IT"

And he hugged him and kissed him on his forehead, showing his immense appreciation of his idea.

At the time of his departure, Harbans told them that he did not like farewells, as they are really painful. So, he took a Rickshaw and left for the station. He was somewhat dismayed that nobody had cared to drop him in his car.

When he reached the station, everybody including Pinki was already there to see him off. He was much touched and now he knew why he had to travel all alone in a Rickshaw. When he was almost going to board the train, Pinki said, "Do I have to give birth to a child after every few months to make you visit Amritsar quite often."

"I have already given you my promise."

And then Mr. Bhandari gave him a cheque, "It is not safe to carry so much cash . . . . it's your share of profit from the shop."

When he boarded the train, a coolie placed a huge trunk, on the railings above his seat, before he could ask anything, Mr. Bhandari said, "A few presents from all of us."

"But you never gave me even a hint."

"To let you create a fuss! We have saved you from being beaten by us. *Baliya* [dear one] we are your fathers and you are not our father," said Mr. Bhandari.

There was a loud laughter which startled other passengers.

When the train started moving, they waved till they could not see each other anymore.

Harbans started talking to himself, *Oh, Amritsar . . . . my dear, dear Amritsar . . . I can never forget you . . . the nagri of the great Gurus.*

When they were having tea at Vijay's house, Bakshi sahib said," Bhandari Sahib, I dare not ask why you took the decision to hand over the cheque to

Harbans . . . you are the head of our small clan . . . . but you always said that we should keep this money for his eventual future security."

"He does not need it any more . . . he is not going to look back."

"How could you conclude it?" Pinki asked.

"You must have noticed his life style, but the foremost idea came to my mind when I had a look at his chain, it's quite a heavy one, must have cost lot of money, that made me take this decision," replied Bhandari Sahib.

"Oh, yes." Everybody agreed.

"Now I understand," Mr. Bakshi said.

Harbans invited the sisters and their families to his house and did not let Mataji cook. He placed the order with a caterer friend of his for a sumptuous dinner. Till then, he had not opened the trunk with the presents he brought from Amritsar. He wanted to show the large-heartedness of his folks at Amritsar. Like a child who wants to show off his newly acquired toys to his friends given by some dear one. When he opened the trunk, he found three beautiful Banarsi saris, of the same design and of pink colour for the three sisters, and three suit-lengths for the three brothers-in-law and a white silk sari and a very expensive Kashmeri shawl for Mataji. Besides, there were gifts for each and every child. Of course, there were many gifts for him, but the gifts for his family in Delhi delighted Harbans the most.

Everybody was of the opinion that they loved and cared for Harbans immensely.

"Only a fool won't like our Harbans,"Ayodhya said, "Why?"

Everybody was surprised at his change of heart for Harbans. His utterance, 'Our Harbans' connoted that he had shed his animosity toward him.

Actually, Ayodhia had well thought of that. It was of no use to be a one-man army against Harbans. The old maxim, 'if you can't fight them, join them,' perhaps made him change his attitude towards Harbans.

Together they had a worth remembering time.

Mataji chose a girl for Harbans named Sat Bharai, which in Punjabi meant 'a sister of seven brothers,' though her parents had lost three of their sons in their infancy. A friend of a friend of a friend had suggested about this matrimonial alliance. She was plump but quite good looking. Her father Des Raj Kharbanda worked as an Assistant Engineer in the Municipal Committee of Delhi. He lived in style and could afford it, because under his official jurisdiction, he never allowed any work to be done unless his palms were greased. Only for that purpose he was polite, soft spoken, understanding which means he had the qualities of a born crook. A day before the engagement his folks from Amritsar arrived and when they asked him, 'How does she look?'

He replied, "I have not even seen her so far."

They urged him to show them her photograph.

"I don't have any, Mataji has chosen her for me. Must be good looking." It was his plea.

They decided to go to Mr. Kharbanda's house to have a 'see' at the girl.

They were treated by the Kharbandas nicely, but somehow they neither liked the girl nor the family, but they suppressed their feelings and did not let Harbans know it. As a matter of fact, they had chosen a beautiful girl from a known family for him, and before they could even inform him, they got his telegram. It was not to be and it saddened them and they put a stone on their heart.

CHAPTER 22

On his first night, Harbans Lal felt awkward and was at a loss as how to make the first move. He had not even kissed a girl all his life, what to talk of a kiss he had not even shaken hands with any female. Many of his friends had volunteered of their own to guide him how to have sex on the first night. 'It is the night when you have to kill the cat; if you are successful then the girl will be your slave all her life and if not she would always rule over you.' But nobody had told him how to make a conversation.

They did not talk to each other what seemed to be an eternity.

Suddenly, his wife started weeping.

"What happened," Harbans asked worriedly.

"Oh, thanks Vaishno Mata. You are not what I thought." She closed her eyes and prayed for two to three minutes.

"I am not . . . what is that, which you thought?"

"What I foolishly thought."

"But what is that which you foolishly thought?"

"Which I thought which you are not . . . . oh, please forgive me."

"I will forgive you! But for what?"

"It is for being so stupid."

"I simply can't understand what you are talking about."

"I am talking about my lack of sense."

"But you have hardly talked to me."

"How could I talk to you what I thought was wrong?"

"What wrong you thought?"

"What I should not have thought. After all, my father chose you for me and he is so intelligent."

"So, there is something wrong in the selection."

"Not the least. How can my mother and father be wrong in their selection?"

"If you are not going to tell me right now, what you thought, and what is wrong and what you should not have thought . . . . I am going out for fresh air."

"Oh, no . . . please . . . . first let me apologize."

"Okay."

"I thought you are deaf and dumb. You were not talking to me and I thought that was why you never tried to meet me even stealthily before our marriage."

He hugged her and started laughing.

She asked for his permission to change, as her *saari* was very heavy and she was not feeling comfortable. She also requested him not to look at her as she would feel embarrassed, which clearly meant, 'do it, but don't make it too obvious.'

She took off her saari, and by and by began discarding her clothes. He felt fascinated looking at her big boobs.

She came to him and he embraced her . . . . *'Why he is not kissing me? He is too naïve . . . . and . . . . My, my, he is so handsome.'*

'Please don't do any mischief . . . . I am yours all my life . . . Why should there be any hurry?" She said softly in his ear.

"Okay, as you please, we can wait."

Ah! Which man listens to his wife's pleas on the first night . . . . they are out to grab her, crush her? Men are like that, she thought.

"I can't understand what do you really want?"

There was a silence.

"I want you to own me, fully." She said in a husky voice.

This made him bold and he denuded her. His unpaid advisers had told him that no bride takes off her clothes of her own during the first few days. It's always the man who has to do it. She let him do it and went against her own plans to make mild protests to show her bashfulness. In a way she helped him to do it.

Now he felt really excited but his Sex Guru, his Munshi had time and again reminded him not to get excited and had advised him that he should count one to hundred during the act, and avoid looking at her and keep his mind away from sex. Once he was inside her, he hardly knew anything about foreplay, neither had his Guru told him anything about it, perhaps he did not know himself about its importance. She shrieked and began making some eerie sounds, as advised by her married friends to prove her virginity, which she was. Her weird sounds astonished him, as nobody had ever talked about it, not even Kishan Lal. Suddenly, he realized that he had already counted up to 143 instead of 100, by now she had stopped making those sounds, both of them forgot about the advice of their instructors and started enjoying the fun and felt great, and reached the climax simultaneously.

She felt that it was the best day of her life. She thought that amongst all her friends and cousins, she had the best husband; so virile, gentle, caring and handsome yet somewhat naïve.

"Was it very painful?"

"Extremely!!" *A virgin must show that it was a very painful experience.*

Then they started chatting. He was mostly listening. She talked so much about her mother and father, for they were her role models. And then she suggested that better they sleep as it was quite late in the night. He agreed, went to his cot and soon was snoring.

She was very annoyed with Sumitra, Kanta, Sheila, Leela and Gurdeep for their joint advice not to agree for the second trip and must make him beg for it before agreeing to it. She profusely cursed them. At the same time she was not angry with him, as with her womanly instinct she had realized that he was so innocent and child-like and totally inexperienced in sex related matters. She felt proud of him.

The very next night she made another folly and like an expert she told him that they should not do love-making till she was relieved of her pains. Before she could think of any device to arouse him, he was fast asleep. His sleep was always like switch off, switch on pattern. *This was advised by her mother; she was angry with her but didn't curse her.*

Next day, when she was talking to him, he started feeling sleepy and slept.

On the fourth night, Harbans felt as if somebody was scratching his back. Or was it a dream?

He got up and she giggled.

"Oh, it's you?"

"Yes, it's me . . . I am not getting sleep."

She had decided to be open and bold with her naïve husband. She asked him to switch on the lights.

"Why?"

"There is a surprise for you, my lord."

He did likewise. She was wearing his shirt and it was unbuttoned.

"You are looking so cute . . . . so alluring."

"It is the duty of every woman to titilate her husband."

He rushed to her, took her in his arms and while kissing her, said, "I can't wait any longer."

"Have patience . . . . this time we will go slowly . . . . and today I have no pains," she said coyly.

He agreed.

"Firstly, some foreplay . . . ."

"And what is that?"

"You haven't heard of it?"

"No, I know of play, but not foreplay. Is it some slang?"

."No," she chuckled, "Like first kissing . . . embracing, fondling and sucking . . . ."

"And sucking?"

"You have never desired to suck the breasts of a woman."

"But that is for small babies."

"They are also for men, my green-horn?"

And she delicately put her one breast in his mouth and nestled him passionately. He started sucking it devotedly and found it exciting and lascivious.

And they slept much after the cock crew in the morning.

"I don't like my name, Sat Bharai . . . . you did talk about it but still you have not given me a new name."

It was customary to give a new name to the bride chosen by her husband or at times chosen by his mother, at times it was not done if the husband liked her maiden name.

"Will Rani do . . . ."

"Yes, my emperor."

Before leaving for the shop, he said, "Teach me more about fore play . . . I really liked it."

"And what will you like to have for your services?"

"Only you."

CHAPTER 23

Harbans Lal decided not to have any intimate relations with any member of his in-laws family. He observed that they were crafty, mean, unethical and manipulative. On the dining table, they tried to outdo each other in filling up their plates, and in case of some non-veg dish, their hunger was insatiable, unmindful of others, they were simply uncouth and inconsiderate of others' requirement. As far as he could, he avoided having meals in their house. He kept just cordial relations with them, as it was important to him to have a happy married life. Sat Bharai adored her parents and admired her brothers. She could never analyze their cheap and detestable behaviour. Only on this score her intelligence failed her.

His three brother-in-laws borrowed money from him with the promise that it will be returned on the first day of next month i.e. on pay day. They never returned him the money, though it was not big money and Harbans never reminded them of it, because it was bliss for him to keep them away from his system. He was spared by the fourth brother as he was working in Ahmedabad, a far off place. The rest of the three were studying and their elder brothers were their role-models.

One day he told Rani that he felt like going to Amritsar and wanted her to accompany him.

"Oh, I will see the Golden Temple . . . it has been the greatest wish of my life," she said excitedly.

It was their first outing together after their marriage. Going out to some place on one's honeymoon was not in vogue in that era. People hardly used the word 'honeymoon', and many did not even know its meaning.

They had a great time in Amritsar and this time Rani was liked by everyone. They found her open, vivacious and full of fun. Actually, they had not liked her parents and this must have gone in her disfavour and they became opinionated against her.

On the second day itself Pinki touched her belly and asked, "Is there something?"

"Yes."

"Carrying for how many months?"

"Two months."

"God may bless you with a son."

Rani kissed her both cheeks and thanked her and they became close to each other, as if they had known each other for a long time. Most of their conversation was about sex and sex-related jokes.

"How is my brother in the bed?"

"He is like a stud."

"Any experience with a stud."

"You are really shameless." And they giggled.

"Okay, performance wise, how many marks out of ten."

"Eleven."

And they laughed like hell.

"And how many marks for Vijay Bhai Sahib's performance?"

"I think more marks should be given to me."

And they could not stop laughing for a long time.

Harbans and Vijay had never talked about their sex life. Not even a nickel of it.

Back in Delhi, he was very happy that everyone had liked his wife. It gave him immense satisfaction and he became all the more attached to her.

Whenever they had their petty spats, Mata ji always took Rani's side, which in a way pleased him and when just out of fun he complained about it, she told him that to keep peace and harmony in the house a *saas* [mother-in-law], should always be biased in favour of the *bahu* [daughter-in-law] and not her son.

"I don't see the logic."

"*A bahu* waits for her time to show her true colours, if she is not treated nicely . . . . and later on she starts showing her coquetry . . . . tantrum, it is because of a bride's inherent insecurity. I learnt it from my saas."

"Mataji you are so intelligent in the ways of the world, so virtuous. I am really proud of you."

"I told you that I learnt it from my *saas*, she was exceptionally intelligent, though she never went to school. As a matter of fact, on the first day of the school, she cried so much that her parents never sent her to any school again."

Then Mataji proudly told him that she had studied up to class 6th.

His business was picking up by leaps and bounds. He was smart, tough but always forthright in dealings. He never undermined anybody. If some customer found defect in the goods, he immediately returned the money and apologized for the inconvenience. And with two or three more complaints, he blacklisted that particular supplier. And because of that his suppliers were always cautious, as they knew that under no circumstances he would compromise on quality. At times he suffered some losses because of that but in the long run he was a big gainer. This way he won over his customers for ever.

Once he decided for a price, he never budged from it, but he treated his major buyers lavishly. Many of them became his close friends. One of them was a leading contractor of Delhi named Hasmukh Choksi, a Gujrati *bania*. Traditionally he belonged to a clan of jewelry businessmen, but some how this profession did not appeal to him, though he owned a jewelry shop in Dariiba near Chandni Chowk, which was run by his eldest son. His youngest son was settled in America working for an MNC. He was popularly known as *Bhai* [brother].

One day he was damn surprised when Bhai asked him to join him in his construction business.

"I work for n . . ."

"Nobody, I know it."

"'Even then you want me? I am surprised."

"I have not made my hair grey in the sun . . . I offer you 2 annas share, and you won't have to invest any of your own money."

"I can't leave this shop. It is like a place of worship for me."

"Please don't, you can still work with me."

"You can ask your son . . ."

"Never . . . I love my son and he is very, very dear to me. But so for this business is concerned I don't allow him to come close to me. Only for the reason, he tends to delay in making the payments and is not a man of his word and is very shifty. And I don't do business like that. It is unethical. And it is totally unacceptable to me."

"I hardly know anything about construction work."

"I know."

"Still you want me?"

"Yes."

"Strange!!"

"You never knew anything about timber merchandise."

"Who told you?"

"I have my ways."

"I will let you know in four or five days."

"Son, always omit this word 'or', in business."

"Two days."

"Why you need two days, with more days at your hands you will get confused."

Harbans began pouring another peg.

"Not for me. I don't take more than two pegs. I am now 73 and before the age of 70, I never took more than three pegs."

"It's scotch."

"I know. I only take scotch or *Desi* [country liquor] . . . . it reminds me of my hard days."

"Okay, I will consult with my elder brother-in-law."

"I think he must know me. Remember, I must know it after two days. After that, it's all over."

In the morning, he went to meet Mahesh and told him about Mr. Choksi's offer and asked him if he knew him. Mahesh told him every businessman of some stature knows him and he was a class by himself. And he added that he liked him immensely, a thorough gentleman . . . . cultured, soft spoken, never backs out of a deal and was a man of his word.

"You have assessed him correctly . . . but I am a tough Punjabi, aggressive by nature."

"True, he is not aggressive by nature, but when circumstances force him then nobody can match his aggressiveness. And he can be very tough. Amongst you Punjabis it becomes very obvious, but not in Gujrati *Banias*. It is a hidden trait in them."

"Are the Choksis Banias?"

"Yes, and he is a man of steel."

And then Mahesh told him that once a chief engineer of MCD created life hell for him, because of his insatiable greed, he wanted more money from him than the one agreed upon. Mr. Choksi refused to pay him a penny more. He manipulated in getting his payments held up from MCD for months together. And he felt severe financial crunch, but he did not budge from his stand. And when the chief engineer felt that there was no payment of any commission to him also, he got his bills cleared. But just for the heck of it, he got paid Rs. 500 less, on the connivance of the chief engineer, obviously to belittle him. Mr. Choksi wrote a letter to the department for the payment of Rs. 500 and subsequently also sent two reminders, but he got no reply. He filed a suit against him and MCD which went up to Delhi high Court and he won the case, and MCD was asked to pay him Rs.500 along with 12% interest and also awarded him Rs. 5000 for the cost of litigation. Mr. Choksi filed another review petition in the high Court pleading that the MCD was being run on the tax-payers' money, and in that case only the chief engineer was to be blamed, as such this amount should be paid by the chief engineer or should be deducted from his salary. Mr. Choksi had spent Rs. Fifty thousand in this case and he spent another twenty thousand on the review petition. The case was dragged on to the Supreme Court of India, where he once again won the case. This chief engineer had much political clout but now everybody amongst his political mentors shunned him. A pandora's box of complaints got opened up against him. And finally, he lost his job and a CBI inquiry was initiated against him.

"So, my dear wife's very dear brother, try to understand, these Gujrati businessmen appear to be mild like lambs, but where business is concerned they are hard task masters, they are known for their quick decision making and they indulge in no hanky-panky."

"But he has offered me just 2 annas partnership."

"And what is going to be your investment?"

"Zero over zero is equal to zero."

"Incredulous. Jump on this wagon, we will manage the shop."

"In the very first place I told him that under no circumstances I am going to abandon the shop. It is sacred to me."

"So, that is the hitch, this problem can be solved."

"No, he had no objection to it, he rather admired me for it. It was in his eyes."

"I hope I am not having a dream," he pinched his hand. "No, it's not. 2 annas share means a profit of a few lakhs. One day you are going to out rich all of us," he laughed, "One day we may have to borrow from you."

"Borrow from me! Brother, you don't know this Harbans Lal of Mintgummery. He can shed his blood for this family."

After two days he went to Mr. Choksi's house. It was a small three bed room house with a spacious L shaped living room. It was built on a 1000 yards plot. There were flower plants and a *neem* tree on the front side and on the back side he grew seasonal vegetables. He never had to go to the market to buy vegetables. The house was simply decorated, on the wall there was a family photograph with his parents and on another wall there was the photograph of the great martyr, Shaheed-e-Azam Sardar Bhagat Singh, who was hanged by the British Empire when he was only twenty three.

"Welcome, I knew you will come. Your brother-in-law must have approved of me."

"How do you know? But it's true."

He told him that he had not made his offer on an impulse, he had made all the necessary inquiries.

"They are your parents?" Harbans said pointing towards the photo on the wall.

"Yes. They were great souls."

"And you like Bhagat Singh."

"I admire him the most. He is my role model against injustice."

"I am surprised that there is no photograph of Gandhi ji. He was also a Gujrati."

"And a Gujrati bania like me, sorry, I don't think much of him . . . . he was a failed bania because of his failed and muddled policies. You will see that there would be more chaos in the country. And There Would Be More Corruption. These Gandhi-capped, dhoti clad leaders do not have the talent to run the country."

"But you do wear a dhoti."

"I am not ruling the country . . . . I am a business man . . . . and I do not wear their cap." He laughed.

"I have this funny feeling that you admire the British."

"Yes, I do, for their administrative skills and ability."

"And what are your views about Nehru?"

"I do like him."

He opened a bottle of scotch and poured whisky in two glasses. Harbans looked at the glass in his hands and asked, "Why bigger peg for me?"

"You are a Punjabi . . . Robust, that is why and I am a Gujrati, mild and frail . . . . but the ultimate winner." And he laughed like a child.

"Cheers for our new association!!"

"Cheers!!"

"When do you expect me to join you?"

"From today itself . . . . there is no tomorrow for this Hasmukh Veerji of Surat."

He brought the papers and asked him to read them and sign. Harbans Lal without reading signed the papers immediately.

"You should have read them . . . . it is childish and unprofessional."

Harbans touched his feet and said, "A son should never doubt his father. With others I don't behave like this."

He embraced him and showered his blessings on him.

His wife came rushing in and told him that he was much more lovable than he had described him.

"For him, please serve Punjabi meals and for me, Gujrati."

"Punjabi meals and Gujrati meals?"

"*Arre baba*, the meals are the same . . . . we put a little sugar in every vegetable dish . . . . aren't we funny people?"

"And also very lovable."

He gave him the third peg but lingered on his second peg and told him that when he first met him and the way he said, 'this Harbans Lal of Mintgummery,' he felt endeared to him and now whenever he was excited or felt challenged, he uses 'of Surat', with his name.

And then he started discussing business with him. At no point he did waiver, he was sure of what he was talking about.

Hasmukh was born after sixteen years of the marriage of his parents. He was connoisseur of their eyes, but his father never pampered him and they bestowed on him high moral values . . . 'What in Hinduism is called *Sanskaras.*' His father was a jeweler but honest to a fault. They were neither poor nor well off. They named him Hasmukh which means a smiling face. He was a brilliant student and did his M.A.[English] from Bombay University on a scholarship. He yearned to be a lecturer, but after many efforts when he could not find a job in Bombay, he came to Delhi to try his luck. Here also he could get no opening as he had no political or bureaucratic clout. Finally, he accepted a job of an English teacher in a private school. As he did not want to further burden his doting parents, but they put a condition that they will pay him only 60% of his salary, and the rest will be given to their ashram; obviously the rest was to go to their own pockets and they started discussing about his salary amongst themselves. Hasmukh simply walked out.

At long last, he got a job of an accounts clerk with a Gujrati builder. He was hard working and a fast learner. Soon he was able to make his mark. When his employer found that he was getting offers from other builders, he made him a one Anna partner, as he was not ready to lose him under any circumstances. He worked for him for another five years and then left him on moral grounds, and he started as a builder with very little money and resources, But He Never Looked Back.

CHAPTER 24

Harbans was now the father of three children. The difference between the two sons was just eleven months, it was because he hated to use the condom, as it took half the fun away when one felt aroused, and one has to put on this mechanical device. Actually, at that time very few people used the word condom and it was popularly known as the French leather.

Fun or no fun he decided not to have another child too soon. It was hell of a job and a great ordeal for Rani to raise two young babies. Actually on the birth of their first child, Vijay and Pinki made a list of fifteen names, then it was cut to ten and finally it was short listed to Vipin, Vikas and Vivek and it was left to Mataji to make the final selection and she preferred the name Vivek. On the birth of their second son, Mata ji consulted a pundit who after consulting some holy books, told her that it would be auspicious if the name starts with the first letter of 'K', so she got him named Kulbhushan.

One day, Mataji decided that she wanted to spend the rest of her life in the holy city of Haridwar, far away from the materialistic world. They bought a two room house for her and appointed a maid to look after her and to give her company.

Six months later they got a letter that Mataji had expired. All of them rushed to Haridwar. The maid told them that Mataji told her that she was going for ever as her time had come. And after that she started praying.

"Why did you not call a doctor?" Harbans asked angrily.

"Then she rested in lotus pose . . . . there was such a glow on her face, I thought she is feeling fine."

"You never called a doctor?" The eldest son-in-law fumed.

"When there was no response from her to my calls. I rushed out and called a Sadhu whom we knew."

"You went to a Sadhu, when you should have consulted a doctor! Had you gone mad?"

"He was once a famous doctor before he renounced the word. It was he who sent you the telegram."

They felt relieved and came to the conclusion that Mataji had a peaceful, saintly death.

The last rites were performed by Harbans and they came back from Haridwar after immersion of the *phools* [her ashes] on the fourth day of her death, in the holy river of the Ganga, and the *Kirya* [last rites ceremony] was performed in Delhi. As she never used a cot during her stay in Haridwar, they were saved from performing certain rites at Kurukashetra, which is essential amongst the traditional Hindus if the death occurs lying on the cot.

After another seven days, Harbans went to the house of Mahesh Mittal and told him that he had made arrangements for an accommodation in Karol Bagh. "I will hand over the keys of the house in the evening."

"Who has asked you to vacate?"

"I have already paid two months rent as advance."

"You took the decision without even consulting me?"

"There are two others, they may not like my continuous stay in this house."

"We want you to stay here till you have built a house of your own. All of us, three daughters and three sons-in-law are of the same opinion . . . . don't you dare insult us again . . . . at least for the sake of Mataji's sacred memory? YOU WERE A SON TO HER."

"Elders always pardon the younger ones for their misdeeds." He lowered his head in shame.

"Take it easy."

Mahesh then hugged him and they smiled.

"You are going to have lunch with us . . . . I'll go to the office late."

"But Rani is waiting for me."

"That is her punishment for not stopping you from taking this ignoble decision."

Harbans did not protest. He was always in awe of his eldest brother-in-law.

Mahesh told him that they had decided never to sell this house. "We have wonderful memories of its four walls. It will remain a sort of family house and always remember, you are a part of the family."

They never sold it, or gave it on rent, even when Harbans built a house for himself in New Rajinder Nagar, a predominantly Punjabi locality.

Rani gained much weight after every delivery, and started having indifferent health. When her younger son was four years old, she gave birth to a daughter. They were really delighted with her birth, as they wanted a sister for their two sons.

She was named Sapna [dream], as their dream to have a daughter was fulfilled. After her birth, she gained even more weight and most of the time she remained ill. Doctors were of the opinion that the root cause of her illness was her obesity, and she must put efforts to lose weight, but she had great love for food, especially the spicy one and she was least health conscious and that was her ruination. Harbans consulted top doctors, but there was hardly any improvement because no doctor could properly diagnose her disease. She was mostly given the drugs on trial and error basis. Finally, he lost all faith in allopathic system of medicine and took her to Hamdard Dawa Khana, which is famous for their treatment of age old Unani system. There was some improvement. The treating bearded old God-fearing Hakim had told her that she should have bland diet with very little ghee, and no spices at all, as spices were poison for her and she should eat lot of fruits. His medicine really suited her and she started improving.

After some days, Rani reverted to her old eating habits; she did not follow the old maxim that prevention is better than cure. Her health started deteriorating again. They again went to that noble Hakim who after checking her, took Harbans aside and said, "Nothing is in my hands now. Only Allah can save her."

After that she was totally bed ridden. Harbans hired two nurses for her, who looked after her for twelve hours each. After two months she died. She was only thirty two.

At the time of her death, Vivek was twelve years old, Kulbhushan eleven and Sapna only seven. His life was shattered, whenever he looked at his children he felt heart-broken. She had died when the kids needed their mother the most. He hired a cook and an ayah to look after his children.

He became over indulgent towards his kids and was too keen to satisfy their every whim; right or wrong, as he did not want them to feel that life has become for them unbearable after their mother's death. Previously, he could hardly give of himself to his kids because of his tight schedule, for their proper growth and particularly for his two sons. Before that he was too naïve to realize it. Now his sole aim in life was to make them financially very secure, so that they do not to have to fight for their way out in the struggle of life, which he had gone through. Once again, he devoted all his time for his business, and there was not enough time for his growing children. His sons could never have the opportunity to be close to their father as they were in awe of him. He could never find time or the urge to take them out, as such his sons drifted away from their father. They hardly communicated with him. But it was different with his daughter, who always chattered with him, and when he returned home from a hard day's work, her closeness to him made him forget fatigue due to the hectic activities of his business. She was simply his darling, the connoisseur of his eyes. Besides, she was his tatter-tale, and because of that her brothers did not like her.

Time passed. His sons were now in college. They were above average students, though not brilliant. Sapna was studying in class 8th. In her teenage, she never turned into a gawky young girl, but day by day she blossomed into a real beauty. When he came back in the evening from his work, she had always so much to tell him about; it gave him real solace.

One day, he and Mr. Choksi were having country liquor, which he liked to take off and on as it reminded him of his days of struggle which he cherished. Suddenly he said, "Look Harbans, I am now seventy eight and two months old and am unfit to work anymore. I want you to buy me out."
"What?"
"I mean it."
"Never in my life, can this happen."
"So, you want me to die with my boots on. I am not a soldier, but a decrepit old man."
"I am going to complain to aunty."
"She whole heartedly agrees with me. My eldest son is doing well as a jeweler. My youngest son is well settled in America and has no interest in this business. He is happily settled there with his American wife. She is a wonderful woman. We have easy communication with her and both of us are very fond of her. It is she who insisted that our grand children should have Hindu names. The son is Arjun and the daughter is Meera. Whenever we are in America, we never see her in any other dress but a saari. What to talk of meat, even eggs can't enter her house during our stay in America. I am addicted to bed tea, I have to never ask for it. When I get up in the morning, it is always there for me. Her day starts by touching our feet. I must have donated pearls in my previous birth that God has blessed us with such a wondrous daughter-in-law. She never talks about her father or mother . . . why . . . I don't know." And he started laughing, "See, I have started digressing, have gone miles away from the topic I intended to discuss with you. This shows I am getting senile. So, better we agree for three years more."

Harbans could not think what to say in reply.

"By the grace of God I still have clear thinking. You won't have any profit from the company for three years. That way you will buy me out. But, here are the duplicate keys of the safe . . . . whenever you need any money you can have it, but you will never tell me how much you have drawn . . . ."

"Never will this Harbans Lal of Mintgummery accept any dole from you."

"I am your father . . . not like your father; I know you lost your father, now I am your father. This Hasmukh Veerji of Surat will not allow his son to disobey him."

And he gave him a slap in mock anger. It was a clinical slap and an intentional one on his part. For a thick-set Punjabi like Harbans, this Gujrati slap was like a flower had hit his cheek.

"I will prefer death than to disobey you, Father." Then suddenly, he started crying.

Then he told him in depth what happened to his family for the independence of India.

Mrs. Chhaya Choksi was listening to it standing behind the curtains; she was sobbing but had put a corner of her saari in her mouth for she did not want to be heard.

CHAPTER 25

After their graduation, first Vivek and then Kulbhushan decided not to pursue their studies any further and they joined their father's business.

Both of them were smart and hard working and strongly believed that honesty is not the best policy, it looks good in the books only. Having studied in a prestigious public school of Delhi, both of them were out and out westernized and somewhat hustlers. They found their father old fashioned and his business functioning and tactics outdated.

Often they had tiffs with him which lasted only for a few minutes because of their father's overpowering personality. His sons then kept quiet and made sullen faces, much to the dislike of their father. The younger brother always backed his elder brother even when he was being unreasonable. As a matter of fact he behaved as if he was his tail. And the elder brother was very protective about him. Such was their closeness that they could sleep with the same girl without any qualms and discomfort.

Their major differences emerged when they wanted to appoint a young, beautiful and smart girl as a secretary in the office; they had already selected a few girls for this post, just giving their father a hazy idea. When they told him that they have chosen a few girls and were going to interview them on coming Monday, Harbans Lal put his foot down and rejected their idea out right, saying that he was not interested in any fashion show, plus she would be a distraction. They further drifted away from their father and it seemed that their differences were going to be unbendable. They started to talk to him in short sentences and the father and the sons felt assuaged to avoid each other. There seemed to be no love lost between the father and his two sons.

Finally after a tumultuous period of disharmony and bickering which continued for about a year, Harbans Lal opened a new concern solely to be run by his two sons.

The first thing the two brothers did was get their new office decorated by a well known interior decorator, which was liked by their father, but he could not stand the fabulous amount paid to the interior decorator but he decided to keep quiet. But he was smart enough to thrust on them the accountant of his choice, Ram Persad, his trusted man, and he asked him to give him weekly report about everything without the knowledge of his sons.

They appointed a smart and attractive secretary. After that the father never visited their office for months together.

When he came to know that they were making good profit, far more than his expectations, he felt relieved and now the weekly reports were curtailed to monthly reports.

They lived in the same house but in reality rarely met each other even on the dining table. They became strangers to each other.

Vivek married a girl of his choice at the age of twenty four and all the money spent on the marriage was borne by the father and nothing by the son. After just three months of his marriage, he announced that he wanted to live separately. He cajoled his father to buy him a three bed room independent house in Patel Nagar, and when his father refused to pay any money for the decoration of the house, the son as per his usual practice made a sullen face.

After failing to woo any girl time and again, Kulbhushan agreed to marry a girl of his father's choice. Harbans spent more money on his marriage as he had pleased him to marry a girl of his liking. A few days before the marriage, he asked him if he would also like to live separately like his elder brother.

"If you don't mind, I will prefer that, but of course with your permission."

Harbans Lal was simply shocked. He was sure at least one of his two sons would stay with him to look after him. Sapna was also listening to it and she remained stunned for quite some time.

After just four days of this talk, Kulbhushan told his father triumphantly, "I have found a four bed room house in Rajouri Garden. It's a beautiful house. You will simply love it . . . the price of the land is cheaper in Rajouri Garden than in New Rajinder Nagar as well as in Patel Nagar that is why I have chosen a four bed room house for myself."

"As you like it, it's your choice."

"Great. I have promised to pay the *bayana* [the initial money] within five days."

"Then do it."

"I don't understand."

"What is there to understand?"

After what seemed to be a long forced silence, he said, "When are you going to give me the money . . . today or tomorrow? I don't want this deal to slip out of my hands."

"Then don't."

"And the money . . . ."

"What money?"

"The one I am going to pay as bayana."

"Then give it. Who is going to stop you?"

"But you are going to give me the money."

"I never promised it."

"That means you are not going to give me the money."

"Your presumption is correct. No money I am going to give you."

"It is funny."

"No, it is not."

"It is discrimination."

"It is not."

"Then I am going to cancel this marriage."

"It's okay with me."

"This is ridiculous . . . you bought a house for Vivek . . . but in my case you flatly refuse. IT IS SIMPLY RIDICULOUS," he protested by thumping his foot.

"Don't raise your voice . . . . otherwise, I have a strong hand and you know it. And there is bloody no discrimination. The ownership of that house in Patel Nagar is under the names of Vivek and Kulbhushan Pasricha. You are going to stay there as a matter of right." And he stormed out of the house.

"Sapna, dear sister, you must try to make him understand. I am sure, father, will never say 'no' to you . . . I have already informed my fiancée and she is gaga about it."

"Hell to your fiancée. AND DOUBLE HELL TO HER GAGA."

And she left him alone.

The marriage was performed nicely, with Harbans Lal's money, with no contribution from his sons. As already had been decided by her, Sapna wore internally a very simple dress sans any make-up. Still, she looked beautiful.

CHAPTER 26

Harbans fixed the marriage of her daughter with a boy working in an American company as an Assistant Manager. The boy was tall, fair and presentable. They were gregarious, fun loving and outgoing and the best part of it was that they never talked about any goods or any cash for dowry. The other consolation was they belonged to the same caste system. But just a month and a half before the marriage, they gave him a list of items to be given before the marriage, with the clause, 'if you don't mind'. He readily agreed. After seven days he got another list with the same clause. He did not like it, but nevertheless agreed. Then he got one more list, then another, and then another. Now they had omitted the clause. They felt since Harbans Lal was rolling in money, he would be too ready to spend as much money as per their desire on the marriage of his only daughter, especially when he was not close to his sons, about which they had come to know and that had inspired them in their greed. And just about a week from the marriage, they demanded a brand new imported car.

This was the last straw. He was furious but kept his cool. He invited both father and the son to his house.

When they came to his house, he greeted them very warmly. They became sure the car was theirs. Better we demand the best in the market. He told the father that he wanted to talk to the son alone. The father agreed readily. He asked the son to follow him to his bed room.

"So, you want a car."

"It is a small thing for you."

"And an imported one."

"To match your stature and prestige."

"In case I refuse."

"Then the marriage is . . . . ," the boy was reluctant to complete the sentence.

"Then it is off?"

"I can't go against the wishes of my parents."

"Before I agree to your request . . . I want to know one thing . . . . can I open up with you?"

"By all means."

"How long is your dick?"

"What are you talking about!?"

"You heard me!!"

"It is six inches." The boy replied, *after all he was getting a car, an imported one.*

"You are lying, show me."

"You are insulting me. Remember, I am going to be your son-in-law."

"You are not going to be even my bastard-in-law."

And he slapped him.

"How dare you!?"

He gave him another hard slap with the back of his hand and then hit his stomach with his fist. The boy was in real pain. He started seeing stars during day time.

"Do as I tell you." Harbans said in a menacing tone.

The boy unzipped his pants with trembling hands and showed him. He was now really scared for his life.

"It is too pricey even for an imported toy-car." And he spat on it.

"Now call your father, I am to discuss some Arithmetic with him and also to exchange some pleasantries with him."

He dragged him by his collar near the door and then kicked him hard on his arse. The boy stumbled and the father saw it. They literally ran out of the house.

When they were on the street, they were caught by a toughie by their neck, and squeezing them, he warned them, "Return everything including the cash by this evening, otherwise I will cut your balls, and will put one in your mouth and the other in your pocket. This I will do in your home in the presence of your family members."

He freed them only when they promised to do likewise.

He was Harbans Lal's man for all seasons.

They lived up to their promise.

All their acts of greed were undertaken on the instigation of the boy's maternal uncle, who was sort of an uncrowned head of their community. The boy beat him mercilessly and then left his home, severed all his ties with his parents for ever. Later on, he married a girl from a very poor family without accepting a single item of dowry.

Sapna was least upset over the breakup of her marriage. Whatever step her father took, in her opinion, was always in the right direction as she loved and revered him. *Her father could do no wrong.* In a way she was happy, as she had a fancy for the brother of one of her closest friends. It was her secret which she had revealed to none and that included her friend. After the death of her mother, she had become very close to her eldest *bhua* [father's sister] as she grew up, who always behaved like a mother to her.

She went to meet her.

"Bhua, I have to talk to you on an important matter."

"I know you are very upset about this break up."

"No, bhua, I am not, not the least."

"That means obviously you are in love with someone else."

"A boy likes me."

"And you?"

"I also like him immensely."

"So, you have been dating him without our knowledge."

"In a way, we have never met."

"You have never met! That is a puzzle to me."

"You are going to solve it for me."

"But, first let me know, what is it?"

Sapna kept quiet.

She laughed and then said, "Oh I see, that means the boy has expressed his love for you.'

"In his own particular way, yes."

"Oh, stop this 'in a way'," she said with a smile on her face, "Okay, on phone, or by writing a love letter or through a friend?"

"None."

"For God's sake, don't be mysterious."

"He conveys it through his eyes."

"And you?"

"I do it by lowering my eyes . . . and by smiling."

"Since how long has this been going on?"

"It is for more than a year."

"Is he sweet to you when he talks to you?"

"We have not said even hello to each other."

"How did you meet him?"

"He is my dearest friend Payal Mehra's brother . . . she is very beautiful."

"Is she, more than you?"

"She is."

"It is hard to accept."

"Believe me bhua . . . . after the death of my mother, it is only . . . . you."

"I am your mother. Our *Lado* [darling] is going to marry this boy . . . even your father cannot stop me."

Sapna embraced her.

"Let's celebrate it by going to a movie."

"Sure, bhua."

In the evening Sarita told her husband Mahesh everything verbatim.

"Our Sapna is so sweet and innocent. Leave everything to me. Trust me, I shall accomplish it."

The very next Sunday, they went to Payal Mehra's house, the door was opened by the boy.

"You are Vinay Mehra, if I am not wrong." Mahesh said it very politely.

"Yes sir, you are right."

"We have come to meet your parents."

"Please, come in."

His parents and sister were already sitting in the living room.

"Papa, they have come to meet you."

"Sorry, I have not recognized you."

"You are going to . . . and you are Payal."

"Yes, hello, I am Payal."

"You have a friend name Sapna . . . . Sapna Pasricha . . . she is our niece."

"Oh, welcome *ji*, most welcome," said Mr. Mehra.

The mother said something in her son's ear and he rushed out.

Both Sarita and Mahesh were sure that the mother had guessed for what purpose they had come.

"Is your son doing some business?"

"No, he is working as a Section officer in the Ministry of home affairs." Mr. Mehra said proudly.

As they could not find a topic to talk about, they started talking about the weather.

Vinay brought sweets and *namkeen* and cold drinks from the market, which was nicely placed on the centre table by Payal and her mother.

"If you prefer tea . . . ," said Mrs. Mehra.

"No, cold drinks will do," said Sarita.

"Uncle, why have you not brought Sapna?"

"We want to bring her to your house for ever," said Sarita.

"We have come to ask for the hand of Vinay for our niece, but of course the final approval will be that of her father." Mahesh said politely.

The mother started praying silently.

"Actually, my wife has talked about this alliance to me several times. But we were hesitant to approach . . . we are not rich. We belong to middle class."

"It is not a crime to belong to middle class." Mahesh said with a smile.

They straight away went to Harbans Lal's office, and asked him to come out. And then they told him that they have seen a boy for Sapna, and they have really liked the boy and the family. Sarita told him with great enthusiasm that it was a real good match for Sapna.

"Of course, I have told them very clearly that the final approval will be yours." Mahesh said.

"You are insulting me and very badly."

"The boy is really good, tall and handsome. Sorry, we did not consult you before hand."

"Yes, again you are insulting me and *bad-o-badly*," Harbans said with fake anger. "When the boy has been liked by my eldest sister and brother-in-law, then who is this bloody Harbans Lal to give his consent. Hell to his consent!" And then he laughed and hugged both of them.

"You are a real drama," Mahesh chuckled.

"Let's go to their home."

"Our *bhai* is always in a hurry."

"He never likes to miss his train."

"You have not asked what the boy is doing."

"He has been approved by both of you. Even if he repairs shoes, I am not bothered."

Sarita was dying to convey this news to Sapna.

They went to the market and bought sweets and fruits and went to Mr. Mehra's house.

And when they saw fruits and sweets in their hands, the mother thanked God for listening to her prayers.

"Now, I know why Sapna is so beautiful you are sooooo handsome." Payal beamed.

"Please say it again, I love to hear it."

They roared with laughter.

Mrs. Mehra let them enter the house, only when she poured mustard oil on the two sides of the door.

It was a gesture of warm welcome.

Harbans emptied his purse and gave money to each member of the Mehra family, and just kept one rupee in his purse, being a businessman he was whimsical about it that the purse should never be empty.

Suddenly, Mr. Mehra interrupted, "I must make it clear beforehand that we are not rich . . . . we belong to middle class."

"When I landed in India I belonged to mud class."

The walls trembled with their laughter.

Money was also given to all of them by Sarita.

"Please give me a photograph of the boy, I want to show it to my daughter."

There was quite a fuss in the selection of the photograph. Finally, Payal chose one and gave it to Harbans.

They chatted for quite some time and there was fine tuning between them.

When they finally left and Vinay was sure that they were not within earshot, he jumped and roared, "Hurray!"

"Have you gone mad?" Payal teased.

"It is even more than that! I have won a battle."

It was Mahesh who informed Harbans' sons that their sister Sapna's marriage has been fixed. They came running to their father along with the younger daughter-in-law.

"Whenever you need some money, please let us know, but in advance." Vivek said.

"Your very presence at the wedding will oblige me and I don't need any money from you." Harbans replied curtly.

"Aarti, my sister-in-law and I will help Sapna in shopping," the younger daughter-in-law said.

"I will let you know if that is required."

Vinay, during lunch hours, when nobody was around, rang up Sapna.

"Hello, Sapna darling, how are you?"

Sapna hung up the phone.

He was surprised and bewildered, never expected such behaviour from his fiancée. Then on second thoughts, he came to the conclusion that she had not recognized his voice, as they had never talked to each other on the phone. And he decided not to call her 'darling', as she may not feel embarrassed on his being so open.

"I am Vinay Mehra. Please don't put the receiver down."

"Oh, I am sorry." She said meekly. She wanted him to call her darling again, but he did not.

"So, how are you?"

"I am fine."

He could not think what to say next. There was silence.

"Are you there?"

"*Ji.*"

"Do you like me?"

No answer.

"You have not answered."

This time, she giggled.

"That means you don't like me."

"NO."

"Then start liking me." He laughed.

"No is not no, it is yes."

"So, you like me."

"Very."

Again, there was an awkward silence.

"Are you there?"

"*Haan ji,*" she said softly.

"Say something."

"You say."

"Right now nothing is coming to my mind."

"Say anything."

"Anything, are you sure?"

"Yes," she said dreamily.

"Right now, I am thinking of telling you the story of the latest film I have seen. Should I?"

"Please do."

"Better we meet somewhere. Then I will narrate you the whole story."

"Naa *baba,* papa won't like it."

"But otherwise you will like to meet me."

No answer.

There was a long silence.

She became edgy, thinking that she had annoyed him.

"*Ji*, are you there?" This time, she gathered the courage to ask.

"Sure." He assured her.

"Say something, please."

"Well, I am going to say. I LOVE YOU."

She blushed and became nervous. Her whole body was beyond her control.

"Do you love me?"

"*Haan.*" She said it rather timidly.

Again, there was silence, but for a short period.

"I want to hear it from your mouth."

"I am yours." Her voice became hoarse.

"You have a lovely voice." He uttered his well-rehearsed dialogue.

"Thank you." She managed to say.

"Please sing a song for me."

"I don't know how to sing."

"Just do it for my sake."

"Please."

He continued persuading her for five minutes. At last, he was able to persuade her. She sang, *Shyama aap baso Vrinda Ban mein, meri umar beet gayee Gokal mein*, a devotional song.

"You sing so well."

"You are joking. Listen, I have started knitting a cardigan for you. Do you like the pink colour?"

"Oh, it's my favourite colour."

He had hardly any liking for the pink colour.

Vinay surmised that she was so hesitant to talk; so bashful. Decidedly, she is untouched and a virgin. HE FELT PROUD OF HER.

From the office, he straight away went to Connaught Place and bought a shirt and a t-shirt of pink colour and got himself photographed wearing them and managed to send it to her through his sister, promising her a grand treat.

In the evening, she went to Karol Bagh and spent more than two hours to buy three shirts and two t-shirts of different shades of pink colour.

The photo got soiled because of her numerous kisses.

All the shopping was done with the help of his three sisters. After two months, the marriage was performed with great pomp and show, which was resented by his sons and daughters-in-law for wasting so much money, they did not say it overtly, but it was written large on their faces.

The Mehras did not belong to middle class anymore.

CHAPTER 27

Hasmukh decided to spend rest of his life in home town Surat. He wanted to be in the company of his own people, all his life he had missed to speak in his local Gujrati dialect. He had his ancestral house in Surat which he got renovated by the help of a son of his cousin.

Harbans kept in touch with him through letters. He was never comfortable to have a long chat on telephone and neither was Hasmukh.

After three months of his stay in Surat, he was surprised to find Harbans at his door.

"What a surprise! Any special reason for coming to Surat . . . ."

"No, I just missed you."

He had decided to stay there for three to four days, but he prolonged it to twenty days.

He mixed with the local people very easily. He found them soft spoken, affectionate and marvelous in hospitality.

After eight months Hasmukh returned to Delhi with bag and baggage and told him, "The trouble with me is that when I am in Delhi I miss Surat, and when I am in Surat I miss Delhi. Besides, I feel bored without work. So, I have decided that I will attend office daily for two hours and not more than that."

"Even two hours will be a great help to me," Harbans said excitedly.

He fell ill. It was just fever and no serious problem. He died at the age of eighty four due to old age and general debility.

Everybody was surprised to find a huge number of people who attended his funeral. Many of them were from down-trodden and very poor families; Rickshaw pullers, cart drivers, plumbers, scavengers, road-side barbers, etc. They were genuinely crying as they had lost a father figure. Whenever any one of them needed money, he never came empty-handed out of his home.

After the funeral, some of them left for their home, and some went to a nearby park to hold a meeting to mourn the death of their saviour. Speaker after speaker showered their eulogies on him in their typical dialects and all of them vowed that they would pay back the last penny to his family, of the loans they had taken from him from time to time, and each of them swore by the name of their deity which was most revered by him.

To drown their unspeakable sorrow, most of them had bought bottles of illicit liquor, called *Panni,* from a fat Rajshthani woman sitting near a drain full of stench. They did not have many glasses, but they were shared and there was no problem, as they finished the entire panni in one or two gulps. The more they drank, the more they cried shouting his name in pain and agony.

Some got drunk, some got dead drunk. Some could not even stir, being totally blacked out and fell on the cozy grass and fell asleep. It depended on their luck whether they would continue sleeping there or would be thrown out in the wee hours of the morning by the police or the chowkidars.

Others staggered back to their homes. Some beat their wives and some were beaten by their wives. Some forced themselves on their wives, and some were not allowed even a touch and were pushed back. Some were allowed but could not get an erection and cursed their wives for being cold. Some docile wives raised their legs up towards their tiny huts and urged their man, 'do it, and do it fast', as they were feeling very sleepy. And some remained asleep during the act.

Nobody was going to live up to his promise to return the loan, as they had no means and capacity to pay back. They were too poor and always needed another loan. They were going to pray for another Hasmukh Seth to emerge on the earth.

Their number as well as poverty was increasing day by day and by leaps and bounds. It was because of them, India *was the biggest democracy in the world. It is The Greatest one.* They are the pillars of the Indian democracy and the Indian democracy was going to thrive because of them. Above all they are very, very dear to the Indian politicians, who are ready to do anything for these destitute people; mostly on paper and in their speeches, always. They have bags full of tears for them, CROCODILE TEARS.

CHAPTER 28

Harbans Lal decided to go to Pakistan to get some news about the whereabouts of his youngest sister, Guddi. He was very annoyed with himself, why he had not thought of it earlier. He managed to get the Pak visa through a travel agent by paying much more than the actual visa fee.

He was welcomed in his village by open arms. They were very happy to find him alive, as at times they thought perhaps he was also killed somewhere, as they did not find him in his home. Rehmat Ali decided not to tell anybody how he had helped him to escape, for that he was guided by his instinct. Later on many Mujaheedins had settled in their village, having occupied the houses of the Sikhs and Hindus and had grabbed their lands and cattle. Not a single Hindu or Sikh family remained in the village after the partition. For the fear of the Mujaheedins, who hated everything about India and the Indian, he kept his escape as a secret.

Some of his friends wept when they hugged him. And felt very sorry for the loss of his family.

He went to his house and stood there feeling deep remorse and he prayed for his parents and sisters, he had altogether forgotten how to pray, as he had stopped praying after he left his village forever. He wanted to go inside his house, but decided against it.

For two days, none gave him any news about Guddi.

They pretended that they knew nothing about her, as knowing about it would be very painful for him because they knew that if they disclose it, it would hurt his feelings immensely. They wanted his trip to be full of joy and fun.

Ultimately Rehmat Ali decided that it was better to tell him the truth. He told him that Guddi was found lying dead behind the trunks. Perhaps, she died of shock.

In a strange way, Harbans felt relieved that her younger sister was not dishonored and did not have to face the torture of being killed and above all was not forcibly converted to Islam. That hope against hope that one day he would be able to find her, proved to be otherwise, and that devastated him.

He wanted to donate his house and his lands to Rehmat Ali and went to some offices of the government of Pakistan, but he found that the *babus* [officials] of the government of Pakistan were the worst. Some of them even laughed at him. So far, corruption is concerned, he found that India and Pakistan are still culturally very strong.

He wanted to cut short his visit, but his old friends literally begged him to stay for a few more days. Their pure, simple and selfless love made him very emotional, and his hatred for the politicians and particularly those who created a rift between Hindus and Muslims and were responsible for the partition of India and the ensuing murders, lootings, rapes, abductions and arson grew much more.

While departing for India, he was given many presents by his friends, most of these he left in Rehmat uncle's house. He also gave him Rs. fifty thousand and his gold chain, which the latter accepted with much reluctance.

Many of his friends came to the Railway station to see him off and took a promise from him that he would come to visit them again.

When the train departed, tears flowed on his cheeks.

During his journey in the train, when his fellow passengers came to know that he was a Hindu from India, they were extra polite and courteous to him. They offered him food also but his friends had packed food for him which was enough for ten people.

I would always cherish the warmth and the hospitality of my Muslim friends.

I can never forget the land of my birth, of my ancestors. LONG LIVE MY VILLAGE.

He could not hold his tears.

CHAPTER 29

Vinay Mehra proved to be a wonderful son-in-law, as a matter of fact he never behaved like a typical Indian son-in-law. He really cared for his father-in-law and respected him and Harbans loved him. Both Sapna and he made it a point to visit him off and on to enquire about his health and welfare. Harbans liked the entire Mehra family, though they did not have much money, but they had high moral standards and were 'Givers' by nature. They never demanded anything from him. Harbans could not strengthen his ties with Amrit Lal Mehra, because he was a teetotaler. So they always met for lunch. They never gave any chance for Sapna to complain, rather Harbans often jokingly used to tell Vinay that if Sapna created any nuisance then he must inform him and he would set her right. Sapna loved this joke and then afterwards always said, 'see how great my father is.'

Harbans felt very lonely after the marriage of his daughter. He started drinking daily, yet never became a drunkard. He always drank within limits. He became very close to his servant Duli Chand who was very loyal to him. He started giving him a peg or two as he needed company but never more than two, and Duli never asked for more. They started eating on the same table, though Duli was initially very reluctant to do so, but Harbans insisted and started treating him as a friend. And from the clothes he now wore, no body on earth could imagine that the poor chap was a mere servant. So to raise his morale, he raised his salary four times. Duli used to tell him anecdotes of his life in his village near Dharamshala, in his simple but inimitable style, which Harbans immensely enjoyed.

Once Sapna came to him and told him that she was going to stay with him for three to four days, as Vinay has gone out on an official tour.

"Did you take your father-in-law or mother-in-law's permission to stay with me?"

"No, but what is the necessity?"

"Then I have to teach you a lesson, my dear child. You must go back with the same feet, you have come here. And never dare to belittle the elders of your house."

And he closed the door on her with a heavy heart. Turning out his dearest daughter really upset him, but he was least dismayed by the step he had taken.

Barely after five minutes, there was a knock at his door and he was surprised to find the entire Mehra family including Vinay, laughing and clapping.

"Sapna has won the bet," shouted Payal jumping like a child.

He embraced his daughter and kissed her hair and said, "She is my koh-e-noor ka heera [the diamond of koh-e-noor]." And Sapna looked at her father with pride.

Waiving off their protests, he took them to Ashoka Hotel for a treat. When Harbans Lal of Mintgummery decided about something, then even devil could not stop him.

He had no truck with his two sons, though they continued coming to him and just before leaving asked for some money which they needed for their business, of course always in the guise of loan with no intentions to return.

And when on the fourth such occasion they asked for the loan, which was more than the total amount he had given them on the three previous occasions, he flatly refused and remarked, "And don't forget, I have not written off the previous loans."

They made a sullen face and it had no effect on him.

"You are refusing your own sons when they are in desperate need of money?" Vivek said bitterly.

"Try your luck with your father-in-laws. You are very close to your in-laws. Rather more close to them than me."

"They are more concerned about us than you, our own father." Kulbhushan said sarcastically.

"Then go and lick their feet, but go there properly dressed and before asking for money from them, first you must have the permission of your respective wives," and he added with effective remorse. "I have my doubts, if they would be kind enough to bestow it on you."

This further soured the relations between father and the sons. They stopped even giving him a tinkle.

When Vivek's wife gave birth to a son, it was Kulbhushan's wife who informed him on the phone. He went to the nursing home along with Sapna and Vinay. When Sapna realized that Vivek was all attention to his wife's family only and least bothered about them, she quietly told her father it was better to leave. They once again congratulated Vivek and left.

For months together, the father and the sons were not in touch. Harbans started feeling pangs of emotions for his grandson, Anurag who was now eight months old. *'He must be crawling now'.* He craved to listen to his baby-noises. He put his ego aside and went to see him. On the way, he bought many expensive toys for the child.

His joy knew no bounds, when the baby cuddled in his lap made chortling sounds. He decided to patch up with them for the sake of his grandson. *Let bygones be bygones.*

He found that his toys were welcome, but with him they showed lukeworm warmth and hospitality. Incidentally, on that day his younger son and his wife, Namrata were also present. So was a friend of theirs named Satnam Singh.

Namrata asked the servant to prepare tea for every body. Just then the phone bell rang and it was picked up by Vivek's wife, Mohini.

He was busy playing with the child, but still heard. 'He is from Bombay ... oh fine. No problem .... he is most welcome, the more the merrier .... lot of work to be done for tomorrow's party.' She cursed herself for uttering, 'tommorow's party'. *We are not going to invite the old man in any case. He is so crude and a spoil-sport.*

After they had tea, Satnam Singh got up and said that he was to meet somebody, "See you uncle in tomorrow's party."

"Let's see," mumbled Harbans.

"Uncle, you must have been the first to whom they gave the invitation card."

"I have not been invited."

"Actually, we have invited a few intimate friends only .... and we find that you don't feel at home in these parties .... and my in-laws don't like outsiders .... I mean ... I think I have used a wrong word ... My father-in-law is a snob. He does not mix up easily ... but ... I mean .... if you want to come, you are welcome." Vivek said trying his best to be diplomatic.

"Time permitting, you must come ... we know you are always so busy, but still try to come," Mohini added with a tongue in the cheek smile.

By this time, the servant had brought the tea. Harbans pushed it aside, got up and left.

Mohini ran after him and caught him by the elbow near the gate. "What are you doing ... going away like this ... without having tea? What will our friend Satnam think? It is high time you learn to behave."

Harbans Lal freed his arm from her hold with a jerk, did not utter even a syllable and left. It suited Mohini.

Mohini entered the house in a huff. "I must say Vivek, your father is a very difficult character . . . How did your mother live with such a man? He always enjoys hurting others. He cares two hoots for the respect we show him."

"I can't change him in his old age . . . . we must accept him for what he is."

"You may do it, being his son. I simply can't. I am not his bloody sold-by-money-slave. And that is that."

"Please try to tolerate."

"I can't. I can't. I'll say it hundred times," and she thumped her foot on the ground and then began crying, none had liked her tirade against him and they felt disgusted with her cheap histrionics. When nobody attempted to console her, her cries became louder. Vivek had now no choice but to console her but she was unstoppable. At last, Vivek had to condemn his own father to quieten her and she stopped her wailing there and then and said in a clear voice without a trace of her earlier howling, "My one aim in life is, and God knows it, to make you happy and be a devoted wife."

Satnam Singh was listening to all this attentively. "You have not invited your own father, Strange!" He said with suppressed anger and disgust.

"Try to understand Satnam. He does not fit in this circle. He is a loud character. After two pegs he starts speaking in English, which is fun for others but very embarrassing for us. And he thinks he is being very impressive. Ridiculous!"

"My seventy year old *daar ji* [father] in our parties, sometimes starts dancing Bhangra or comes out with old Punjabi folk songs, some even bawdy. Sometimes he also sings English songs in a heavy Punjabi accent."

"It must be very discomforting to all of you." Kulbushan said sympathetically.

"No, we enjoy every moment of it, to the utmost. He is the most important person to me than the entire world because I am not a mother fucker like you and I don't wear my wife's petticoat like you do."

And with one swipe of his hand, he threw away the crockery. It got broken to pieces and it soiled their clothes.

"How dare you?" The two ladies shrieked.

"I am a Sardar, if a Sikh cannot dare, he is not a true Sikh." He looked at them with disdain. "And you bloody sister's penis. Vivek better start wearing a saari. You bastard, third rate cuckold!"

He put two hundred rupees on the table. "It is for the damages. You bloody cunt-licker slave!"

He really was in a frenzy; it was unbearable for him that an old man was humiliated by his own sons, it simply maddened him. His parents had taught him to always respect the elders even if they are not known to him. He took out his watch and banged it against the wall. "Time will teach you, you must be having a limp penis that is why you have become your woman's stooge!"

He spat on the ground and walked out slowly with a swagger. *It was his challenge to come after him.*

Vivek started weeping and his brother and his wife began consoling him.

"I must say that your father is a kill-joy. A bad omen! Our party is going to be a failure." Lamented Mohini venomously.

And it was a failure. Because back home, Satnam Singh had one passionate zeal to narrate the whole episode to whomsoever he could circulate. As a result of that most of the invitees boycotted the party. In the Indian milieu, if someone tries to dishonour or discard his parents, then socially he is considered as a rotten rat. *There is a Punjabi saying, he who cannot be true to his parents, how can he belong to us.*

Harbans Lal was deeply perturbed. While driving the car, he was not in full control. Everything appeared hazy and blurred to him. He felt emotionally drained and his mind was not working. He was simply not able to drive and even had lost sense of direction. He parked his car outside a walled colony and requested the security guard to watch for his car and gave him a hundred-rupee note. He took a taxi to go home.

He was in a suicidal mood, life seemed meaningless to him. He felt mentally weak, and he hated himself for being so. He was feeling very lonely. He gave a ring to Sudan. "Come to my home. I need you badly."

He opened the bottle and decided to drink, then changed his mind to wait for Sudan, who came after thirty minutes.

Sudan found him disheveled and extremely distressed, but decided not to ask any questions.

When they were taking their second peg, Sudan could not check himself from asking, as he was making hardly any conversation.

"Something is troubling you?"

"Yes, it's because of a friend of mine. His sons find him socially awkward and not fit enough to invite him to a party in their home, where their in-laws are present. For them, their father is no better than a street mongrel."

"It's too bad."

"It is better to be childless than to have sons like that."

"You are right."

"What would you do if you were in that man's position?"

"I would disown them and have no regrets for my decision."

"There can be other ways . . . ."

Harbans was quite for a long time, lost in his thoughts, and they continued drinking sans any conversation. Then it was Sudan who was talking most of the time and Harbans was half listening.

Harbans was in no mood to stop drinking and it was Sudan who ordered his servant to serve the dinner.

After they had their meals, Sudan told him that he was not going home as it was too late and he informed his wife accordingly and told her that because of certain reasons he had decided not to let Harbans be alone, and who for a change did not grumble, as he had told her that he would tell her later on why it was important for him no to let Harbans be alone and she had readily agreed. Everybody in their home had great liking for Harbans.

"It is your own home." He asked the servant to give Sudan a night suit.

They retired for the night. After some time, Sudan felt the urge to go to the bathroom. He saw the lights in the living room on. He went there and saw him drinking. He snatched his glass and threw the whisky in the wash basin and dragged him to the bed. Harbans did not protest.

In the morning, Sudan told him, "It is your own story."

"Yes, I knew you will guess it . . . . Still tried to hide it. Now, what do you have to say?"

"Avoid them, but don't disown them."

"You are changing now."

"Well, you see . . . between father and sons . . . Well, I am in a very awkward situation."

"I can understand. Sorry, I troubled you."

"Not at all, rather, I feel honoured that you thought of me only. A friend in need is a friend indeed. Always do that."

And he left.

A fortnight later, Satnam Singh came to his home, which really surprised Harbans. Actually, he had got his address from Kulbhushan, who could not dare refuse him, as all of them were now really scared of him. Without beating around the bush, he straight away said, "You are a Mona [A Hindu] and I am a Sikh, can you still accept me as your son? I have severed all relations with them. I hate to utter their very names."

Harbans hugged him, there were tears in his eyes. He could not even say anything. Before he could say anything, Satnam took him to his home. His family gave him a warm welcome without making it too obvious, they knew the whole story. Gradually Harbans and Tarsem Singh, Satnam's father became great friends. There was not a function in their home where Harbans was not the most important guest.

A fortnight later, Sudan gave him a ring and told him that he was going to buy a flat in Vasant Kunj as he liked the locality and he wanted him to accompany him for the selection of the flat.

"We will purchase two, one for me."

He did not want even a chance meeting with his son, Vivek who was staying at a close distance from his house.

They bought two flats of their liking which were only at a distance of a few blocks from each other.

He shifted to his new house within a few days of its purchase. He still felt very lonely and down-hearted, but still thought that it was a good idea to shift from that house. Sad memories outnumbered happy ones of that place. He had totally rejected his two sons, yet could never forget them and that tortured his very soul. He thought that they became by dispositions so, because they lost their mother when they were very young. When they were kids, they were simply lovable. To his good luck, his daughter and son-in-law were very devoted to him. But in India, no matter how close are a daughter and a father, they cannot talk freely to each other and many matters cannot be discussed between them at all, there is always a strange kind of distance and formality between the two of them. There just cannot be any real intimacy between them.

Amazingly, he never neglected his work.

After a few months, Sudan abandoned his government accommodation and shifted to his new house in Vasant Kunj. With the companionship of Sudan, life became worth living for Harbans. There was something in

Harbans that women liked and had sisterly or motherly affection for him, and Sudan's wife was always very nice to him. Yet he could never talk freely with her or any other woman, Pinki was the sole exception. Even at his age, his ears became red while talking to a woman. Though grumbling was Mrs. Sudan's basic nature, but she never complained when Sudan and he had their drinking sessions.

CHAPTER 30

A chance meeting with Swami Bharat Kumar, a yoga acharya, revealed to him the importance of yoga in one's life which is good both for physical as well as mental health.

Swamiji originally belonged to Andhra Pradesh, but he had lived all his life mostly in Punjab and later on in Delhi and spoke Punjabi fluently. He was a linguist, he knew English, French, Urdu, Punjabi, Sanskrit, Telugu and Bengali. He never talked about his life before he took sanyas. He was in his late seventies but could sit erect for hours in meditation. There was a saintly glow on his face and he looked much younger than his age. His famous saying was, 'Yoga is enjoyment and not torture; so always do it according to your physical capacity and strength.' He was not sober or sedate as is expected from a holy man, but was always rather full of humour and told captivating anecdotes. He discouraged others from renouncing the world and emphatically spoke in favour of *Grihisth Ashrama* [Family life]. Once, somebody asked, "Then why did you, Swamiji, not marry?"

"There is only one reason, simply because, I was an extremely irresponsible man. And I would have been a bad role model as a family man. Thus I have saved the life of a woman to become miserable."

The way he said it, everybody in the congregation felt amused.

He mixed up with women freely, but the only woman he talked about was his mother. He lived in a one room accommodation built by his followers and had bare necessary belongings, but lots of books on different subjects. He never allowed a female to enter his house unless she was accompanied by her father, brother or husband.

Harbans Lal was highly impressed by Swamiji, and thought of joining his yoga class, but did not pursue it.

One day, Sudan suggested that they should start going for a morning walk daily. Harbans agreed.

They went to a well maintained park, there on a board it was displayed that entry of dogs, and playing of cricket or football is strictly prohibited, but this rule was regularly flouted.

There they found a yoga class being conducted by a yoga acharya [guru]. It attracted them and they began watching them. Then one of the practitioners approached them.

"Why don't you join us?"

"What is the fee?" Sudan asked.

"No fee and no donations."

"I am surprised."

"It is a heavenly sent blessing, as such there should be no charges."

His name was Kimti Lal and it was his mission in life to coax more and more people to pursue yoga. If somebody agreed to his proposal, he felt highly obliged and felt joyous like a child. The name of their organization was, The Akhil Bhartiya Yoga Sansthan and their motto was 'to live and to give life to others.' The very next day, they joined the yoga class. They gave them a plastic sheet and a *duree* to spread on the ground. They sold it on cost to cost basis, and if somebody could not afford it, they gave it for free and nobody could know who paid for it.

Just after a week, Harbans was able to do all the major asanas properly, but it took Sudan almost a month.

Just after four days, he happened to notice that a woman was looking at him keenly and when he also looked at her, she gave him a cute smile. Harbans felt strange, why should an unknown woman smile at him? *May be she has a smiling face and he was getting wrong meanings.*

After another three days on a Sunday, after the yoga session she was talking with some people and regaling them. She had an easy laughter and was the centre of attraction. She was sexily voluptuous. Harbans Lal was standing aloof. She went to him and said, "Why don't you join us, Mr. Harbans Lal? Nobody is going to eat you."

He was flabbergasted how this woman knew his name with whom he never had any contact. His ears turned red and legs started shaking a bit, but he did join them.

"Why are you always so quiet? We all like you. You are a good learner . . . perhaps the best new comer."

"Thanks." He felt a little reassured.

"It does not cost anything to say hello!!"

"Hello."

"Hello." She smiled, she had a bewitching smile. He felt attracted to her but did not let it show.

"We are going to my house for breakfast . . . in Vasant Vihar . . . . it's close by . . . . and you are going to join us."

"Better excuse me . . . . some other time." His legs started shaking even more.

"We are not going to devour you. There are other three men to protect you from me," and than she addressed a man standing close by, "Khanna sahib, Harbans will be going in your car."

Now his legs stopped shaking. She had not invited Sudan, so he slipped away. On the way he was thinking, *'First she called me Mr. Harbans and now only Harbans!! Quite Strange. She is bold . . . there is something mysterious about her . . . . but nothing cheap, rather, she has class.'*

Different kinds of Paranthas, of potatoes, cauliflower and radish along with bowls of curd were laid on the dining table by a servant in fine livery. There were also pickles of different variety. Harbans was the only one who put sugar in his bowl of curd. And when he put the third spoon of sugar, every one looked at him with curious eyes. Aashoo who seemed to be the closest friend of hers could not check herself from saying, "You seem to be not concerned about your level of blood sugar."

"A month back I got it examined, my friend Sudan forced me, and it was 80/112. I did not consult any doctor."

"You don't have to, rather, the doctor should consult you," said the portly Mr. Khanna.

"Oh, marvelous, unbelievable!" were some of the other comments.

Harbans was no more feeling awkward in their company.

"You don't seem to be overweight. Not at all," Aashoo said. "How do you check it?"

"Why it is so, I will show you next Sunday. We are going to have some fun."

After the breakfast was over, she went out to see off her guests.

"I understand that you are a builder," said the lady.

"Yes, I am."

"Then I have to discuss something with you. Why not right now?"

Harbans could see through that she was intentionally trying to detain him and he could not find a way to escape, as she was so nice to him, this further reddened his ears and his legs began to shake.

When others left, she said coyly, "You don't want to know anything about me?"

"How do you know me?" He tried to ask curtly, but his voice was weak.

"Just as I know Vijay . . . . Prof. Vijay Puri and his wife Pinki." She spoke looking straight into his eyes.

"Just a minute . . . you are Priya?"

"Yes, and you thought that some flirt is trying to chase you."

"No, never." He lied. He became excited and was almost going to hug her, but could not. He felt timid.

She took him inside her bungalow, and they chatted for another hour. Now he was totally relaxed.

They started meeting quite often. Priya observed that he was never comfortable in a five star hotel. So, she made it a point to go to those restaurants, where food was good, but they were not hi-fi.

Harbans started day dreaming about her, but he did not even touch her; there was not even a shaking of the hands.

Priya had lost her husband about two years back. He was mild-mannered, generous and very intelligent. And loved living in style. His one obsession in life was to earn more and more money and for that he was very ambitious. He was very hard working and was always pressed for time, at times he ate sandwiches in his car for breakfast. He always neglected his health, though he was free from any serious ailment. He loved his wife and two very good looking sons. The younger one was very fond of riding on a bike, he had no liking for a car, though his father could buy him a car of his choice. His love for speed cost him his life. He rammed his bike into a truck and died on the spot. His elder son was settled in America and he was married to an American girl. Two days after the first death anniversary of his son, he was found dead with his hand stretched while sitting on a sofa by his servant. It seemed as if he was relaxing after having solved some problem. A business channel on the TV was on, unaware of his death.

Priya was utterly devastated, first with the loss of her younger son and then with the death of her husband. The elder son was very devoted to his mother, but felt disgusted with India, because of filth, corruption and frequent outages of power supply. He pleaded with his mother to stay with him in America for ever. But to Priya, America was like a golden jail and she always got bored there after a few days and yearned to return to India.

It was just about six months back that she had started moving out and mixing with people socially.

She was very close to her American daughter-in-law, Janice. When she was just twelve years old, her mother abandoned her husband and married a man much younger than her age. And she never fought for the custody of her two children; Janice and her seven year old son. After four months, her father remarried and she had just cordial relations with her step mother, and it ended there. So, she valued her relations with her mother-in-law, who was a mother to her in the real sense. She was always genuinely too eager to please her. At times, she behaved like a mischievous but lovable teenager with her. It pleased her son immensely.

With her woman's instinct, she knew that Harbans was head over heels in love with her, but was not coming forward to propose and she was in this context too Indian to propose herself and even to give an obvious hint. She could not even confide with anyone, as it was a very tricky matter for an Indian widow, who is supposed to live the rest of her life in the memory of her husband. To have any carnal desires is an unpardonable sin for her, even if she becomes a widow at a very young age.

Priya and her daughter-in-law were not only close to each other but also very frank and intimate with each other. So, one day, she decided to talk to her. She told her over the phone that there was a man in her life, whom she loved when she was a teenager. In the end she told her not to tell anyone about it, particularly her son Vikram, because he might have become Americanized but was still an Indian at heart. It would be too hard for him to digest that his mother had fallen in love with a man at her age.

Janice could understand all the complexities in this matter, as she was an Indologist of some repute.

Priya was dismayed that for days, Janice had not called her back. She was in a big dilemma.

After twelve days when the bell rang, she picked up the phone.

"Mom, I am coming to India."

"Please let me know your flight number and the time of arrival. I will myself come to the airport to pick you up."

"Don't worry. I'll come on my own."

Her bell rang and the gate was opened by their trusted servant Chandru, who had been working for the family for the last twenty-five years and was always treated kindly, rather like a family member.

He was surprised to find Janice standing there. She asked him to tell ma that there was a beggar at the door who wanted to meet her and she gave him a ten dollar note, which he took reluctantly.

"*Didi* there is a beggar at the door."

"Ask him to budge off."

"The beggar wants to come inside and talk to you."

"Ask him to get lost."

"The beggar won't agree."

"Then shoo him away."

"I can't."

"You can't! What the hell you are talking about!"

'Because the beggar is too indolent . . . . you must meet him personally."

"Then throw him away."

"I can't."

"Why you can't, let me listen."

"Because, there is something in this beggar, I like him."

"Is he your mother's maternal uncle that you are pleading for him?"

"No, but it hurts me even to listen even one word against this beggar."

"Then go and touch his feet, but leave me alone."

"I can't till you meet this beggar."

"Then go to hell!"

"I am ready to go to hell for this beggar."

"I think you have gone mad, that is why you are pleading for this beggar."

"The very presence of such a beggar brings luck to one's house."

She got up and said angrily, "First let me tackle this beggar . . . . then I am going to break the legs of your luck. Damn it. Can't you use pronoun for the beggar, Beggar, Beggar!"

She took a cane and rushed out in a fury and when she saw Janice there, her mouth remained open for quite some time. She threw away the cane.

"So, you are the beggar?"

"Yes, I am."

They hugged and kissed each other.

Chandru was standing there smiling. He took her baggage inside.

"So, you prompted him to say so."

"Of course, ma."

She gave Chandru five hundred rupees saying, "One hundred for befooling me, one hundred for your marvelous acting and three hundred for enhancing my joy."

Janice took her face in her palms, "Let me look at you . . . Janice is so lucky . . . . Jesus has blessed her with such a beautiful mother."

The next day she gave Harbans a ring and told him that his daughter-in-law had come from the USA, and she wanted to meet him and if he did not mind they intend to come to his house.

"You are most welcome."

Harbans was both puzzled and glad as to why her daughter-in-law wanted to meet him and that also in his own house.

Both of them arrived punctually at the decided time of 7.30 pm in the evening.

Janice found that there was hardly any furniture. There was just a centre table and three ordinary chairs. The walls were bare but for a calendar. It was, to her mind, a typical bachelor accommodation with no taste for decoration and who was leading a bohemian life. Perhaps the man was not doing financially well.

Harbans Lal told them that his servant was not feeling well. He offered to treat them for dinner at Ashoka hotel.

When he went to a room to inform his servant that he was going out for dinner, Priya told Janice, "He is taking us to the Ashoka hotel for your sake, otherwise he does not like the five star culture, he feels uncomfortable there . . . . and I don't know why."

"Even I don't like that and I know why, it is so phony and full of show-off."

After some discussion, they decided to go to hotel Diplomat in Chanakya Puri, a diplomatic area.

Janice had the knack to make other persons friendly and to open up. It was a god's gift to her, like for a fish how to swim.

When Janice started speaking in Punjabi, he was amazed and liked her all the more and felt very comfortable in her company. To his astute mind, he thought that she ardently loved her husband and Priya and the Indian culture attracted her. Though Janice was not really fluent in Punjabi, but could manage to communicate without difficulty.

He ordered rum for himself and cognac for the ladies, as suggested by Janice. This was the first time that Priya drank wine in his presence. The way she was drinking he could observe that she was not used to it, but just to impress her daughter-in-law that she was quite modern, she took it. The food was good and they had a nice time together. Janice was really impressed when he got the food packed up for his servant also. *He has a human heart,* she thought.

Back home, she told that she had really liked Harbans.

"Ma, he is the man for you. He is so handsome and has a humane heart and there is nothing hanky panky about him."

Before sleep could take her over, Janice started thinking about her next move. She was the kind of a woman who was always in a hurry.

The very next day at 8 pm, she was at his door step. The door was opened by Harbans Lal himself. He was taken aback to find her there like that.

There was an awkward silence. His legs became unsteady but his ears remained normal.

"Won't you ask me in? I'm not going to kidnap you." She smiled.

"Oh sure." He led her in.

"How is your servant?"

"He still has fever."

"What will you like to have, tea or coffee?"

"Coffee with milk, but without sugar."

He went inside his kitchen to prepare coffee. Now his hands also began trembling. Just when the coffee was ready, he thought that he was not all alone in the home, his servant was there. His hands became steady, but not the legs. While sipping coffee, she said, "I've come to talk about mom and you. I guess both of you are very fond of each other."

"That's true." Now he had no hurry-scurry. His body was in full control.

"And in love?"

"Well . . . Hun . . . I . . . me . . ."

"You don't know how to express your love for her?"

"You are right there . . . yes, I am in love with her."

"This is what I wanted to listen . . . . one can always learn and you're going to. I must be going now. Ma does not know I'm here. She must be worried."

"You are quite a girl!"

"I am. Will you please drop me home? I want to save on the taxi."

"Can I dare say no to you?"

She gave a ring to Priya. "I'm coming home with a friend and he will stay for dinner. His name is Harbans."

"You are quite a funny girl."

"To create fun and mirth in life is my hobby."

Then she told him, "I've come all the way from America with one aim to be your daughter-in-law."

And she touched his feet with both hands in the Indian tradition.

Harbans felt touched and was speechless.

"Do I have to seek your permission?"

"Never . . . . now I have two daughters, I will like you to meet my other daughter, Sapna."

"Oh, I'd love to."

Once back home in Vasant Vihar, Janice said, "Both of you're clinically shy. The coin will decide who is going to propose."

She took out a coin. "Well Harbans, I am too ready to propose to you myself. You're sooooo handsome. I wish polyandry was legal . . . what a fun to have two husbands!" she laughed at her own joke. It amused Priya but Harbans felt somewhat embarrassed.

"Heads or tails?"

"Heads," Harbans said laughingly.

She threw the coin in the air. And heads it was.

"Don't feel awkward, I'm going out for fresh air. I'll be back after three minutes."

It was Harbans who attempted to propose. "I want . . . . you see . . . . what Janice . . . even I thought so . . . . but lacked guts . . . I want you . . . . Be Mine."

"I am yours." She kissed him lightly. Three minutes was a short time.

Exactly after three minutes Janice came. "So, who proposed?"

"That is our secret," said Harbans.

"That means it is you who proposed. You wanted ma to be the winner."

"Your guess is correct."

"You are a Real man!"

Harbans confided with Sudan and Priya with her closest friend, Aashoo, both of them were of the same opinion that marriage should be solemnized on the auspicious day of Maha Shivratri [Lord Shiva's birth day], which was going to befall after ten days. It was decided to have a simple, quiet marriage and to throw a party later on, where only close friends and kith and kin would be invited.

When Janice informed Vikram about it on the phone, he seemed to be very disturbed.

"Who gave mom this funny idea?"

"Her name is Janice. Try to understand, basically she is very lonely."

"She can stay with us permanently."

"You very well know it that whenever she comes to America, for a few days she is fine, and then she starts missing India."

"She will adjust by and by."

"Never, she has strong roots in India . . . . let her live her own life. She needs a companion and then life in India is not safe for a single woman, particularly so if she happens to be rich."

"Don't expect me to come . . . . I'm too busy."

She wanted to tell him that with the death of your father her sexual urge had not died, but she checked herself from making him aware of this fact, because of his typical Indian mentality, he would have lowly opinion about her mother. Besides, it would create great misunderstanding between the two of them also.

She never wanted Vikram to attend the marriage, who would keep a long face during the ceremonies. She knew her husband that he was liberal and broadminded where others were concerned, but where his mother was concerned, he was damn conservative and not open-minded and had anachronistic ideas. In short, he also had double standards, like most of the Indians.

CHAPTER 31

When Harbans Lal's sons came to know about his marriage through Janice, they were really agitated and wanted to prevent the marriage at all costs, by hook or crook. Janice thought that his sons will be very happy for their father getting settled, but it proved to be her undoing. Though, she was an Indologist, yet she lacked to understand the Indian ethos, which is difficult even for the Indians to understand because of innumerable variety of cultural values and sense of social ethics and taboos.

The same evening when they heard this news, they decided to have a conference in Vivek's house. His wife's parents and Kulbhushan's father-in-law also came to attend. Her mother-in-law could not make it because her spiritual guru was to address a congregation, who lived in a cave for eight months in the Himalayas, and nobody knew his address. And above all, a devotee was to present him an imported car, and she was very keen to have a *dekho* of the car and then clap for that ardent devotee. *These golden moments rarely come in one's life,* she thought. For her guru, she could abandon anyone.

Vivek's father-in-law Gulzari Lal Trikha was most vociferous in his condemnation, but checked himself from being abusive. At the end of his each sentence his wife Phool Kamal, with a big shake of her head uttered, "Aha, he is right."

There were suggestions and counter suggestions. Kulbhushan's father-in-law, Chaman Lal Bagga was mostly reticent. At times he just uttered, 'too much' or 'it's too much', when he did not like an idea at all, he said, 'too much' and when he despised it he said, 'it's too much.' Throughout he maintained his monotone.

They were unable to reach a consensus decision. Finally, Mohini, the younger daughter-in-law said that let's report the matter to the police.

"It's too much." Chaman Lal said.

"He is very rich, well connected, I guess even politically well connected. Police won't do anything. They may even garland him. This idea is simply ridiculous." Gulzari Lal said vehemently.

"Too much."

Finally, Gulzari Lal came with a brilliant idea that they should call him a day before his marriage and keep him as a captive till he agrees to cancel it."

"You don't know our father, when he gets his chance, he will break our nose." Vivek interrupted.

"It is too much."

Since everybody had immense love for their nose, so this idea was out rightly rejected.

They then started condemning him and decided to create a *hangama* [scene] at the time of the marriage.

"It is both much and too much."

"You have not suggested anything so far, please come out if you have anything to say." Gulzari Lal said sarcastically.

Chaman Lal got up from his seat, cleared his throat noisily and then addressed them like a leader on his election campaign, "Look, so far this marriage is concerned, I am against it and I am with you wholly and very truly. Whereas condemnation of Harbans Lal is concerned, I am not with you, not at all. I condemn this condemnation wholly and truly. THIS IS TOO MUCH. Now listen to my plight, I have three daughters and no son. After my death, my eldest son-in-law will have an eye even on my coffin and will like to grab my property. My middle daughter's father-in-law has taken loan from me six times. SIX TIMES. ALWAYS, gave me the promise that he would return it after seven days. And it is ALWAYS SEVEN DAYS AND NEVER FOUR, FIVE OR SIX. Now, he has stopped coming to our house, after I showed him my inability for any further loan. AND HE NOW CONDEMNS ME. That is why, I condemn condemnation. And now he has the temerity to tell all my relatives that his son, Khairati Lal that is the name of my son-in-law, has married into the most stingy and meanest family. WE ARE THE MOST STINGY . . . WE ARE THE MEANEST . . . . WE THE BAGGAS . . . . the famous cloth merchants of Sargodha, now in Pakistan . . . THIS IS MUCH, TOO MUCH. Whereas, Harbans Lal ji, never demanded anything from me and DO YOU KNOW, when I suggested giving some radio-shadio, furniture-shurniture as dowry on the marriage of my youngest daughter, do you know what did he say, 'Chaman Lal ji, have a round of my house, do you think I need anything?' Of course I gave a double bed sheet, a very costly one, and he accepted it with great difficulty . . . We the Baggas, the famous cloth merchants of Sargodha, now in Pakistan, WE can be anything, MEAN . . . STINGY . . . . ANYTHING . . . BUT NEVER UNGRATEFUL, we the famous cloth merchants of Sargodha, now in Pakistan, will prefer to get drowned in a well than to be ungrateful."

He raised his index finger high, did a little bit of Bhangra and left, holding his head high, after his successful oratory.

There was pin drop silence for what seemed to be a long time.

"I must say Namrata, your father has behaved like a traitor." Mohini spoke with disdain.

"WHAT!?" Namrata shrieked.

"Yes, like a rat!"

"Like a rat!?"

"See the dictionary for synonyms, the word for a traitor is also a rat."

Namrata started yelling at the top of her voice. "You eater of husbands! May your mother's cunt burn . . . . you have the gall to use such words for my angelic father. You call him a rat . . . . well, your father is a lizard."

And she slapped Mohini with full force.

Mohini was taken aback, she had least expected it. She composed herself and then slapped her with equal force. They started fighting like wrestlers. Soon, they were in a tight embrace and began hitting each other with their palms. When they found hitting with palms was too mild, they began pulling each other's hair.

Phool Kamal, Mohini's mother jumped in the fray to separate them, but offering advantage to her daughter, which was quite obvious. Namrata saw through it that she was trying to give her daughter an upper hand. Phool Kamal hit Namrata on her belly with her elbow, pretending that it was not deliberate.

Suddenly, the old lady started jumping and made a loud and continuous wail. Accidentally, Mohini's hand fell on her mother's head and she had pulled a tuft from her head, thinking that this was Namrata's head. Phool Kamal's shrieks and thumping her feet on the ground, was akin to Kathakali dance. When Mohini saw a tassel of grey hair in her hand, she shrieked even more loudly.

Suddenly, the battle was all over. Namrata raised her right hand as the victor of this bout. They went to their seats, and their breasts started heaving vigorously, up and down.

Phool Kamal continued sobbing, uttering again and again, "Hai, I am dying." Her husband did not even console her because she had intervened without his permission.

The brothers secretly enjoyed the fun, because often their wives created life hell for them, particularly Vivek was very happy at the plight of the old woman, as she was the most interfering mother-in-law. *I wish I could give some prize to Namrata.*

Kulbhushan felt proud of his wife.

The conference ended in a fiasco.

Later on, the brothers came to know through their sleuth, that the woman their father was going to marry was herself very rich, living in a sprawling bungalow in the posh locality of Vasant Vihar. They held a meeting amongst four of them that they should try to find ways and means to have good relations with their step mother-in-law; the two sisters-in-law had buried their hatchet and were again friendly with each other, as if nothing untoward had ever happened between them because of the common cause.

CHAPTER 32

Finally, they decided that the marriage would be performed in Priya's bungalow, on the auspicious Maha Shivratri day, and the same evening they will throw a party in a five star hotel, where only those who are very close to them will be invited.

Janice thought differently and she argued, as there was not going to be a very small gathering, so let the party be held in the lawns of Priya's bungalow and they would engage the services of a well known caterer. She always advocated being economically wise. Besides, they would have better fun and would be at liberty to make a lot of noise. She also suggested that the party should be held the coming Saturday after the Shivratri. She wanted the newly married couple to have their fun and to feel at ease during the party. Also to save them from unsavoury comments of which she had her apprehensions. She could never forget when his son, Vivek retorted on the phone, 'our father has become shameless. We won't let it happen.'

After some discussion, Janice's proposal was accepted; Aashoo was her chief supporter.

Just an hour before the marriage, Harbans gave a ring to Sudan. "Sudan, I need you . . . . there is a big surprise for you. I am sending my driver to bring you to Vasant Vihar."

"Right now, I am very . . . ."

Harbans did not let him complete and he put down the receiver.

On the way, the driver told him nothing, as per instructions given to him, although he asked him a few questions. But the driver seemed to be cheerful. *So every thing must be right. But what is the mystery . . . .* thought Sudan. *This Harbans always gets on my nerves, one day I am going to set him right, but what to do he is such a lovable, great friend.*

When Sudan entered Priya's bungalow, he found Harbans, Priya and a foreign woman sitting in the lawn and a priest was busy making preparations for a wedding to be performed.

"What is the mystery?" Sudan asked.

"I am getting married!!"

"Oh, that's great news!" And he embraced him.

The two ladies were decked like brides.

"Which one of them are you going to marry?" Sudan asked with a twinkle in his eyes.

"I am not the lucky one. I am already married. No chance." Janice replied and as usual laughed at her own joke.

Harbans introduced them and they shook hands.

After half an hour, Aashoo came along with her husband Avdesh Khandelwal.

Only then Harbans realized the non-presence of Kamla, Sudan's wife.

"Why Kamla bhabhi is not here?"

"Did you tell me to bring her along?"

"You should have used your common sense."

"Damn it, I did not even know that you are getting married!!"

"Okay, don't be angry. Ask my driver to fetch her."

Kamla was least prepared for this occasion. There was no time to even to go to a beauty parlor. She took half an hour to decide which saari to wear, another twenty odd minutes for the selection of the jewelry. Then she took her bath and started getting ready. She took another twenty five minutes to decide for the hair style. And then she hurriedly started getting ready. As time was running against her, she took only forty minutes for the makeup. She was still not satisfied, as they had not given her ample time to get properly ready and she had to rush. *One has to compromise, there was no time to work on the eye lashes.*

By the time, she reached the marriage venue, Harbans and Priya were already pronounced husband and wife.

She was very angry with her husband and she compensated her wrath by not letting him come near her for ten days.

After the marriage, they discussed for half an hour where to go for lunch. The caterer did not turn up, he must have got some more lucrative assignment, which is not unusual in India to let down at the last minute. Nobody even thinks of suing them as the cases linger on for years and years. In case one wins, the expenses for litigation are invariably much more than the actual expense. At last, they decided to choose one of these three places; Oberoi Intercontinental, Maurya Sheraton, and The Ashoka, all five star hotels. Harbans wanted to have no say in this matter, personally, he would have preferred a *Dhaba* where they could have some nice food. He never liked five star hotels, where one has to show manners and etiquettes to establish that one has class. One has to show respect even to the waiter! Surprisingly, Priya also did not participate in this discussion.

"Priya, you are so quite . . . . have not uttered even a word . . . it's your day. Let us know your choice."

"Actually, I want to go to hotel Diplomat. It was here we came close to each other."

There was no further discussion, everybody agreed to go to hotel Diplomat.

"Of course, we can go to some five stars for the dinner." Priya said.

"No outing for dinner tonight. I don't want you to feel tired on your first night," Janice winked.

Everybody laughed and Priya blushed feeling somewhat embarrassed. So did Harbans and his ears became red.

Before leaving for lunch, Harbans rang up Vijay and invited him for Saturday's party.

"What is the occasion?"

"It is my marriage."

"Hey chum, it is great news. You have taken the right decision. So, you are getting married on this Saturday?"

"Not on this Saturday."

"Then why you want us to come on this Saturday?"

"I got married a few minutes back."

"And you are informing us after getting married!" And then he shouted for Pinki. "Hey Pinki, our greatest wretched fool Harbans got married, but did not think proper to invite us. Of course, he is informing us now." Vijay said bitterly.

"I had hardly invited anybody. It was a very simple marriage . . . . try to understand."

"Go to hell!" Vijay shouted, "You are lucky you are not standing close by, otherwise I would have strangulated you."

Then Pinki snatched the phone from him.

"Hi, Harbans, congratulations!!!!"

"Thank you and drag him to come to attend this party on Saturday."

"We are coming."

"You did not ask who the girl is."

"Oh, yes, please tell me."

"Her name is Priya, she is from Amritsar and you know her. Please let me know the date and the arrival time of the train, I will personally come to pick you up. And please cool him down for my sake. I will explain everything when we meet. You two are the most important persons in my life. And Vijay is the most lovable son of a rifle." *He then realized that the word is gun and not the rifle. How does it matter?*

Pinki took quite some time to recollect who Priya was. And then she almost jumped.

"Vijay, you know whom he has married. It's Priya. What a surprise!"

"Who is this Priya?"

"She is the daughter of our first landlord . . . . But where are you going?"

"To the railway station, for advance booking . . . though I feel like killing him."

Pinki smiled. *One look at him and you will melt down, I know you, you husband of mine.*

CHAPTER 33

Janice wanted to decorate the bedroom, but Priya told her that Harbans did not like any ostentations and show off, as he was too simple minded for all that and he was still a rustic at heart and his rustic charm had attracted her in the first place. She left for Jaipur for sightseeing, as she wanted them to be left alone, moreover she was fascinated by the ancient culture of Rajasthan.

On their nuptial bed, Harbans felt too awkward to start any conversation and Priya knew that it could happen. He felt a burning sensation in his ears. It was Priya who broke the ice.

"I hope your friends approve of our marriage."

"You don't know them, they would go to any length to make me happy. It is I who often get on their nerves and being the youngest member of our family circle, I often take the advantage."

"What about Indu, I hope she is not jealous."

"You mean Pinki, it's funny I had almost forgotten her real name. She is like a sister to me, rather more than that . . . . she loves to mother me and even once she beat me as she thought I was going against my own interests."

"She once beat you, I can't believe that!" Priya said it by checking her emotions against her. *Once I meet you, on one pretext or the other I am going to beat you blue.*

"When they saw that I was well established in Delhi and there was a very dim chance of my returning to Amritsar. They decided to sell the shop and asked for my opinion."

"First they decide to sell the shop and afterwards, they ask for your opinion, I am surprised." She was really now annoyed with their behaviour.

"What I am going to tell you next, it is going to surprise you all the more. The shop was in Vijay's name, as he had got it allotted against the property owned by his father, and all the money, I repeat all the money, invested in the shop was His Money. I contributed nothing, as at that time I had hardly any money. I had just two hundred odd rupees during that time. After the shop was sold, they tried to give me half the money. I refused as I had morally no right on it. All of them wanted me to accept it but I flatly refused, and then Pinki got very angry and started beating me with her fists, she has such soft hands, and I giggled and said, 'Please call a doctor to treat my wounds, otherwise I am going to faint,' and then the matter was referred to Bhandari uncle, who had always favoured me, whenever we had some dispute."

"Who is he?"

"He is the patriarch of our clan. A man with a golden heart."

"And what was his verdict?"

"He said, 'As it was basically all his planning, and the business flourished because of his business acumen and hard work, so Harbans should get a little more than 50%. I know Vijay too well, he would have run the business at a loss.' But I put my foot down and at no cost I was going to agree to their offer. Actually, I had defied Bhandari uncle never before and felt bad."

"What happened then?"

"Then Bakshi uncle intervened, 'First let him have his food, he has all the way come from Delhi,' and the food had lot of chillies, but I thought it unwise to complain and in between at least four times I asked for the water and they always said,'we are just bringing' but they did not give me the water, which I desperately required. I got very angry and when I tried to go out of the house to find some water somewhere and I was dying for it, two strong muscled police men did not let me go out and they laughed, 'Sir, we are ready to lay our life for you, but won't let you go out' and then Pinki brought a thick stick and challenged me, 'try to go out and I will break your legs with this stick,' then shouted at me, 'I mean it, you idiot,' whenever she fights with me like that I feel my sister Durga is fighting with me whom I lost with all of my family members for ever. It makes me very emotional."

He kept quite for some time and checked himself from talking any more on this subject. He forced a smile on his face and said, "I had to agree, only then they gave me water and then she threw a jug full of water on my head in celebrations. Then I had to sit with them to eat again as I had kept them hungry all this time with my obstinacy."

Priya felt very sorry for him and also felt bad that she had formed a horrible impression about them without knowing the full version. *I have learnt a lesson, one should not be opinionated.*

She decided to change the topic, "the name of your shop was Top O' Top General Store, but do you know by what name the girls used to call it?"

"By what name, it is news to me?"

"They called *it sohne mundia di dukan,* and later on only *Sohnia di dukan.* Once a friend of mine dragged me to your shop and when we came out, she sighed, 'Hai, aren't they very handsome, especially the younger one, isn't he?'

Then she laughed. I replied, he is just okay . . . actually, the way she uttered *HAI* for you, I felt so jealous that I wanted to break her nose."

"You were almost going to break my nose with your hand movement."

"I am sorry."

"Please don't."

There was some awkward silence.

"I can't believe my luck that I am your wife. I am going to be wonderful with all of them because they love my Harbans so much."

"I will always feel obliged to you."

Abruptly, she got up and went out of the room and came back after about ten minutes.

"Here is a necklace for Indu, my mother-in-law, Pinki." She laughed like a child.

"I will cherish this gesture of yours all my life."

"I want to buy something for my dear daughter-in-law, Janice. Will a necklace do or something else?"

"She will appreciate if it is something typical Indian."

"Okay, together we will decide."

She chuckled and out of the blue said, "I don't even know your caste."

"Why? It is Pasricha."

"And I don't even know your date of birth. This I want to know to wish you on your birth day."

"Nobody bothered in our village to note down the date of birth of their sons and daughters."

"I can't believe it."

"It is true," Harbans said, "My mother used to say that when I was born it was the season of oranges." He laughed and his awkwardness evaporated, his ears had become normal by now.

They kept quiet for a little while.

"When I invited you to my house for breakfast, why were you so nervous?"

"No, I was not."

"Even my friend Aashoo noticed it."

"If she had noticed it, then I was." Both of them laughed.

"When I was alone with you, you were really tense."

"I thought you may not rob me."

"Do I look like that?"

"Not at all, Priya."

"One day I am going to rob you."

"By all means . . . . I will close my eyes." He chuckled.

"I have already robbed you by making you mine."

He felt turned on.

"When you told me I am Priya . . . . I . . . . I wanted to hug you."

"Why didn't you?"

"My legs trembled." They laughed and laughed.

"If I had done that, would you have thought badly of me?"

"I would not have gone against your wishes. *I would have become your slave.*" And then she remembered Janice's parting words before she left for Jaipur, 'make him relaxed.' She put her head on his shoulders and he began playing with her hair. He felt totally relaxed now.

"Actually, I wanted to embrace and kiss you."

"I can't believe it. In Amritsar when you knew that I was in love with you, you took so many days even to look at me with full open eyes."

"Honestly, I thought you may not take it otherwise . . . you may not think that I am not a gentleman."

"Which I wished so longingly . . . . Why didn't you?"

"To tell you the truth, I lacked guts . . . . whenever any girl talked to me, my ears used to become red and my legs trembled . . . . it happens even now sometimes."

"I know it that is why you were trying to avoid coming to my house, when I invited you after the yoga class."

"You are not wrong there."

They were now shedding their inhibitions and were quite open and candid with each other. It was obvious to both of them, that apart from being husband and wife, they yearned to become close friends.

"Harbans, do you remember when I met you in the corner of our street in Amritsar?"

"I can never forget it."

"And I gave you a flower."

"I was thrilled."

"Do you know what I expected, what I yearned for at that moment?"

"Please tell me."

"NO, I can't."

"You must."

"You guess."

"I will like to hear it from your mouth."

"I feel shy."

"Please do tell me."

"Ay some other time?"

"Tell me right now."

"I don't find it easy . . . I promise I will tell you but not right now, I feel too shy."

"You are now my wife. Throw away this shyness in thin air."

"Oh my my, I should not have brought this topic."

"I feel obliged that you reminded me of it. Please tell me. I am all ears for it."

"I thought you would take me in your arms and kiss me."

He took her in his arms and kissed her tenderly. "Like this?"

"Yeah!!" She said in a husky dreamy voice.

By now, he got very excited and took her in his lap, and started kissing her passionately and she kissed him back with full lips. Soon, there clothes were lying scattered on the floor and passionately they made love to each other.

She found him very virile and she was too keen to please her man. They threw away their inhibitions. They behaved like teenagers, full of vigour and passion. All night they chatted and made love to each other. They had so much to talk about and share, they talked at length about Amritsar and both of them were of the opinion that life in Amritsar was much better, with full of fun, joy, fraternity feelings and friendly concern for each others welfare, they became even sentimental about the potable water of Amritsar which is nectar and is really good for digestive system and decided to stay over there for at least a month every year.

And the morning became night for them to sleep for long hours.

Love is the ultimate winner. It is a force to reckon with against all odds. Life is too short for love, how and why people find time for hatred.